MADISON KLEIGH

and the
Onyx Stone

JEFFREY DAVID MONTANYE

For information:
Jeffrey Montanye
PO Box 148
Bullville, NY 10915
845-361-2029

ISBN: 978-1-951801-03-8

Copyright © 2020
Montanye Arts Publishing, Bullville, NY
www.jeffreydmontanye.com
4 – 05/27/2020

For Julia, Emily, Timothy, and Oliver

1

Launch Day

Madison studied the drawings as if she knew every artist personally. Every inch of the dry-erase board had been filled with sketches of varying colors. Everything from monkeys in space suits to shuttles orbiting the Earth dotted the stark white background. The simplistic artwork, with its anatomically incorrect figures, made it evident that young children had created them. Others were the work of older kids with more skill, like herself.

"Are you coming?" her mother asked.

"In a minute," Madison answered without taking her eyes off the board.

Her mother sighed and turned away. "Don't dawdle too long," she said as she continued to the observation room of NASA's launch control center. "There are too many ghosts in these drawings."

The echoes of her mother's footsteps faded as she turned a corner. Standing alone in the hallway, Madison stared at the whiteboard for a while before slowly touching the glass that preserved the delicate erasable ink. Under her fingers was a crude drawing of a man in a spacesuit, waving. This sketch had been drawn at the bottom of the board, where a seven-year-old could reach. The artist had placed a big smile across the spaceman's face, and the message, "Be safe, Dad," was written above his head. Madison slid her hand to the bottom corner where the artist had signed his name with the awkward print of a second-grader, *Michael Kleigh*. Madison's eyes glassed over as she whispered, "Dad."

A pain rose in Madison's chest as she read the date on the brass plate mounted at the bottom of the display. It was January 26, 1988, the day the shuttle, Olympus, had exploded on the launch pad. She had never been given a chance to know her grandfather.

Stepping back, Madison glanced down the stark white hallway, which gave her the feeling of being in a sterile hospital. The only break in the monotonous white were the colorful collages hanging end to end as far as she could see. Each one represented another mission NASA had sent into space while the astronaut's family watched from the observation room. She took in a deep breath and continued in the direction her mother had gone.

Though her mother was able to ignore the drawings, Madison could not. She took note of the dates and mission numbers etched on the brass plates at the bottom of each board as she moseyed past. The dates continued in succession: 1989, 1990, 1991, until she recognized one of her own drawings on a board with a 2011 date. It was a stick-figure of a dog wearing a space helmet. Madison had been five years old at the time of her father's first mission.

As Madison followed the line of whiteboards around the corner, the excited voices and laughter from the observation room became louder. Hesitating in the doorway, she glanced inside before entering. Madison had been in this room before, but this time she was old enough to comprehend the dangers fully. She took in a deep breath and let it out slowly.

Though a couple dozen people were meandering about, Madison felt alone as she crossed the room. Their faces blurred as they laughed and conversed with each other. Their voices became incomprehensible echoes inside her head as she passed by. On the opposite side of the room, Madison stepped up to one of the large windows that made up the entire outer wall of the observation room. Her worried reflection stared back at her as she glared out over the Banana River.

Three miles away, NASA's latest rocket stood on its launch pad, ready to go. She could barely make out the tiny capsule at the tip of a massive booster where her Dad and the two other astronauts sat waiting for the final countdown, sitting there on top of millions of pounds of highly volatile rocket fuel.

As Madison watched through the glass, another reflection appeared behind her.

"Are you going to add a sketch to the board?" the man asked, speaking with a heavy German accent. "It's filling up."

Madison took her eyes off the rocket just long enough to look over her shoulder at the new, fifty-inch touch screen TV hanging on the wall. A few of the other children stood in front of the device, taking turns writing with a stylus.

"I was wondering how they were going to fit more drawings in that hallway." Turning back to the window, she continued. "I prefer drawing the old way. With a pencil and paper. Then hand it to the person I drew it for."

The man's eyes followed her stare until he, too, was gazing at the rocket. A flock of seagulls flew past, glistening in the sunlight. "Worried about your dad?"

Madison looked up at him. He was a tall man in his early fifties, wearing an outdated striped suit that was a little too small, "You must be the veteran astronaut

NASA assigned to our family," she said, turning back to the window.

"Yes, I'm Dr. Lauro Alazar."

"No," Madison said, finally getting around to answering his question. "I'm not worried," she continued, though she knew it was a lie. "My dad does this all the time."

"You know," Dr. Alazar continued, "You're not making my job very easy. I'm supposed to be guiding you through this day. You've been avoiding me all morning," he said, ending with a forced grin.

"Well," she said, shrugging, "I don't know why they have to assign us a helper. We've been here before, you know."

Dr. Alazar laughed. "Helper? I'd like to think I'm more important than that. I've been up there myself a few times. I understand what you're going through."

"I know," Madison said in an apologetic tone. "It's just that... well, what more can you do?"

"Let's start with what's bothering you." Dr. Alazar pulled a chair over and sat down, leaning forward on his elbows.

"I don't know," Madison stared out at the launch pad on Cape Canaveral. "I don't want him to go."

"Someone has to go," Dr. Alazar's eyes wandered back toward the rocket. He appeared to have the same concern for her father as she did. "If we want to know what's out there." He slapped his knees and spoke louder, "And your Dad is the best one for the job. That's what happens when you're good at what you do. You get chosen. But that's not a bad thing. Your Dad's a hero," he said, stretching his arms out.

"No, he's just my dad," she answered without taking her eyes off the rocket.

Dr. Alazar nodded. "That's not what the rest of the world would say," he said in a low voice.

"What missions did you go on?" Madison asked.

"What?"

Madison turned to the veteran astronaut. The man looked surprised at the question.

"I said, what missions did you go on?"

"Oh," Dr. Alazar rubbed his chin. "I was a mission specialist on two shuttle launches back before you were born. I studied the effects of zero gravity on different objects." He laughed. "Basically, I threw tennis balls around the shuttle. I made everybody mad at me. I'm a physicist with the European Space Agency."

Madison turned back to the window, sighing. "Oh," is all she said. She thought about her father and how he was about to make the most important space flight in Earth's history.

Dr. Alazar sat back in his chair. "Here," he said as he pulled a round embroidered patch from his pocket. "I saved one of these for you."

Madison took it into her hands and studied it. The NASA mission patch depicted the first crewed flight to Mars. In the center was an image of the new Excalibur, an Orion class spacecraft with Mars in the background. The names of three astronauts encircled the patch: Mission commander Brad Hankins, pilot Francis Beckman, and mission specialist Michael Kleigh. She stared at her father's name, rubbing the patch between her fingers.

Dr. Alazar glanced over at Ida, who was checking her watch. "Your mother seems a bit distracted today."

Madison looked over her shoulder again. Sitting in the last chair closest to the door, her mother fiddled with the pearl necklace adorning the front of her blouse. Madison always felt her mother dressed a little too classy. It attracted a lot of men. "She's worried about missing her hair appointment," she said.

Dr. Alazar laughed. "I guess you two are more used to this than I am. Has the magic worn off already?" Madison shrugged her shoulders, then glanced over at the chair beside her mother, where her backpack sat. It was a dark purple color with metallic blue and yellow designs depicting the twelve zodiac constellations. She never went anywhere without it.

"Excuse me," she said to Dr. Alazar and strutted across the room to retrieve her art supplies from the pack.

Dr. Alazar stood to follow but hesitated when the speaker system inside the observation suite sparked to life.

"T-minus ninety seconds and counting... All systems are go in about ninety seconds..." a monotone voice cracked.

Ida rolled her eyes when she heard the announcement. "Finally," she complained as Madison approached. The launch was supposed to have taken place two hours earlier, but some unexpected wind had kicked up that morning.

As Madison rummaged through her backpack, a waiter carrying a tray of hors d'oeuvres bumped into her mother's chair. Ida's purse fell to the floor, and the man picked it up. "Sorry, ma'am," he said as he handed it back to her. "Would you like a piece of goat cheese bread?"

"No, thank you," Ida replied as she glanced at her watch.

"As you wish," the man said. Madison noticed him slip something into his pocket as he stepped away, but didn't give it a second thought. Eager to begin her sketch, she began pulling her drawing pad and pencil set from her backpack.

Ida purposely looked the other way when Dr. Alazar approached, hoping he wasn't going to speak to her.

"Can I get you anything, Mrs. Kleigh?"

"Oh," she said, turning to the veteran astronaut. "Please, call me Ida." She glanced toward the windows.

"No, I'm good."

"You know, I don't feel like I've been doing my job very well. I'm supposed to be helping ease you through this difficult time."

"Oh, don't be foolish," she said politely. "We've been through this before. We know the drill." She turned and smiled at Madison.

"But your husband will be gone for almost a year this time. That's got to make you feel a little uncomfortable."

"Well—"

"T-minus sixty seconds and counting..." the announcer's voice came back over the speakers. Ida was glad for the interruption. Her smile fell away as soon as Dr. Alazar turned toward the viewing windows.

"Show's about to start," he said.

"Transferring power to the Excalibur's internal fuel cells at this time..." the announcer continued. "Coming up on a go for auto sequence start..."

Most of the people in the suite took their seats; some stood up near the windows. Ida glanced at her watch again.

Madison scurried back to the windows and hunched over her pad on the floor. After taking a quick glance at her subject, she began to sketch. She had drawn so many rocket launches, she could have filled an entire sketch pad with them, but this one was special.

During this mission, her father would become the first man to walk on Mars.

Dr. Alazar crouched to look over Madison's shoulder as she drew. "I've heard you like to draw. That's a very impressive likeness. I'd like to see some of your other work."

"Mm-hm," Madison replied, trying not to break her concentration.

Dr. Alazar sat back down in his chair and let out a puff of air. Madison did her best to tune him out. The announcer's voice continued to buzz over the speakers. "We have a go for auto sequence start..." Madison could feel her heart begin to race in her chest. She wanted to ignore the anxious feeling and continue her drawing, but she couldn't take her eyes off the launch pad where clouds of white vapor began pouring out of the rocket's engines.

"The Excalibur's onboard computers are now in control of all the vehicle's critical functions..." the voice announced. "T-minus fifteen seconds and counting..."

"Do you think we'll get shock diamonds?" someone asked. Madison looked to her side. It was Jason, the youngest son of one of the other astronauts. He had made his way from his seat to lie next to Madison near the windows. "I've always wondered what they did with the diamonds after the rocket launches. My brother says they use them to pay for new rockets."

"Shock diamonds aren't real diamonds," Madison said. "They're—"

"Ten... nine..." the announcer began, and the rest of the attendees in the room joined in. "Eight... seven..." Madison watched as sparks shot out under the rocket engines, burning off the excess hydrogen. "Six... five... four... Start..." A second later, the booster engines ignited. "two... one... booster ignition... and... liftoff."

Madison's eyes went wide as she watched the tremendous white plume of vapor shoot out from under the rocket engines as the craft slowly lifted off the pad.

"What do you mean, they're not real diamonds?" Jason asked.

Madison pointed at the rocket. "Look at the fire coming out of the engines. It crisscrosses itself, making diamond-like shapes."

The room suddenly filled with loud applause as corks popped from champagne bottles. Madison dropped back down to her drawing pad and began sketching again. The excitement in the room helped to alleviate her fears. She could hear Jason whining to his brother as she feverishly drew the launch. Beneath the rocket in her drawing, Madison began sketching diamond shapes.

"Matt, you lied to me. Shock diamonds aren't real. That's not how they get the money to pay for new rockets." Jason's little voice was lost in the chatter of the other attendees as he chased his brother through the crowd.

Madison could feel the vibration of the launch in her chest. Though they were inside the control center, the roar of the engines was still loud as the rocket ascended into the sky, picking up tremendous speed. She glanced out the window, imagining her father sitting inside that thing. "Be safe, Dad," she mumbled to herself.

The rocket rose into the sky, getting smaller and smaller as it gained altitude. The long white trail leading away from the space vehicle was already beginning to dissipate near the launch pad. "Solid rocket booster separation confirmed," the announcer called out. "The Excalibur is away."

Madison watched as the boosters spun off to the side. "And bring me back a space stone," she added. "A real one." Within a few minutes, the Excalibur was too small to see, but Madison kept drawing.

Suddenly a pair of stocking legs in high heels stepped up to Madison as she lay, hunched over her sketchpad. "Ready to go home, Maddy?" her mother asked.

"Just a few more minutes, Mom."

"Come now. I'm leaving," her mother said, turning to go.

"Leaving so soon?" the kind voice of Dr. Alazar stopped Ida in her tracks. He reached out with a champagne glass, offering it to her.

"Dr. Alazar, I—"

"Lauro," he said, interrupting her.

"What?"

"Call me Lauro, it's my given name."

Ida shook her head. "Look, Dr... I mean, Lauro," she waved the drink away. "I really have to go. Thank you for everything. You've been a great host." Turning to Madison, she called again, "Come on, Maddy."

Madison dragged her feet as she followed her mother to the door, leaving their astronaut guide behind.

Before they had a chance to exit, Dr. Alazar hustled up behind them. "What about dinner, then?" he called out.

Madison and her mother turned to face him. "You don't give up. Do you?" Ida chuckled.

Dr. Alazar shrugged his shoulders and stammered, "I-I'm just trying to do my job."

Ida finally dropped her ice-cold demeanor and let out a real smile. "Okay, we can have dinner." She lifted her finger. "As a professional courtesy," she said sternly.

Dr. Alazar flashed a friendly smile as he nodded.

As her mother fumbled through her purse for a pen and paper, Madison wandered over to the electronic display. The other children had already pretty much filled the screen with their inspirational messages and drawings. There were pictures of a rocket blasting off, a rainbow, an astronaut cat, and just about anything else a child's imagination could conjure up.

Madison noticed one small space still available to add her comment. It was a small area toward the bottom right corner of the display. Madison lifted the stylus and drew a picture of a man in a spacesuit, waving. She added a big dopey grin on his face and wrote the words *Be safe, Dad* above his head. In the bottom right-hand corner, she signed her name, *Madison Kleigh*.

Dr. Alazar stood by himself in the middle of the group as Madison and her mother left the room.

Idle chit chat and gossip buzzed all around Dr. Alazar. It meant nothing to him. Nothing, until one conversation caught his ear.

"They got this launch ready in record time," one of the other family members said to her guide. "I never saw anything like this happen so quickly before. Are we back in the space race with Russia again?"

"I don't know," the former mission specialist, Jack Spenser, answered. "It's all been hush, hush."

Dr. Alazar glanced away, pretending not to be interested in their conversation.

"I know they might be launching their own craft to Mars in another month or two. Do you suppose it has anything to do with that accident in Korolyov?" the woman asked. "I heard the entire town is a jungle now, literally."

"Whatever it is, they're not telling anybody. NASA has been very tight-lipped with this one. It reminds me of the Apollo days," Spenser went on. "Did you know that Russia had its own Luna program aimed at going to the moon at the same time? They launched Luna 15 three days before Neil Armstrong was the first man on the moon."

"No, I didn't know about that," the woman answered.

"It was an unmanned spacecraft that was supposed to retrieve samples and bring them back to Earth, but it crashed on the surface."

"Hmm," the woman furrowed her brow. "What kind of samples?"

"That's the question everybody's asking now," Spenser answered. "Luna 15 and Apollo 11 were so close at one point, they almost collided. It's a big moon. Too big for that to be a coincidence."

"So, what were they after?"

"I don't know. But now, everybody seems to be after something on Mars." The former astronaut paused to sip from his glass. "It's as if they're racing to get there first. I know one thing for sure. Whatever it was they had brought back from the moon... it was no ordinary rock sample."

Dr. Alazar glanced down at the piece of paper with Ida Kleigh's phone number written across it, then stepped through the doorway himself. Michael Kleigh was involved in something big. The only question was, did Ida know anything about it?

Outside in the hallway, Dr. Alazar stopped at the 1988 whiteboard and examined the drawing of the smiling spaceman in the bottom corner of the collage. Then his eyes darted to the top where another member of another family had drawn a similar picture. Only the astronaut was holding the German flag. The message written was simple: "Go, Dad!" It was signed, "Lauro."

2

The Bridge

Five months later...

Madison ran as fast as she could. The woods were dark, and the trees were casting long shadows across the forest floor. She took deep breaths, jumping over moss-covered logs rotting quietly in the dead leaves where mushrooms took root. She ran through a sea of lady ferns lit up by the few rays of sun that managed to make their way through the upper canopy. Her heart pounded in her chest, but she was determined to make it.

Pausing for a moment, she rested against a tree, looking back over her shoulder. *Did she lose them?* she wondered as she listened for their sounds. High above, thousands of cicadas sang their ponderous song, a chorus of buzzing that rattled through the woods. Though the noise was loud, it wasn't enough to mask the footsteps crashing through the underbrush. They were not far behind.

She hiked her backpack a little higher on her shoulders and pushed on. Looking ahead, Madison could see light at the forest's end. She was almost there. Picking up her pace, she kept her eyes on the ground, being careful not to trip on a rock or fallen branch as she weaved between the Pin Oaks. She didn't see the spider web hung delicately between the branches until it was too late. In a panic, she wiped the webs from her face. A terrified Micrathena Spider hung from her hair. "Ew, gross," she said to herself as she continued her run to the edge of the forest.

The sun beamed around puffy cumulus clouds as Madison burst from the trees into a field full of bright purple Loosestrife. Without slowing her pace, she continued running. Tall grass and wildflowers brushed against her legs as she hastily made her way across the field. She was almost free when she came to the edge of a stream, stopping her in her tracks. She turned in earnest, glaring back to the woods. She knew the boys were following right behind.

Breathing hard, Madison hastily dropped her backpack to the ground and pulled the zipper open to check its contents. Inside, a tiny rabbit, wrapped in a towel, shivered with fear. "Don't worry, little guy. It'll all be over soon," she whispered.

Standing at the edge of the stream, Madison glanced back and forth, trying to decide how to get across. Far to the South, she caught a glimpse of cars buzzing over the Oxford Street Bridge. To the North was a train trestle, which was a lot closer.

"There she is!" someone yelled. Madison gasped, jerking her head back toward the woods. Three boys between the ages of thirteen and fourteen stood at the edge of the trees holding BB guns in their hands. It was Harold Gordon and his gang. One of them was pointing toward her.

Madison closed her bag and pulled it onto her shoulders. Looking up at the train trestle, she made her decision and bolted toward it. Knowing the boys would be running after her, she kept a fast pace. Near the bridge, the briars were thick, pulling on her clothes and scratching her arms as she pushed her way through.

The climb to the top of the embankment was steep, making it difficult to pull herself up. Dry black dirt crumbled under her feet, causing her shoes to slide backward as she ascended the hill. Finally, she stumbled onto the ballast of the railroad tracks where the bridge began. The smell of oil-soaked railroad ties permeated her nostrils, and the stones crunched under her feet as she rushed along. She glanced back in dismay to see that the boys were already making their way through the thickets. Ignoring the danger sign, she darted onto the bridge.

Madison walked as quickly as she could, carefully watching her feet, making sure to step on the blackened ties which crossed under the metal rails. Far below, she could see the creek through the gaps between each wooden tie. Any misguided step could cause her foot to become wedged, instantly ending her plight in a bad way. On each side, rusty metal girders rose high and crisscrossed above her head. The bridge wasn't much wider than the tracks themselves, and there was no walkway of any kind. It was not designed for foot traffic. As Madison hurried across, it became apparent the bridge was much longer than it appeared. She pushed on, hopping over the wooden ties two at a time.

Unable to resist the urge, Madison took her eyes off her footing and glanced over her shoulder. She was almost across the bridge when Harold Gordon and his gang made it to the tracks and began hustling across themselves. Panicking, Madison lost concentration on her steps and miscalculated her next hop, catching her foot between the railroad ties. She went down hard, banging her elbow on the oily trusses. The boy's laughter carried across the bridge, announcing the pleasure they found in her misfortune. Eager to overtake their adversary, Harold and his friends darted forward, hopping three railroad ties at a time only to be stopped fast in their tracks by the sound of a train's air horn.

Madison jerked her head around and watched in horror as a diesel locomotive came barreling around a turn in the tracks with its whistle blaring. She pulled frantically on her leg, but her shoe was stuck fast. No matter how hard she struggled, she was unable to dislodge her foot from the crack. Turning back to Harold and his gang, she saw they were running away in the other direction, heading back to their side of the bridge.

"Guys, help me!" she yelled, but they had no interest in endangering themselves to save the girl who kept foiling their fun. Madison had to think fast. She tried again to pull her shoe free, but it was stuck tight and wrapped snug around her ankle. She couldn't even slip her foot out.

Her heart pounded as fear and panic began to set in, causing her to lose all rational thinking when she remembered what her health teacher had taught her class. When in a crisis situation, keep calm. Take a deep breath and think. There is always an easy solution to any problem. Madison breathed in deeply and tried not to think of the train speeding straight toward her.

The air horn screamed again as Madison tried to concentrate. Then a solution dawned on her. Instead of pulling up, she pushed down hard. Her foot pushed through to the underside of the bridge, taking splinters of wood with it. With her foot hanging free below the deck, she was able to reach between the beams and pull her shoe off. Without the shoe, she was able to lift her foot up through the crack with ease.

She scrambled to her feet and dashed to the end of the bridge, jumping to the side the tracks only moments before the train whizzed past. The engineer shouted something as the locomotive sped by, but she could not make out what he had said. It was for the best. She was sure it wasn't anything pleasant.

Madison sat down in the grass and put her shoe back on as the freight train clanked across the metal rails behind her. It was a long train, providing plenty of time to get away from Harold and his gang. While the boys were stranded on the other side of the stream, she was determined to get as far away as possible. Madison was off and running as quickly as she could tie her shoelace.

When Madison had traveled far enough to feel safe, she scurried behind a thick bush and sat in the shade, catching her breath. She pulled her backpack off and set it in her lap as she rested, then slowly pulled the zipper open. Inside, the tiny rabbit continued to tremble as she gently lifted it out of the pack and set it down in the grass.

"There now, you're safe. Nobody will shoot at you here." She glanced back in the direction of the train trestle. "Those boys won't be able to get across for a long time."

The terrified rabbit crept to the edge of the high grass, then tore off as soon as it felt it could get away from its captor. Madison, of course, had no intention of harming the innocent animal. Her job was to rescue it from becoming the boy's target, but the rabbit had no understanding of such things. It was alive. That was all that mattered to Madison.

As Madison sat in the shade resting, her thoughts turned to her father. He would be landing on Mars soon. At least there was one good thing about being so far from Earth, she thought. There were no bullies to harm him. However, if something did happen, there was no way she would ever be able to help. And that troubled Madison.

While the image of the rabbit was still fresh in her mind, the young artist pulled out her sketch pad and began to draw. Half an hour later, another drawing was added to Madison's collection of illustrated memories. Not realizing how much time had gone by, she peered around the edge of the bush. There was no sign of Harold's gang. *I guess they gave up*, she thought, and headed home imagining the elegant dinner her mother would have waiting for her.

3

Leftovers

Madison slipped off her backpack and tossed it onto the sofa when she entered the house. "Mom, I'm home," she called out. There was no answer. She stepped into the kitchen and grabbed a banana from the bowl of fruit on the table.

"What's for dinner?" she yelled out again. The house was silent. A bright orange sticky note hung from the fridge, catching Madison's attention. She pulled the note off and read it out loud.

"Gone out. There's leftover stew in the fridge. Heat it in the microwave. Don't eat in the living room. Be back later. Love, Mom."

She crumpled the note and threw it over her shoulder. "Yeah, right, how much later?"

Madison pulled a bowl from the cabinet and filled it with sugar puffs, added milk, and headed for the living room. She pulled her legs up onto the couch, crossing them in front of her as she relaxed into the cushions. Clicking the remote, she surfed through the channels until she found a cartoon. With her eyes fixed on the screen, she pushed a spoonful of sugar puffs into her mouth.

It was after midnight when Madison's mom pushed the front door open, giggling as she fidgeted with the key in the lock. Madison had fallen asleep with an empty box of sugar puffs at her side. Ida Kleigh laughed as she stumbled into the house, her boyfriend grabbing her waist so she didn't fall. Glancing into the living room, she noticed Madison sleeping on the couch and held her finger to her lips.

"Shhhh, she's asleep," she slurred, followed by drunken laughter. The two of them stumbled into the kitchen. "Would you like a nightcap, Jimmy boy?" she asked as she pulled a bottle of wine from the cabinet, almost dropping it on the floor.

"I think you've had enough," Jim laughed as he grabbed the bottle before it fell.

Ida threw her arms around his neck to keep from tumbling over. "I think I'd better sit down."

"I gotcha," Jim said as he pulled Ida into an embrace. Their lips barely touched when she noticed Madison standing in the doorway.

"You should be in bed," Ida said as she pulled herself to her feet, trying her best to be the mature grownup, a somewhat challenging undertaking when one was drunk.

Madison found it difficult to take her mother seriously in her current condition, but she knew it was pointless to argue with her now. She rolled her eyes and headed up the stairs to her bedroom. In her room, she could hear the muffled sounds of chatting and laughter coming from down the hall. Turning over onto her stomach, she pulled her pillow over her head, holding it against her ears to drown out the noise. As she lay in her bed, her thoughts drifted to her father, thirty-five million miles from home.

Once a week, her mother would drive Madison down to the NASA command center, where she was able to send a video message to her father. At first, they had been able to hold a conversation with only a slightly annoying delay, but later it had taken more than fifteen minutes for the signal to travel one way, which meant waiting over a half hour for a response.

Her mother did not like waiting, so she had begun to make Madison send her message, then leave without waiting for a reply. This had left her feeling empty inside. It had felt more like leaving a recording on an answering machine than having an actual conversation. She would not be able to listen to her father's response for an entire week.

While lying in her bed, Madison thought about what she would say in her next message. She would tell her father how she had foiled Harold Gordon's plans to shoot the rabbits, and about her adventures she had been having with her friend, Lou, in the woods behind their house. As Madison drifted off to sleep, she thought about the experiences her father would have on Mars and the many sample rocks he would bring back to study.

In her mind, she could see him in his white NASA space suit walking on the surface of Mars. He had that big dopey grin on his face, like the one she had drawn on the electronic whiteboard. Madison giggled in her sleep. She watched as her father bounced across Mars in the lighter gravity, taking long clumsy steps as he walked.

Suddenly, something terrible happened. A humungous twister swept down, scattering dust and sand into the thin atmosphere. Madison's father was struggling against the wind, unable to make it back to the lander. He fought the storm, one step at a time, reaching out for help. The ground began to shake, and large boulders tumbled from the mountains. One headed straight for the ship. Madison tried to yell out, but there was no air to carry her voice. The boulder came crashing down and crushed the lander as her father fell to his knees. He reached toward Madison for help, but she couldn't move. An apple-sized rock was heaved by the wind, knocking into the side of her father's helmet, shattering the shield, and exposing his face to the toxic carbon dioxide of Mars' atmosphere. She could see him gasping for air as he tried desperately to breathe.

"Madison, help me," he yelled out, but Madison couldn't answer. She tried desperately to respond to his call but was unable to get her breath. She gasped, struggling to get air into her own lungs. Finally, she jumped up from her bed, tossing the pillow off her head.

Her heart pounded in her chest as she filled her lungs with air. Sitting up, she wiped the sweat from her forehead as she looked around the bedroom. The red lights on the digital clock read 3:42am. The room was silent. There was no wind, no storm at all. She was safe in her bedroom in Florida on Earth. *But what about her father?* she thought.

Madison lay down on her back, staring up into the darkness. With thoughts of her father spinning in her head, she was unable to fall back to sleep, so she reached over and switched on her virtual planetarium. Above her, an emulation of the universe danced across the ceiling. Her eyes searched through the sea of thousands of tiny lights until she found Mars.

"It was just a dream, Madison," her mother said in frustration as she mixed up a batch of pancakes. "There was no accident. We would have been told."

"But it was so real, Mom," Madison insisted. "It was as if I were actually there."

Her mother poured the batter into the frying pan and pulled three plates out of the cabinet. "That's why they're called nightmares, Maddy. They *always* seem real."

Madison furrowed her brow. "Why three plates?"

"Oh, Jim's going to eat with us."

"He's coming back this morning?" Madison asked suspiciously.

"Not exactly. It was late, honey. I told him he could sleep here. It's just for one night."

"What would Dad say about that?"

"Nothing, he's not going to know."

"What if he finds out in his next video message?" Madison said, challenging her mother's actions.

"That's enough!" Madison's mother slammed her hand on the table. "I've had enough of your mouth, young lady. You don't know what it's like, sitting here alone day after day, waiting for him to come home while you go out and prance around with your friends. What do you expect me to do? Sit here and wait?"

"Yes," Madison answered matter-of-factly. "That's exactly what I expect. It's what I'm doing."

"You're just twelve," her mother said, stressing her voice. "You have no idea what it's like!"

"Don't tell me I don't know what it's like," Madison yelled. "I miss him too. Last night I dreamt that he died."

"Maybe that would be a good thing. Did you ever think of that?" her mother blurted out.

Madison leaped up, knocking her chair over. It fell backward and crashed to the floor. "You hate him," she cried out, letting her emotions get the better of her. "You don't love him like I do... I hate you." She bawled as she ran to the front door, repeating those hurtful words. "I hate you."

"Madison, I'm sorry. I didn't mean—." Madison cut her off, slamming the front door. She plopped onto the steps to brood.

"What's all the commotion?" Jim asked, coming down the stairs.

"Madison's upset."

"About what?"

"She doesn't like... She's not happy about..." Ida struggled with the words. "She's very attached to her father."

"Oh, I get it," Jim said as he put the pieces together. "She doesn't like me."

Ida shrugged her shoulders. "It's not that. It's just..." She shook her head. "It's a bad situation for all of us."

Jim reached over to give her a hug, but she pushed him off. "Maybe we should cool it for a while," she said, looking toward the front door.

Jim tried again. "That doesn't mean we shouldn't—"

Smoke began pouring out from under the pancake. "Damn!" Ida cried out and ran to stove, pulling the pan from the burner. She hit the switch to turn on the hood fan. "I hope you like burned pancakes."

"I'll grab a bite on the road," Jim said and kissed her on the cheek. "See you tonight?"

Ida dropped her head back and groaned.

"I'll take that as a maybe," he said as he made his way to the front door.

Closing the door behind him, Jim stepped around Madison on the front steps. She threw him a dirty look as he hurried down the front stairs. Halfway down the walkway, he turned and stepped back toward her. "You know, you could have a little more consideration for your mother. She's going through a tough time right now."

Madison looked deep into his eyes and thought for a moment. "What do you do for work?" she asked.

Jim looked to the side and back as he shifted his weight to one leg. "What does that have to do with anything?" he asked in a snobbish tone.

"Because if you had an important job, you would have answered me with pride. My Dad is a space explorer." She pointed into the sky. "He's up there right now, risking his life for all of us. Maybe you should have more consideration for him."

Jim let out a huff and shook his head. There was nothing more for him to say, so he simply turned and walked to his car.

4

Soccer

Madison walked down her street and rounded the corner near the old road heading to the soccer fields at Deerwood Park.

A girl with black hair cut very short, wearing a baseball cap backward called to her. "Madison! Over here."

"Hi, Louise," Madison answered.

"That's Lou."

"What?" Madison asked, holding her hand up to block the sun from her eyes.

"Call me Lou. I'm not Louise anymore."

"Okay... Lou, why didn't you sign up for gymnastics this summer?"

"That's girl stuff."

"But... you are a girl."

"Just because I look like a girl, doesn't mean I am a girl."

"Um... Yes, it does, unless you grew a wiener overnight, and I don't think you did."

"Well, I'm signing up for softball instead. You should too."

Madison grimaced. "No, I don't like softball."

"What about soccer, then? Lots of girls play soccer."

"I don't know."

"Come on. It won't be fun without you there."

"Okay, I guess. I don't mind playing soccer." Madison looked across the field at the other kids kicking soccer balls around disk cones. "As long as we're on the same team."

"We will be. They get us as a pair, or they don't get us at all." Lou locked arms with Madison and dragged her off to the signup table.

"Name?" the teenage boy asked as Madison stepped up to the table.

"Madison Kleigh," she answered.

"Grade?"

"Um, seventh."

The older boy looked at her funny.

"Going into eighth," she corrected herself.

"Seventh," the boy said out loud as he jotted the information onto the sheet.

"Phone number?"

Madison rattled off her home phone.

Lou stood by, stiffening her legs in excitement and hopped slightly. "This is going to be great!" she said.

"Next," the teenager called out, and Lou stepped up to the table. After recording her information, the boy pointed to a group of children. "Go over and wait in that line. The coach will tell you what to do... Next," he called out. A dark-skinned girl with black hair stepped up, and the boy continued with his mundane job. "Name," he asked the girl as Madison and Lou stepped away.

The coach blew his whistle to get the group's attention. "Okay, everybody, I want two lines here," he yelled as he motioned with his arms, signifying two parallel lines. Lou made sure that Madison was in the same line she was in, pushing another kid out of the way. The redheaded girl scowled at her.

"Sorry, this is our place," Lou apologized.

The girl stepped away, revealing the face of Chad Baggett in the other line.

"What is *he* doing here?" Lou asked.

"Who?" Madison didn't need an answer. She saw him the moment she turned around. "Oh, no! Not Chad Baggett. I guess they let anybody play here. He was with Harold Gordon on the bridge the other day."

"On the bridge?" Lou asked.

"I'll tell you about it later, she said," glaring at the boy.

It was at that moment Chad noticed Madison looking at him, and his face went sour. "What are *you* doing here, Madison? Going to save the soccer balls from being kicked around?"

Madison sneered back at him.

"All right, listen up," the coach instructed. "I'm only going to say this once."

Madison and Lou craned their necks around the line of kids to see what the coach was doing.

"You're going to take this ball, pass it between each cone, then dribble it down to the cone at the end. Turn around and kick it back to your teammate. Got it?"

Nobody said anything.

"Good." He tossed the ball to the first kid on line and chirped his whistle. "Go!"

The kid stopped the ball with his foot and began kicking it through the disk cones. The first kid on the other line did the same. They followed each other side-by-side down the field, dribbling their balls through the cones. At the last cone, they turned and kicked it back to the next person in line.

"Are you staying over tonight?" Madison asked Lou as they waited for their turn. "I have the tent all set up."

"You bet. I have my sleeping bag ready to go."

"Do you still have that game we played last time your cousins came to visit?" Madison asked.

"Yeah," Lou answered. "Do you want me to bring it along?"

"Yes. We can play it if we get bored."

"What do you mean *if we get bored?*" Lou contended. "What do you have planned for us to do?"

"Well, I think we should—,"

"Heads up!" the boy yelled after he kicked the ball to Madison, who wasn't paying attention. It was her turn, and the ball rolled right past her. Lou charged after it, kicking it back to Madison, who began her run.

She tapped the ball up to the first disc cone, then rolled it across around the second one. Spinning about, she caught it before it rolled off and kicked it lightly around the third cone. *This is easy,* she thought as she dribbled the ball around each cone. She hadn't noticed that it was also Chad Baggett's turn in the other line. He was dribbling his ball through the cones at the same time, keeping up with her.

Madison was just about through the cones when she heard Chad yell out a sarcastic "Oops!" His sudden shout took her by surprise, causing her to look over at him. He had kicked the ball as hard as he could directly at Madison. The ball whipped through the air, heading right toward her head. Without thinking, she instinctively raised her hands to protect her face and ended up slamming the ball back to him. This took Chad by surprise, since touching the ball with your hands in soccer was forbidden. The soccer ball came back at him so fast, it smacked him in the left cheek before he had a chance to block it, leaving a bright red welt that didn't go away for the rest of the day.

Though her hand was sore, Madison felt good every time she got a look at his face.

5

Shooting Star

The front flap of the tent blew gently in the summer breeze, providing an unobstructed view of the stars from Madison's back yard. The two girls lay on their sleeping bags with their faces peering out through the front of the tent, gazing up into the night sky.

"Which one is Mars?" Lou asked as she searched through billions of stars.

Madison lifted her hand and pointed toward one of the constellations. "See that group of stars?" Without looking, Madison could sense Lou's nod. "That's the Sagittarius Constellation." Madison shifted her arm to the left, pointing at a bright light that stood out from the others. "That's Mars, right there."

"Is your Dad there now?"

"No, but he should get there any day now. They've been talking about it on the news a lot. My Dad sent some pictures back, but they're all the same red mountains and craters you always see. Kinda boring, actually." Madison sighed.

Lou shifted on top of her sleeping bag, seeking a more comfortable position. "You must get tired of hearing about it all the time."

"Yeah, it's no fun seeing it only in pictures. I wish I could have a stone. One that actually came from another planet. That would be so awesome."

The girls lay in silence as they took in the immensity of space. Madison fantasized about being the only kid in school with a space stone. Everybody would want to see it.

"It's so weird," Lou spoke up. "I mean, your Dad is actually out there. One of those specks of light could be his space ship. Way out there, millions of miles away."

"Thirty-five million miles to be exact," Madison corrected her friend.

"When will he be back?"

"Sometime in December. I can't wait. I really miss him."

"Yeah, I know what you mean. I miss my Dad, too."

Madison sat up, shooting Lou a disgusted look. "You're Dad lives across town, just ten miles away." She reached down and grabbed Lou's smartphone, which had been lying between the two of them on the floor of the tent. Shaking it in her face, she continued, "You can call him right now if you wanted to."

Lou snatched the phone from Madison, "I know. I'm just saying... I know—"

"You know what? What it's like to have your father thirty-five million miles away, and he can be killed at any time? I don't think so." Madison dropped back on her sleeping bag and continued to glare into the sky.

"I just know what it's like, you know... When your Dad isn't home with you. No matter how far away he is, if he's not home, it might as well be thirty-five million miles."

Madison couldn't appreciate Lou's profound remark. To her, having your father actually that far from home was far worse. She lay on her bag staring at the bright light just to the left of the Sagittarius Constellation. Their conversation fell silent once again.

As if she would miss something important, Madison tried not to blink as she watched the tiny speck that was Mars. Suddenly a bright streak of blue broke through the darkness, carving a scar of light across the night sky. The girls simultaneously hopped to a sitting position.

"What is that?" Lou asked as the newly formed light in the sky lit up their faces.

"It's a meteor!" Madison answered, almost yelling from her excitement. "A humongous one, coming through the atmosphere."

The girls watched in amazement as the blue ball zipped along growing larger as it got closer.

"It looks like it's going to land in our back yard. Run!"

Madison and Lou leaped from the tent and ran as fast as they could across the dew-covered grass to the protection of the house, screeching as they went.

"Hurry, before it hits the ground," Madison yelled.

Stopping at the back door, the two of them turned just in time to see the light disappear behind the trees surrounding the back yard. There was a brief flash that could barely be seen through the branches, and then— nothing. Madison breathed hard as she stared across the yard into the woods. The night sky seemed darker now than it had been before the meteor went by. "That was close!"

"What are you two screaming about?" Madison's mother spoke through the screen door. The girls jumped at her unexpected appearance. Pulling the door open, they ran inside.

Out of breath, the two girls competed to get their story out. "You should have seen it," Lou gasped.

"Yeah, Mom, it was the biggest meteor ever!"

"We thought it was going to hit our tent!"

"It was so bright, it lit up the whole yard!"

"No, the entire town was lit up!"

Madison ran to the kitchen counter and pulled open the drawer closest to the broom closet and frantically rummaged through it.

"What are you doing?" her mother yelled, annoyed at the over-excited girls.

Madison spun around, holding two flashlights in her hands. "We're going to find the meteorite," she said as she backed into the drawer to push it closed. It screeched on its metal runners before crashing shut. Madison was halfway to the door before her mother could get a word in.

"Oh no you're not."

Madison spun around in disbelief that her mother did not share in her enthusiasm over finding the meteorite. "But Mom!"

"No buts," her mother insisted. "You're not going tramping through the woods in the middle of the night looking for rocks!"

Madison gestured toward the back yard. "But, this isn't an ordinary rock."

"No, it's dark, and you two need to get into your sleeping bags."

Madison began to whine as she continued to make her case. "But the meteorite will be glowing. We can find it easier now."

"I said No!" her mother yelled out over the girl's excited voices. "Do you want to sleep in your room tonight?"

"No," she said with an attitude, her shoulders drooping as she slunk to the door. "Come on, Lou," she said as she handed her one of the flashlights.

"What are we going to do?" Lou asked.

"It looks like we're not going to do anything," she said, giving her mother a sideways glance.

Lou followed Madison across the back yard to the tent, but Madison didn't stop there. Her sauntering turned into a gallop as she trotted over to the edge of the woods where trees met manicured lawn. Stopping just before going into the shadows, she switched on her light and beamed it into the darkness.

"Madison Marie Kleigh! What did I tell you?" her mother's voice boomed from the back door.

"I'm not going into the woods. I'm just looking!" Madison yelled back without taking her gaze off the circular spot of her flashlight. Her mother rolled her eyes and went back into the kitchen, mumbling something the girls couldn't hear.

Feeling uneasy about being in the middle, Lou had to say something. "We should go back to the tent, Maddy. You're Mom's going to be mad at us."

"She'll get over it," Madison answered as she peered into the woods.

"What do you think you're going to see from here?"

Madison didn't answer right away, but she kept searching the woods with her flashlight until... "Found something!"

"What?"

Madison grabbed Lou by the shoulder and pointed her flashlight at a rotting log. "Look right there, near the bottom of that old tree. See them?"

"See what?" Lou asked.

"Those lights."

Lou lowered her head and squinted. "Those two tiny lights?"

"Yeah, do you see them?"

"What are they?"

"I don't know, maybe pieces that flew from the meteorite when it hit the ground."

Madison panned her light left and right until she saw two more tiny lights. "Look, there's more!"

Aiming her light further to the left, she spotted two more. "They're all over the place," she chattered. "They must be from the meteorite!" The two girls stared intently into the woods, trying to make out what the tiny lights could be. Finally, Madison took a step off the lawn.

"Madison!" Lou called out in a loud whisper.

"Don't throw a fit. I'm not going far," Madison said as she crept further into the woods.

Lou nervously looked back toward the house. "Your Mom's never going to let us sleep outside again." When she turned back, Madison had disappeared behind a bush. "Madison!" Lou called out. "Wait up." Finally, getting up the nerve to enter the woods herself, Lou caught up to Madison just as she was bending down to get a close look at one of the shiny objects on the ground.

"Can you see what it is?" Lou asked as she crept up alongside. Madison was about to reach out and touch the object when Lou let out a deafening screech. A split second later, Madison noticed it too. The girls screamed, jumped up, and ran back to their tent.

Madison flew open the flap and dove into the comfort of her sleeping bag, burying her head deep inside. Lou followed right behind her, hiding in her own sleeping bag.

"That was the biggest spider I've ever seen!" Madison cried out from beneath the covers.

"That thing was as big as an apple!" Lou concurred as a chill ran through her spine, causing her to shiver.

"Ew! I can't believe I almost touched it. I didn't know their eyes glowed like that! I'm not coming out of my sleeping bag until morning." Madison curled her legs up and held them tight against her chest.

The two of them lay quietly for a while until Lou finally spoke up. Her muffled voice emanated from her sleeping bag, "Maddy?"

"Yeah?"

"What if one of those spiders crawled into one of our sleeping bags while we were outside?"

Madison let out a scream as she threw off the covers. She sprang out of her bag and unzipped it all the way to the bottom, tossing the top part over, exposing the entire inside of the bag. Lou did the same, shining her flashlight onto every inch of the fabric. The two girls bumped heads as they floundered with their bags. They rolled back on top of each other and laughed uncontrollably.

"Maddy?" Lou barely got her words out between gasps of laughter.

"What?" Madison giggled.

"Your..." Lou had trouble speaking through the laughs. "Your..."

"My What?" Madison laughed.

"Your Mom's here," Lou said, pointing to the frowning face peering into the tent.

Madison sobered up instantly as she sat up and faced her mother.

"Enough," her mother spat out. "I don't want to hear another word. If I have to come out here one more time, both of you are coming into the house. Do you hear me?"

"Yes, Mom," Madison said softly as she rolled back onto her sleeping bag, accidentally letting out a giggle.

"I mean it!" her mother said, trying to keep a stern face. "Here, I brought these out for you."

Madison's eyes widened as her mother handed her a small wooden box with Blue Jays and Cardinals carved into the lid. It was about twelve inches long and eight inches wide. "Thanks, Mom!"

"Now be quiet," she said as she turned to head back to the house.

"What's in the box?" Lou asked.

Madison smiled wide. "You'll see."

She undid the brass clasp and slowly lifted the lid to reveal several cut minerals set inside cutouts in foam. "My father gets these for me."

Lou's face lit up. "Space stones?"

"No, it's illegal for him to bring anything home that was collected in space. He gets these from mineral shops that he visits."

Lou crawled over to get a closer look. "What are they?"

Madison held up a light blue stone cut like a diamond. "This one is topaz."

Lou took it into her hands. "It's beautiful."

"My Dad got that for me the day before he went to the moon." Madison reached into the box and pulled out a pyramid-shaped stone of many bright colors. "This one he brought back after training for the Mars expedition. It's opal."

"These are all so wonderful. How long have you been collecting these?"

"Ever since I told my Dad that I wanted a space stone," Madison answered. "Since he couldn't get me a real one, he gets me these instead. He says the stones here on Earth are much more beautiful, anyway."

Madison pulled out a smooth, shiny black rock about the size of a large egg. It was a deep black that seemed to absorb all light.

"What is that one?"

"This is one of my favorites," Madison said as she admired the stone. "My uncle gave it to me a few years ago. He said it belonged to my great grandfather. Both he and my great grandmother were archeologists. He found it on a dig in South America. My uncle told me it was onyx. I've never seen anything so black in my life."

Madison held the stone up to the sky so that Mars glistened behind it. "These stones help me to remember my Dad when he's gone."

The black rock blended into the night sky as if it were a hole in space, engulfing the stars behind it. "It's like the stone sucks in all the life around it," Madison said. "Storing everything inside until its ready to burst out with life."

Lou looked on in amazement. "Do you think you'll ever get a real space stone?"

"Maybe, someday," Madison answered as she looked deep into the stone, allowing her imagination to take over. *Maybe, someday,* she thought to herself.

6

The Visitor

Madison's heart leaped when the little guy poked his face under the tent flap.

"Razor! Come in, boy," Madison spoke in a high pitched voice. A scruffy-looking ginger tabby cat pulled himself under the tent flap and flopped down onto Madison's sleeping bag, purring like it was the happiest moment of his life.

"You named him Razor?" Lou asked with a smirk.

"Of course. Because he has razor-sharp claws and teeth, like a mountain lion, right, my little friend?" Madison rubbed him all over, from his head down to his tail. His purr was so loud, she bet it could be heard across the yard.

He seemed happy, though she feared he was starving. Madison could feel his ribs, for he had no fat on his body at all. "He hasn't been getting enough to eat, the poor little guy."

"Why don't you adopt him, since you love him so much?"

"I want to, but my Mom won't let me." Madison continued to stroke Razor's fur as she spoke. "She hates cats. She won't even let me feed him. She says it'll just make him hang around all the time, and he'll poop in her flower beds. I told her that it's good fertilizer, but she just got mad."

Lou reached over and petted Razor on the head. He stretched out on the blankets and closed his eyes, soaking in the love and affection he rarely received.

"I have an idea," Madison said eagerly. "Are you hungry?"

"Kind of, why?"

"Let's go in and make tuna fish sandwiches."

Lou twisted her face and scrunched her forehead in disgust. "I don't like tuna fish."

Madison gestured to Razor. "You do tonight."

Lou rolled her eyes. "Can we also make PB and J?"

Madison clucked her tongue. "Sure," she said reluctantly.

Madison unzipped the tent, and the two of them slipped outside. Turning back to Razor, Madison said sternly. "You stay!" and the girls ran up to the house.

Being as quiet as she could, Madison pulled the screen door open. They tiptoed through the kitchen and began pulling things from the cabinets and refrigerator to make their sandwiches. Working in the dim lighting of the kitchen night-light, Madison slipped a can of tuna fish into the electric can opener and pushed down the handle. The machine whirled into action, making a much louder sound than she remembered. "Why is everything always so much louder at night?" she murmured.

"Madison, is that you?" her mother called from the living room.

"Just getting something to eat, Mom," but her mother didn't answer back. Madison froze. She knew that silence meant her Mom was coming in. Suddenly the overhead light flashed on.

"You're opening a can of tuna fish?" her mother asked in a grumpy sort of way.

Madison cringed.

"You don't even like tuna fish."

"Yes, I do... sometimes," Madison answered.

Her mother pulled a dish from the cabinet and picked up the jar of mayonnaise. "Here, use this bowl," she said as she opened the jar.

Trying to act convincing, Madison stammered. "I-I don't want mayonnaise."

"You're going to eat it dry?" her mother asked with a suspicious tone.

Madison nodded, "Mm-hmm."

"Okay, she said as she replaced the lid and set the jar back down. "Make it yourself, then." Turning to Lou, she continued, "What would you like, Louise?"

"I'd like a PB and J sandwich, please."

Madison's mother was pulling out two pieces of bread for her sandwich when Madison chimed in. "Could you make one for me, too?"

"I thought you were going to have tuna fish?"

"I am, but I want PB and J, too."

"That's a bit of an odd combination. What are you up to?" Her mother asked.

Madison noticed the squint in her eye. "Nothing," she lied, hoping to alleviate her mother's suspicion.

Madison's mother shook her head in frustration. She scooped out a glob of peanut butter and began spreading it across the bread, then went for the jelly. All of a sudden, a thought occurred to her. She stopped what she was doing and banged the end of the knife on the counter.

"You're feeding that cat again, aren't you?" her mother said, sounding annoyed.

"No," Madison answered, though she could tell she wasn't fooling anybody. She knew her mother could see right through her as if she was made of glass.

"Don't lie to me. I know you are." Pointing toward the back door with the knife, she continued. "That mangy thing will never go away if you keep feeding it.

I don't want that animal getting into my flowerbeds again. Besides, I won't have you wasting food." On that note, she handed the knife to Lou and turned to get a plastic container from the cabinet for the tuna fish. Lou stood there staring at the unfinished sandwiches, worried she might not be able to have one now. Madison tapped her on the shoulder. "Quick, spread the jelly on so we can go."

The girls finished making their sandwiches and high-tailed it out the back door leaving her mother to clean up the mess.

Returning to the tent, they found the cat sitting up, waiting for them. "Here you go, Razor." Madison dumped a handful of tuna onto the floor of the tent, which Razor happily scarfed down as fast as he could.

"How did you get that?" Lou asked in amazement.

"I scooped it into my hand when my Mom's back was turned," Madison answered.

"You're such a sneak."

Madison snickered as she scrunched her shoulders. "I can't help it."

In no time, Razor had eaten all the tuna fish and looked up to Madison for more.

"I'm sorry, Razor," Madison said, making her voice as sincere as she knew how to. "That's all I could take without my mother noticing." She looked at her sandwich. "Do you like peanut butter?" she asked as she peeled the bread apart. Razor licked the slice with the peanut butter clean while Madison dined on the one with jelly.

Lou lay across her sleeping bag, reclining on her elbows. "Why do you like animals so much, anyhow?"

"I don't know." Madison watched as Razor scratched behind his ear with his rear paw. "I just do. They need us."

"For what? Wild animals get along fine without us."

"That's just it," Madison pointed out. "They would be fine if it wasn't for people. It's people that make things hard for them."

"Like Harold and his gang?"

"Exactly," Madison answered as she crawled up beside Razor and parted his fur down to his skin. Several fleas scattered, burrowing themselves deeper into his scraggly coat. "Do you have that little comb with you today?"

Lou reached over and fumbled through her bag, pulling out a little red comb with fine teeth. She started to hand it to Madison but suddenly pulled it back. "You're not going to use it on him, are you?"

Madison reached out her open palm, "Just give it to me."

Lou grunted and handed her the comb. Madison ran it through Razor's fur, then pulled it up to examine the teeth. A half dozen fleas found themselves suddenly ripped from their comfortable home. Madison smashed them with her fingernail and flung them outside the tent.

"I guess you don't consider a flea's life valuable, huh?" Lou asked.

"Well, I guess you have to draw the line somewhere."

"So, Harold and his gang draw the line at small animals. You draw the line at pesky insects. Who's right?"

Madison thought for a while. "There is one huge difference, though, Lou."

"And what's that?"

"Those boys are harming the animals for fun. I'm killing the fleas to help the cat."

Lou didn't say anything more. She lay there in silence, watching Madison pull fleas off Razor. "By the way, you can keep the comb," she finally said.

7

The Hunt

Madison rolled over and stretched, letting out a big yawn. The bright morning sun beamed through the trees making its way through the nylon of the tent. She patted her sleeping bag where Razor had been sleeping, but he wasn't there. Sitting up, she looked around for the cat, but he was not in the tent. Lou, on the other hand, was still sound asleep inside her sleeping bag. Reaching over, Madison gave her a shake. "Come on, wake up. It's morning."

Lou rolled over, facing the other way. "Go back to sleep," she grumbled.

"But the meteorite. We have to find it."

Lou immediately sat up. "What about breakfast?"

Inside the house, the girls dressed and gobbled down a bowl of sugar puffs each.

"I hope nobody else is looking for it," Madison said as she poured a second bowl of cereal.

"How do we know where to find it?"

"We look for a big hole in the ground. A meteorite that big should have left a crater."

Lou stared at the back of the cereal box as her thoughts wandered, thinking about the meteorite. Something didn't feel right, but she couldn't put her finger on it. "Shouldn't we have felt the ground shake or something when it hit?"

Madison shrugged her shoulders as she shoveled sugar puffs into her mouth.

After downing her second bowl, Madison pulled out her sketch pad and flipped to a blank page. Lou leaned across the table on her elbows, watching Madison draw out a map of the area.

"This is our neighborhood," Madison said as she drew squares for houses up and down the three lanes that made up their development. "And here's the woods behind my house." Madison circled out an area of trees. Next, she drew in the fields, train tracks, and soccer park. "Okay, we saw the meteorite go down in this direction, right?"

"Yeah," Lou confirmed.

"So, that's where we start looking." Madison's finger landed on the far corner of the woods on the other side of the tracks.

Dead leaves crunched under Lou's feet as she trudged along behind Madison lugging her backpack with her. The underbrush scratched against her bare legs. "Why did I wear shorts?" she murmured under her breath.

"What?"

"I was just asking myself why I wore shorts for this," Lou answered.

Madison stopped suddenly and looked around. The sun bore down through the leaves of the trees in thin rays. Flies and gnats buzzed around her head. A hawk called out from the highest branches. Far in the distance, she could hear the sound of a lawnmower.

"Which way?" Lou asked.

Madison looked left, then right. "This way," she said and continued forward. Before long, they had come to an old rock wall that ran along the edge of the woods, marking the boundary of a large field. The girls crossed the wall and followed it north. The whole time they watched for any signs of disturbed ground but found none.

"I can't see over this tall grass," she complained. "It could be just a few feet away, and we'd never know." The field hadn't been used in years and was overgrown with briars and weeds that blocked their view.

"We have to get somewhere higher up," Lou suggested, but Madison was way ahead of her.

Pointing ahead, she called out, "The train trestle," and the two of them rushed forward through the weeds.

It was a hot day, and the heat rising from the railroad bed caused the tracks to waver as Madison glared across the trestle. She remembered clearly the previous day when her foot got caught between the ties. Looking around, she could see no reason to cross the bridge today. There were no fresh disturbances in the ground anywhere within their view.

The girls sat on the steel rails, feeling dejected that they may never find the meteorite.

"Your Mom's going to say I told you so," Lou spoke up.

"I was hoping we could say that to her," Madison said. She couldn't hide the disappointment in her voice. "I wish she would have let us look last night. It would have been easier to find in the dark while it was still glowing red hot."

"Hey, Maddy," Lou said after pondering things that were on her mind.

"Yeah."

"Who was that man at your house the other day?"

"Just some guy," Madison said as she reached down and clutched a few ballast rocks in her hand.

"What was he doing there?" Lou pressed.

"I don't know, just sleeping over, I guess." Madison tossed a rock across the tracks.

"But why? Your Mom's married."

"I know."

"Are your parents getting a divorce?"

"No!" Madison barked, giving Lou a scowl.

A dark shadow crept across the fields as a thick cloud rolled in overhead. Lou looked up into the sky. "I think it's going to rain."

"We should go back home," Madison said, dropping the stones she had picked up and began scrambling back down the raised railroad bed. The two girls dashed across the field, but not before heavy raindrops started to fall.

Madison slipped off her backpack and held it over her head as she ran into the woods. The trees blocked much of the rain, but the girls were still getting wet. They ran through the thick underbrush and crossed over the back yard of an old house.

"This is the old house at the end of the dirt road," Madison said. "We're still pretty far from home." Madison studied the rundown building. The paint had chipped away, exposing the weathered gray wood underneath. Many of the windows were broken, and the door was hanging half off its hinges. In the short time they had stood there, the rain had turned into a downpour.

"We have to go in," Madison said.

Lou looked into her eyes. Water was dripping down her face. She finally agreed with a nod, and the girls made a break for the broken door.

Inside, the place was dark and dismal. The air was thick with the smell of mildew and wet carpet. An overturned table lay against the wall. Somebody had spray-painted the words "I'm going to kill you!" across the cabinet doors.

The floor was littered with household goods that had been pulled from the cupboards and shelves, then tossed about by looters seeking anything of value. Dirtied from years of dust and rodents, everyday items were now useless junk.

Lou picked up an old toaster, and ants came pouring out. Screeching, she immediately dropped it back to the floor.

"I wouldn't go touching anything in here," Madison warned her.

The girls cautiously meandered through the kitchen. A foreboding chill trickled down Madison's spine, causing her to shiver.

"I wonder what happened to the people who lived here?" Lou pondered.

"I don't know, it looks like they just left, leaving everything they owned behind." Stepping into the living room, Madison pulled open a small door embedded into the wall. Inside were dozens of videotapes.

"Oh, cool," Lou called out. "They're old-fashioned videos. My grandma still has one of those machines that plays these. Imagine needing special equipment just to play a video?"

More junk littered the floor, including an old tube TV that someone had smashed with a rock. Water dripped through a hole in the ceiling onto an old couch sitting in the corner of the room.

"Why would somebody go away and leave all their stuff?" Madison wondered out loud as she glanced around the room. The girls crept through and entered a dark hallway at the other end. Pictures still hung on the wall of a smiling family, like ghosts who haven't the slightest idea that their happy home was now a tomb for memories.

"Maybe the house is haunted," Lou said in an eerie voice, then let out a sound she imagined a ghost would make. "Boooooooooo."

"Stop it!" Madison hissed. "You're freaking me out."

She stared at one of the pictures. A man and woman with a young child who looked to be about five years old smiled back at her.

"What's wrong?" Lou asked.

"These people," Madison cocked her head. "They look familiar."

"You're imagining things. They must be at least eighty years old by now, wherever they are."

At the end of the hallway, they came to a bedroom with windows lining two of the walls. One of them had been completely broken out, and vines now encroached upon the room, with their grabby little tentacles attaching themselves to the ceiling and walls.

This room was also littered with old household items. Clothing, blankets, and books were scattered across the floor. In the corner was an ominous dark closet with its door hanging partially open.

"Maybe space aliens came down and abducted everybody," Lou suggested.

"No, I don't believe in space aliens," Madison said as she stepped over a dirty mattress, partially leaning against the wall.

"That's hard to believe, knowing about what happened in Russia."

"That wasn't space aliens," Madison snapped.

"Are you sure?"

"No, it was vines that grew out of control from some experiment."

"Yeah, vines that your Dad brought back from the moon."

Madison rolled her eyes. "He didn't bring any vines back. It was just rocks. I should know. He is my Dad."

"Yeah, vine-spewing alien rocks," Lou jested.

"We don't know that for sure."

"Maybe," Lou continued, "but you have to admit, our government is involved in some pretty weird stuff. Things that your father probably can't even tell his own family."

"I don't know," Madison argued. "My Dad wouldn't lie to me."

"Well, your father probably didn't know about it. He wasn't there when the vines went crazy and strangled all those people. It grew through the entire town before they were able to stop it, you know."

Madison thought about the meteorite they were looking for. "Imagine if the meteorite that landed here last night was like the one they had in Russia?" She studied the vines now growing through the broken window and began to imagine the accident at the Russian space laboratory. "And now the vines are coming to attack us," she whispered, wide-eyed.

"Quick, grab something to defend yourself." Madison looked around and picked up an old broom handle. She began swinging it at the vines. "Get back, you evil space plants. I have a sword, and I'm not afraid to use it!"

Lou looked around for something she could use as a weapon too. She picked up an old broken bed slat. "Yeah, well, I have a chain saw," she yelled out, making the sounds of a gas motor. "Varoom! Varoom!"

Together the girls attacked the wild plants, pretending they were sentient creatures that were after them. They beat on the sides of the old window frame with their sticks, sending broken leaves and stems through the air.

"Oh, no!" Lou yelled. "It got my chainsaw!" She tossed her board out the window and ran toward the closet. "Quick, run and hide!" she shouted as she grabbed the knob and threw the door open.

As the door flung wide, a giant creature jumped at her, flapping its wings hard. Lou screamed in terror as she fell back to the floor. Madison let out a shriek herself, bending low and covering her head as a humongous owl swooped around the room. Panicking and screaming, the girls huddled in the corner until the monster escaped through the vine encircled window frame.

"Is it gone?" Lou whispered as she slowly lowered her arms from her head.

Madison cautiously looked up and glanced around the room. Her cheeks felt hot, and her heart pounded in her chest. Suddenly she began to giggle. "That was awesome!" she exclaimed as she broke out in laughter.

Lou began to laugh too.

"You should have seen your face!" Madison squeaked out between gasps, pointing at Lou.

"That wasn't funny," Lou said even though she couldn't stop laughing herself. "I almost had a heart attack," she choked out.

The two girls sat on the floor until they were able to calm down enough to continue their quest. They made their way into a second bedroom where the sun beamed through holes in the old curtains.

"I think it stopped raining," Madison said. "The sun's out again." She stepped up to the dirty glass and peered out. Lou followed, stepping over more junk on the floor.

Suddenly, Madison gasped and dropped to her knees. She reached up and pulled Lou to the floor by her side. "Get down," she warned.

"What's wrong?" Lou asked. Her question was answered when she heard the voices.

Hidden below the windowsill, Madison stealthily raised her head to get a glimpse of the outside. "It's Harold and his bullies," she said.

"Did they see you?"

"No, they don't know we're in here."

"Good. I don't want to face them after what happened at soccer practice. They're all pretty mad at you."

"I know. Maybe they'll go away. There are no animals to shoot in here." She glanced toward the bedroom. "Not anymore."

The distinct sound of an air rifle being pumped caused Madison's heart to race. "They must have found something to shoot at," she whispered.

Madison was about to raise her head to look out the window again when the glass pane shattered, spraying shards into her hair. She retreated lower to the floor and pulled Lou down with her. Seconds later, another windowpane blew out.

"They're shooting out the windows," Lou said. "What are we going to do?"

"Quiet," Madison ordered. "I have an idea. Follow me." She rolled over and shook the glass out of her hair as another BB burst through another windowpane. They could hear the boys laughing outside as they pumped up their guns.

Madison and Lou crawled through the living room into the kitchen, out of sight of the windows. There they stood up and scrambled over the twisted back door. Once outside, they ran through the overgrown back yard and into the woods behind the house. The boys never knew they were there.

8

For the Love of a Cat

Madison and Lou walked down the old road together, laughing as they recalled their adventures of the day.

"I can't believe there was actually an owl living in the closet," Lou laughed.

"I know, right? And the rain, what was that all about?" Madison laughed. "It poured for like, five seconds, and then the sun came back out. If it weren't for that, we never would have even gone into that—"

Madison stopped short. Her eyes were fixed on the road ahead. "Razor?" she took one step forward, then another as she gazed at the orange and white fur lying in a heap on the side of the dirt road. She hoped he was just sleeping, or it was some other animal, but deep down inside, she knew. Madison's short steps turned into a run, as her heart pounded. She dropped to her knees beside the lifeless animal.

"Razor?" Madison could feel pain welling up inside her chest as she reached for her friend. "Please, no..."

Lou ran up and knelt beside her. "Is he...?"

Madison ran her hand over his fur. "He's cold." The tears welled up in her eyes. "Razor," she moaned, barely getting her words through her tightening throat. "No!" She buried her hands in his fur. She could feel every rib and his shoulder bone. Razor lay there with his eyes closed and tongue hanging out.

"Maddy?" Lou reached out to her, but Madison refused to be comforted.

"I tried to..." Madison said, gasping for air as her sobs became audible. "I tried, but nobody would let me," she cried out. "I tried!" the tears ran down her cheeks. "All they had to do was give him a little food." She looked up at Lou. "Why was that so hard?" Kneeling in the dirt, Madison kept stroking the cat, wishing she had done something more.

"Maybe it wasn't that," Lou said. "Maybe Harold's gang got him."

"Look at him!" Madison yelled through her sobs. "Do you see any blood?" Her tears dropped down onto Razor's fur. "I could have saved him." She caressed his head in her hands. "You're a good kitty, you are," she spoke to him as if he were still alive. "You're a good boy. You're going to be okay." She slid her hands under his body and cradled him in her arms. "You're going to be okay." He was light, much lighter than she had expected him to be.

"What are you going to do?" Lou asked.

Madison looked up, her face wet with tears. "We have to bury him."

Lou looked around. "How? We don't have a shovel."

"Get me a flat stone." She nodded to the side of the road. "There's one over there."

Madison dug into the ground with a sharp rock, scraping deep into the sandy dirt. "All she cares about is her stupid flowers, and getting her hair done, and her clothes, and other things that don't matter. She doesn't care about anything that matters, like cats that are starving, and people who are traveling through space right now."

Madison sat back and sniffed, wiping her nose. She glanced over at Razor's body. "All she had to do is let me feed him a little food," her voice squeaked.

"Maybe he was hit by a car," Lou suggested.

Madison glared at her. "It's a dirt road to an abandoned house that nobody uses."

Lou shrugged her shoulders, "I was just thinking…"

"Thinking what?"

"That maybe he didn't starve to death."

Madison didn't answer. She gently lowered Razor's body into the hole and covered him up. She took one of the flat stones and scratched his name across the front of it, then stuck it into the ground as a memorial stone.

She could feel Lou's stare, but she couldn't look back at her.

"Maddy?" Lou gently reached out to touch her friend.

Madison turned away to hide her face and started walking down the old road toward their neighborhood.

Lou ran after her. "Maddy?" She grabbed Madison's arm, forcing her to turn and face toward her. Madison was unable to hide her tears. The pain she felt inside was too great. Lou didn't say a word. She just stared back.

Madison covered her face with her hand, turned, and ran. Lou let her go. She stood there in silence and watched her friend run toward home.

Jim glanced around the kitchen, taking note of the closets and drawers.

"You seem preoccupied," Ida said as she picked up her mug of coffee.

Before Jim could answer, the front door swung open and Madison ran inside.

She stopped short on her way to the staircase and glared at them, her face wet with tears.

"Did you find the—" her mother said before noticing her daughter's shattered look. "Madison, what's wrong?"

Madison paused for a moment but was unable to speak without sobbing. She ran up the stairs and slammed her bedroom door closed.

Jim looked across the table at Ida. Right away he could see the concern on her face. "Perhaps you'd better go up and find out what happened," he suggested.

Ida nodded. "I'll be back."

Jim's eyes continued searching the room as Ida left the table and headed upstairs. He could barely hear her voice as she spoke to Madison through the door. "Madison, what's wrong?" Ida asked.

"Just go away!" Madison cried.

Down in the kitchen, Jim stood up from his chair and walked to where he could hear better what was happening upstairs. As he stood in the archway to the hall, he peeked over at the china cabinet. Three drawers lined the front of the hutch.

Nonchalantly, he reached over and pulled one open. Inside were papers and envelopes. Jim glanced quickly up the staircase, then went to work digging through the drawer. Not finding what he was looking for, he went to the next drawer and rummaged through that one, then the third.

He moved stealthily to the hallway closet, like a burglar looking for valuables. After giving a quick look up the stairs again, he pulled open the door and dug through the items on the top shelf, pulling down box after box to search them.

Ida's voice carried down the stairs. "Dinner will be ready in an hour," she said through Madison's door.

"Come down when you feel better, Okay, hon?" Madison didn't answer.

Jim could hear Ida's footsteps and quickly shoved the last box back on the shelf. He closed the door and scooted over to meet her at the bottom of the stairs. "How is she?" he asked, pretending to be concerned.

"I don't know what to do. She's been acting strange ever since her father left."

"That's not surprising." Jim glanced up the stairs. "She misses him."

"I know. I just wish she could adjust. It's tearing her apart inside."

Madison never left her room to join her mother for dinner. Instead, she had fallen asleep in her clothes on top of her blankets, but her sleep was not peaceful. She tossed and turned as nightmares tormented her, racing through her mind.

In her dreams, Razor was dying of hunger. Madison tried her best to feed him, but every can of tuna fish she opened was full of dirt and vines grew out of them as soon as she got the top off. They wrapped themselves around her legs so she couldn't move. Chopping at them with a knife, she was unable to free herself and save the cat. Before her eyes, a giant owl swooped down and carried Razor away.

It was about midnight when Madison jumped awake. She sat in the dark, thinking of the ill-fated cat. The faint voices rising from the TV downstairs were soothing, but she could not get back to sleep.

Across the room, Madison's sketchpad and pencils lay on top of her desk. She crossed in the dim light and clicked on her desk lamp as she pulled herself into the chair. At first, the light hurt her eyes, causing her to squint, but they adjusted, and Madison opened her pad to a blank page. Careful to choose just the right color, she selected a pencil and started to draw.

When she closed her eyes, she could see Razor as if he were standing in the room with her. She remembered every detail—the way his darker bands of ginger fur made a swirling pattern on his sides and formed an *M* above his eyes, the white on his nose and the tip of his tail. She could even see the soft fur over his white paws and how his green eyes sparkled in the sun. She colored each and every detail on the paper, drawing a cat that made you believe it was alive.

The clock glared brightly in the darkness displaying 2:33 AM across its face when Madison colored in the last band of fur. She never noticed that the TV downstairs had gone silent. Sitting back in her chair, she marveled at the picture. It was Razor. Without a doubt, probably the best picture she had ever drawn. But it wasn't enough. Madison picked up a pair of scissors and thought, "Should I?" She did. She cut the image out of the background.

"There," Madison said, satisfied with her work. "Now, you'll live forever."

Ida was awake and making coffee at six-thirty. Still in her bathrobe, she strolled out to the bright yellow newspaper box by the road.

"Mrs. Kleigh?"

Ida heard Lou's voice and turned around. Lou was sprinting across the street toward her.

"How is Maddy?"

"She's still sleeping. What happened yesterday? Did you two have a fight?"

"She didn't tell you?"

"No, she wouldn't talk last night. She just ran up to her room, crying."

"Oh," Lou broke eye contact, looking off to the side. A mourning dove cooed in the distance. "She... she was very upset."

"Upset about what?" Ida asked.

"The stray cat, Razor."

Lou didn't have to say anything more. Ida could deduce what had happened, but she had to ask. "What about the cat?"

"He's dead." Lou took in a deep breath to force the rest of her words out. "We found him yesterday in the woods."

"I'm sorry, Louise," Ida said sincerely. "I'm so very sorry." She glanced up at Madison's bedroom window and frowned. "This is going to be a tough one," she said under her breath.

Looking back at Lou, Ida felt she should say something that would explain herself. "She'd have every stray in the neighborhood living in our house if I'd let her..."

"Yes," Lou said with a nervous laugh.

Ida sighed. "I'll go and talk to her." With that said, she turned and headed back toward the house.

Lou looked up at Madison's window for a moment, then ran off down the road.

Upstairs, Ida slowly pushed open the door to Madison's bedroom. She was sound asleep, tucked under her covers with the cutout of her cat drawing lying on the bedspread at her side. Ida chuckled under her breath. Without making a noise, she walked across the room and sat on the edge of the bed. Madison didn't stir. Ida reached over and gently stroked her daughter's hair.

"You don't realize how much I love you," she said softly. "It's just that... well..." Ida let out a puff of air.

"You can be so hard-headed at times. You take after your father. It's no wonder you love him so much." She sat, watching her daughter sleep. "I promise you, Maddy. I promise you, I love you even more."

Madison sighed as she shifted in her sleep, curling up under the covers. "And... I'll never let any man get between us. Never. I promise you that." Ida bent over and kissed Madison on the forehead. "I love you, Madison Marie... with all my heart."

9

The Gift

The week dragged by, giving Madison time to recuperate from the shock of losing Razor. She romped down the stairs in good spirits, for it was her birthday, and she was turning thirteen.

"When are they getting here?" she asked her mother. Her eyes were wide with excitement.

"I told everybody two o'clock. You have an hour."

Madison grunted at the ceiling. "Why is time going so slow today?"

"Why don't you go in the living room and draw a picture or something," her mother suggested. "Just stay out of my way... unless you want to blow up balloons."

"No, Mom. No balloons. Balloons are for babies."

Madison dragged herself into the living room and plopped down into an armchair. She pulled her sketchbook from her backpack and began to draw. Before long, a beautiful picture of a blue butterfly with orange circles outlined in black filled the page.

Losing herself in her art, she hadn't noticed how much time had slipped past. The ring of the doorbell pulled her back to reality. Tossing her drawing pad to one side, she ran to the door and threw it open.

Lou and her mother stood on the front stoop. Her friend held a brightly colored package in her hands. "Hello, birthday girl!" she shouted.

"Good, you're early." Madison grabbed her by the arm and yanked her into the house. "Let's go to my room."

"Uh, Madison," her mother called out as the two girls raced past toward the stairs.

Madison spun around on the bottom step and leaned over the banister. "Yes, Mom?"

"You have other guests coming. Don't hide away in your room."

"I won't," she shouted as she ran up the stairs. Lou jammed her gift into Ida's hands and followed.

Ida shook her head as she walked to the door to greet Lou's mother, Karen. Like Lou, her mother had dark hair cut short, but she was dressed very much like a woman—a beautiful woman at that.

"Thanks for coming early to help set up, Karen," Ida said.

"Oh, it's no problem. I have to deal with this by myself all the time, ever since Lou's dad and and I split up. You're lucky, this is only temporary for you. Michael will be back in a few months, right?"

Ida gave a nervous smile and nodded her head.

An hour later, seven preteen girls were storming through the house. Karen lifted the cake high as one of the girls rushed past her in the narrow hallway, being pursued by another who was *it* in a hot game of tag.

"Watch it," Karen announced. "Cake coming through." She made her way to the dining room and set it down on the table near Ida. It was a yellow cake with chocolate icing and had a shooting star across the top.

"This was so much easier when she was five," Ida said, reminiscing birthdays of years past. "A few balloons, pin the tail on the donkey, a piñata, and they were happy as can be. Madison turned her nose up at everything I suggested," she complained.

"Just feed them cake and let them go. That's all you can do at this age. They find their own entertainment." Karen said as she hung a giant yellow star from the overhead light.

"What is that for?" Ida asked.

"It's something I read about in a magazine," Karen answered. "Everybody writes down a wish or blessing, folds it up and puts it in this bowl, under the star. After the birthday girl blows out all the candles, she gets all the wishes. She reads each one out loud to everybody. Sometimes they're amusing. Sometimes they're touching."

"How adorable," Ida started to say but was suddenly interrupted by her daughter.

"Mom. Mom!" Madison shook her mother's arm.

"What?"

"Here," Madison handed a piece of paper and a pen to her mother. "We're having a selfie photo scavenger hunt. I want you to write down ten selfie pictures that we have to take while doing something funny or gross." She ran to get more paper to make copies of the list. "And make it hard!"

Ida looked at the blank piece of paper and shrugged. "I don't know what to put on this list."

Karen motioned with her hand, "Oh, oh, put down, *eat a bug.*"

"What? That's disgusting!"

"No, it's fun. They don't have to actually eat the bug, just pretend they are while they take the picture."

Ida laughed, "Okay, if you say so." The first thing she wrote down was *eat a bug*. She tapped the pen against the table while trying to think of another idea.

"I'm not very good at this," she said, gazing at the cake, trying to come up with something creative. Suddenly a giant smile stretched across her face, and she wrote down the second item. "Got it!" she announced.

"What did you write?" Karen asked.

"*Smash cake into your face*," she answered with a snicker.

"Now you're getting it! Here's one, *flying on a broomstick.*"

Ida laughed as she jotted down the third idea. "*Feet can't be touching the floor*," she added.

Karen laughed.

Ida continued adding creative selfies until she had one item left to fill.

"I'm out of ideas," Ida said.

"Let me see what you have so far."

Ida pushed the list across the table to Karen. She chuckled as she read down the page. "*Something sticking out of your nose!*"

Ida stared at the paper star Karen had hung from the light. "Wish upon a star," she said softly. "Selfie pose, selfie pose, selfie pose," she kept repeating, trying to think of an idea. Suddenly it hit her. Sitting up abruptly, she shouted out, "I got it." She snatched the paper from Karen and wrote down the last item.

Madison heard her mother shout and came running into the dining room. "Did you finish?"

Ida passed the paper to her daughter, and she read through the list. "Really, Mom? A selfie with a meteorite?"

"It's on the list. You have to do it."

Madison tipped her head back and rolled her eyes, dropping her hands to her side. She turned to her friends. "Come on outside, everyone," she commanded.

"How are we going to get a selfie with a meteorite?" Lou asked.

"Just get any old stone, she won't know the difference."

From the dining room window, Ida watched the girls run back and forth across the back yard with their cell phones in hand. "That'll keep them busy for a while."

"Good," Karen said. "I can use a break."

That break was short-lived. Before long, the girls were back and ready for cake. Ida lit the candles, and the girls all sang the birthday song. Madison took a deep breath, and every candle was out in one blow.

"Read the wishes," Karen said.

"What?"

"You blew out all the candles. Now you have to read all the wishes that we wrote down for you. They'll all come true now."

Madison pulled the first paper from the bowl and unfolded it, "*I wish that Madison won't get fat eating all her cake!*" She dropped her hands to the table and groaned. "Who wrote that?"

One of the girls giggled as she raised her hand.

Madison looked at her sideways as she pulled another balled up piece of paper from the bowl. She unfolded it and read the note, *"I hope Madison will become rich and famous."* Madison nodded with a smile in agreement with that one.

The next one she read said, *She will get good grades in school and go to college and get a good job.* Madison looked over at her mother. "Thanks, Mom!" she said sarcastically.

Ida shrugged her shoulders. "How did you know that one was mine?"

Madison rolled her eyes, "Really?"

One by one, she read each note. There was laughter or cooing after each wish until there was just one left.

Madison pulled out the paper, folded into a very tiny ball. It took her a while to open the many folds. "Okay, this one better be the best, because it was the hardest to open. Hoping for a good wish, she began to read. "I wish that Razor would—"

Madison stopped suddenly and looked directly at Lou. The room got deathly quiet.

Her mother took the paper from her and finished reading it softly. "—come back to life."

Everybody looked at Lou.

"I didn't know that you would be reading them out loud," Lou said. "I'm sorry."

"That's okay," Madison said. "It was a good wish."

"Time for presents," Ida announced, attempting to snap everybody out of the sullen mood. She carried over the largest present of the bunch and set it in front of Madison.

There was no standing on ceremony this time. She tore right into the wrapping paper and pulled out a lifelike figurine of a horse. "Thank you..." Madison pointed from girl to girl until one of them acknowledged that the gift was from her. Then Madison shouted out, "Lizzy!"

Her mother shot her a scowl as she pointed to the card that Madison ignored. "If you had read the card, you'd have known who it was from."

Madison paid no mind to her mother and tore open the next gift.

Ida looked over at Karen and shook her head. Karen shrugged.

The last present was a shirt. She held it up to her chest for a picture. "Thank you, Melissa," she called out and looked around for more presents.

"That's all of them," her mother said just before remembering the package that came in the mail. "Wait! I think there's one more."

Madison looked up with a surprised look on her face. "More?"

Her mother placed a plain old brown box on the table plastered with strange foreign stamps.

"Who is it from?" Madison asked.

"Now you want to know who it's from. You weren't concerned about who brought your other gifts," her mother moaned.

"Yeah, but I knew they were all from somebody here." Madison looked at the package, "But this is more like a mystery."

Her mother spun the box around to read the address. "That's funny," she said, puzzled.

"What?" Karen asked.

"There's no return address." Ida glanced up at Karen. "Take a look at this." She pushed the package toward Lou's mother. "Are those Russian stamps?"

"I think so. That looks like the Kremlin."

Ida pulled the package back. "M Kleigh," she read out loud. "I'm sorry, Madison, this might be for your father."

"But it came on my birthday. Who would send a package to Dad on my birthday, when he's on his way to Mars?"

Ida sat back in her chair and thought for a moment. "I don't know," she said, shaking her head. "Okay, open it up, and if it's not for you, we'll put it away for your father."

Madison's excitement grew as she snatched the package back and tried to dig her fingernails into the tape.

"That'll never work as long as you keep biting your nails," her mother said as she reached over with a knife.

Madison waited impatiently as her mother cut through the tape. "Don't get your hopes up. This could be boring documents or something."

"I don't think so, Mom. Those come in large envelopes," Madison said as she pulled the cardboard flaps open. Styrofoam peanuts spilled onto the table as she lifted a light blue, plastic chest from the box.

Her mother dug through the packing for a note or card as Madison fiddled with the latch on the front of the chest. She looked over at Karen and shrugged her shoulders. "Nothing," she said.

Finally, the plastic fastener popped free, and Madison lifted the lid. Inside the box, cradled in foam which had been hollowed out to fit the object snuggly, was a black stone about the size and shape of an egg.

"What is it?" her mother asked.

"It's a stone."

"Let me see."

Madison spun the chest so her mother could get a better look. She reached in and pulled it from its pouch. "It's heavy," she said, looking over at Karen.

"What is it?" Karen asked.

Ida studied it carefully. "Just what Maddy said it was, a stone." She held it out for Karen to see.

"It looks like obsidian."

"It's onyx," Madison said. "I have another one just like it. Uncle Robert gave it to me. It belonged to granddad."

Her mother ran her finger over the smooth surface. "It's polished. It would be perfect if it weren't for this chip in it."

"Chip?" Madison asked. "What chip?"

Her mother handed over the stone for Madison to examine. "Do you think it got damaged in shipping?"

Ida poked at the packing peanuts. "I don't think so. It was well packed. That stone was chipped before it was sent to you."

"Oh, here's something," Madison said, lifting a small brown card out of the little chest. *"This is a very special stone. Keep it safe,"* she read out loud.

"Who's it from?" her mother asked.

"It doesn't say."

"Give it to me," Ida said, taking it from Madison. She turned it over in her hand. "Huh," she mumbled. "No name."

"Could it be from Dad?"

"I don't know Madison, maybe we should put it away until he gets home."

"Until he gets home?" Madison whined. "That's not for another five months. It's *my* birthday. Everybody knows I collect stones. Why would they send a stone to Dad?"

"Okay," her mother shrugged. "It's just a stone, but do what the card says, okay? Keep it safe. And I want it back in this box and put in a safe place when you're done with it, understand?"

"Uh-huh," Madison nodded as she took the stone, cradling it with both her hands. The other girls gathered around her.

"Do you think it's a space stone?" Lou asked.

"I'll bet it is. That's why it was so protected inside the foam."

"Wow! Can I hold it?"

"Be careful, don't drop it."

The girls passed it around, each one adding their suspicions as to its origin.

Becoming bored with the stone, Melissa chimed up, "Let's play tag again," and the girls all bolted for the back door.

Once outside, each of them began calling out, "Not it," and ran off. Madison and Lou both called, "Not it," at the same time and ran away together, crying out, "Lizzy's it! Lizzy's it!" Accepting the challenge, Lizzy went off chasing her friends to try and tag them.

Lou and Madison raced around the house and ducked behind a shrub. While hiding, they took the opportunity to study the stone again.

"Do you think this was one of the samples my Dad brought back from the moon, and he was able to sneak it to me? He knew I wanted a moon rock. I practically begged him for one."

"How could that be?" Lou objected. "Weren't all those samples destroyed in the accident?"

"Maybe he got this out *before* that happened."

"Then why didn't he just bring it back with him? Face it, Maddy. It's just an ordinary stone," Lou said with a smirk.

Madison sat staring at the egg-shaped orb, wondering if there was anything noteworthy about it. If she had been more concerned with the game she was part of, she would have heard Melissa's heavy footsteps coming around the house. Lou heard them and crammed in closer behind the shrub to keep from being seen. In doing so, she bumped Madison's arm, and the stone tumbled to the ground.

"Hey, watch it," she said in a loud whisper.

"Sorry." Lou picked up the stone, brushed it off, and handed it back to her friend.

Madison grumbled, "You got it dirty," she said, and took in a deep breath to blow it off.

Lou's eyes bulged as she watched the stone glow a bright blue when Madison blew on it. The chip in the stone snapped and crackled as surges of energy arched across its surface.

Instinctively, Madison pulled her hands away, and the stone fell back to the ground.

The egg-shaped onyx hit with a thud, sending energy waves across the dirt. The area glowed blue for several seconds, then all went dark, including the stone. The two of them stared at the black rock.

"Lou," Madison said without looking away.

"Yeah."

"I don't think it's just an ordinary stone."

As Madison and Lou crouched in their hiding place, they could hear the other girls talking.

"Everybody's tagged except Louise and Madison," Lizzy yelled. "Let's get them!"

"Where are they?"

"I saw them run over here someplace, near the bushes."

Madison looked Lou in the face. "We can't tell anybody about this. Got it?"

Lou nodded.

Madison continued, "Ask if you can spend the night. We'll sleep out in the tent again. We'll figure this all out then, okay?" she said quickly before their hiding place was discovered.

"Okay," Lou agreed.

Madison slipped the stone into her pocket.

"I found them, I found them!" Lizzy yelled as she ran toward the girls. "They're hiding behind the bushes."

Madison and Lou scrambled to their feet and dashed away. On the ground where the stone had fallen, several green stems rose up from the dirt. They twisted and turned, growing fast, reaching a foot tall in only seconds. Leaves sprouted from the stalks and buds sprang out of the tops of each stem, bursting open into bright red flowers with blue centers. In less than a minute, several flowering plants now stood where the girls had been hiding.

10

Late Guest

Ida looked on as Madison and her friends watched a videoed "Happy Birthday" message from her father that NASA had sent over. She was hoping Madison's father would reveal that he had sent the stone in the mail, but that moment never came. Little by little, parents returned to pick up the girls until only Lou and Madison were left. By that time, even Karen had gone home. Madison's fingers drummed the top of the blue plastic box with the stone stored safely inside. It was obvious the girls were anxious to start their sleepover in the tent outback.

"We're going out to the tent now, Mom," Madison announced as the girls made their way toward the back door. Tired from the hectic day, Ida waved them on, and the girls raced to the back yard. When Ida finally had a chance to relax, the front door pushed open, and Jim popped his head in as he knocked.

"Where have you been all day? I could have used your help."

Jim pushed the door closed. "And be tormented by little girls? I don't think so." He pulled a bouquet of yellow roses and daisies from behind his back. "I brought you something."

"Great. Just what I needed, something else to do."
Without getting up, she pointed to the kitchen. "There's
a vase in the cupboard."

"How is Madison doing today?" he asked as he
pushed the bouquet into the vase.

"She's much better. I think she's finally over the
whole cat thing." Ida sat up from reclining on the couch.
"She got a stone in the mail today. That made her
happy."

"Oh," Jim suddenly became very interested. "What
kind of stone?"

"Madison says it's onyx."

"I'd like to see it."

"Good luck prying it out of her hands," Ida
snickered.

Jim glared through the kitchen window at the little
tent set up in the back yard. It glowed in the dark from
the battery-powered lantern inside, casting the girl's
shadows across the side of the canvas.

"Cold, dead hands," he said under his breath.

11

The Power Within

Lou jumped onto her sleeping bag, which was spread out on the floor of Madison's tent in the back yard. "Come on, let's see the stone again."

Madison reached over and pulled the small plastic blue box to her side. She gently lifted the lid and wrapped her fingers around the stone, treating it like a fragile egg as she lifted it from its foam cradle.

Lou snuggled up closer, crossing her legs under and walking on her knees. "Let me see."

"Be careful," Madison warned, anxious that her friend might damage her new gem. She reached over and pulled her original onyx stone from her collection of rocks to compare the two together. "Look," she said to Lou. "They're almost identical."

Lou took the new stone into her hands and rubbed her thumb over the damaged area. "They would be if it wasn't for this chip."

She raised the stone to her mouth and blew on it gently. The side that her breath warmed lit up blue. She spun the stone between her fingers as she blew, attempting to make the entire stone turn color. After blowing around the circumference of the rock, she held it out in her palm and watched in amazement as the blue slowly faded to darkness.

Madison laughed, then took the stone to repeat the action herself. The stone glowed blue for several seconds except where her fingers blocked her breath. "Maybe it's magical," she suggested.

"How would it work?"

The two girls stood on their knees, huddling over the stone. "Make a wish," Lou suggested.

"Okay," Madison took a deep breath and blew until the entire stone glowed bright blue, then began, "Stone, I wish for ice-cream." They sat back, looking around as if they were expecting a brick of vanilla ice-cream to drop from the sky.

Suddenly the flap of the tent pulled back, causing the girls to scream.

"What on earth is wrong with you two?" Madison's mother said in an annoyed tone. "You're going to wake up the neighbors."

"Sorry, Mom, we were just waiting to see what was going to happen. You see, I just—"

"Here," Madison's mother interrupted, "I brought you ice-cream sandwiches."

Madison's eyes went wide as she continued what she was going to say, "—wished for ice-cream."

Madison's Mom went on, apparently not hearing what she had just said, "Be careful not to make a mess. If you get cold, come in and sleep on the living room floor." She pulled herself out of the tent. "And be quiet out here," she said as she stood to leave.

Madison and Lou stared at each other. Two ice-cream sandwiches lay on a plastic plate between them. Madison opened her fingers, not realizing how hard she was clutching the stone. "Do you think?"

"No, it can't be. It's just a coincidence."

"Yeah, just a coincidence," Madison agreed, and the two of them devoured their ice-cream sandwiches.

Madison lay back on her sleeping bag with the onyx stone balancing on her fingertips.

"Maybe it *is* magic," Lou said, hoping with all her heart. "After all, it is from space, right?"

"Yeah, but that doesn't mean anything. After all, Earth is in space, which means all the stones here are actually from space, in a way. And they're not magical."

"Well," Lou interrupted, "I've never seen any Earth stone glow when you blew on it."

Madison held the stone up as the two of them stared at it.

"Maybe we have to say the right thing, like a rhyme or something," Lou suggested.

Madison sat up and held the stone out in front of her. "Black stone that came from Mars, I wish I had a... had a..." She smacked Lou on the knee. "What's something good that rhymes with Mars?"

"I don't know, stars, cars, candy bars—"

"Okay, okay, here goes." Madison swallowed hard. "Black stone that—"

"No, no, you have to blow on it first."

"How do you know? It's not like you ever had a stone from space before," Madison growled.

"Then, why does it glow when you blow on it? Maybe that's how you get its powers working."

"Okay, here goes..." Madison blew on the stone, causing it to glow blue. "Big black stone from space, help me punch Lou in the face!"

"No!" Lou reached over and snatched the stone from Madison, and held it up to her mouth with one hand while holding her friend back with the other. She blew quickly before Madison could snatch it back, and the stone glowed blue. Laughing as she spoke, trying to keep Madison from reaching the rock, she called out, "Stone so dark without the light, help me win this fight!"

Suddenly there was a crackle, and the stone vibrated, sending out blue lightning charges throughout the tent. Lou screeched and immediately dropped the rock. The two girls scrambled out of the tent as fast as they could. Huddled in a heap near the front flap, Madison and Lou stared back inside as the blue static charges slowly faded away.

Madison's heart pounded in her chest. "What the hey..." The girls looked at each other, then scurried back into the tent for the stone.

"What did you say?" Madison asked urgently as she snatched up the stone. "What did you say?"

"I don't know, I just blurted something out before you could stop me."

"But what was it?"

"I don't remember."

"Think..."

Lou looked up, trying to remember what she had said. "Stone so black, in the night?"

"No, you said *dark*. It was the word *dark*."

"Stone so dark in the, in the, without the—"

"Stone so dark without the light," Madison interrupted, trying to be the first one to say the words. She tossed the stone onto her soft sleeping bag before anything could happen while it was still in her hand. But nothing happened. The rock just lay there black as ebony. "What's wrong? Why didn't it work for me?"

Lou rolled her eyes and spoke with a sarcastic voice, "You're supposed to blow on it first." Madison reached over and grabbed the stone. "And... you have to finish the rhyme. What do you want to ask for?"

Madison looked around the tent. They hadn't brought many things out with them. She had her sketchbook and the cutout drawing of Razor. Suddenly her eyes lit up as an idea flashed through her mind. She drew the stone to her mouth, trying to hide a devious smile.

"What are you going to wish for?" Lou asked.

Without answering, Madison blew on the stone, and it glowed a deep blue.

"Wait!" Lou shouted. "Tell me before you make your wish."

"Stone so dark without the light..."

"Madison!"

"I wish my drawings would come to life." She said it quickly before Lou had a chance to stop her. Madison cringed as she dropped the stone on top of her sketchbook. A few faint rays of blue electric shot from the rock and irradiated her drawings.

Lou jumped back, slid into her sleeping bag, and pulled it up over her head.

Madison closed her eyes and rolled back as the stone spat and sputtered blue sparks, then slowly faded back to black. All was quiet as she slowly opened her eyes.

"Is it over?" Lou's muffled voice came from inside her sleeping bag.

"I think so," Madison answered.

Lou slowly pulled the bedroll from over her head. The two of them stared at the pad, which still had a faint glowing blue hue around it.

"What happened?" Lou asked.

"I don't know." Madison carefully reached for her drawings, but before she could touch them, the cover bounced slightly open then closed back up. Madison quickly withdrew her hand, letting out a high pitched squeal.

It felt like an eternity had passed with both girls too scared to go near the pad. They sat there, petrified, staring until the cover finally bounced again. The girls squealed, grabbing each other for protection, but nothing came out of the pad. The pages just wiggled and curled under the cover.

Finally, Madison managed to muster up enough courage to crawl over and open the sketchbook. Inside, the first drawing was of a lizard. It's big, bulgy eyes moved back and forth, looking up at Madison as it pulled hard, trying to free itself from the page.

"They're stuck in the book." Madison's laughter dissolved Lou's fear, and she finally crawled alongside her friend. "They're alive, but they can't get out." Madison laughed. "This is so cool."

"So, if you cut them out, they'll be able to run around?" Lou wondered out loud.

"I guess so. Maybe if I cut them out, like Ra—" Madison stopped before she could finish and looked at Lou. Her face went pale as though she had seen a ghost. She managed to squeak out the rest of what she was going to say as her throat tightened, "...like my drawing of Razor."

The two girls turned slowly to where her paper cat had been lying all evening. But now, instead of lying flat as an inanimate drawing, Razor was sitting up, licking its paw.

"O-M-G!" Madison said slowly.

Curious but cautious, Lou reached toward the paper cat, unsure of how it might react. The creature didn't respond well, swatting at her hand. She instinctively pulled back, cradling her arm. A bit of blood oozed from her finger. "He gave me a paper cut," she cried out. "He's living up to his name."

"Let me see," Madison scooched over to take a look. "It's nothing." Turning toward the cat, she wondered out loud, "How are we going to show it we're friendly?"

"Feed it," Lou suggested.

"Feed it what? It's made of paper."

"Draw some cat food," Lou answered.

Madison scowled.

"I'll try petting it myself. Maybe it'll trust me since I'm the one who drew it." Madison reached out toward the animated picture. "It's okay, picture of Razor... paper Razor... I'm not going to hurt you." Without understanding, the cat pulled back, but this time he allowed himself to be touched. Madison gently slid her hand along the drawing.

"What's it feel like?" Lou asked.

"Like... paper," Madison answered. She withdrew her hand and turned to Lou. "I have an idea."

Sitting up, Madison flipped through the pages of her sketchbook until she came to a picture she had drawn of a mouse. Its beady eyes darted back and forth as it tried to pry itself from the page.

"What are you going to do?" Lou asked, squinting her eyes. She knew Madison well enough to know that she was probably thinking up some crazy scheme that was going to get them both in trouble.

"I'm going to cut out this mouse," she said, pulling a pair of scissors from her backpack.

"I'm not too sure if that's a good idea," Lou cautioned. But Madison's stubbornness won out, and in a few minutes, the mouse was free.

For a second, the paper cutout just stood there on Madison's knee as the shock of being free wore off. Then the fun began. The critter hopped onto the sleeping bag and gradually padded away.

Like a real cat preying on its next meal, Razor hunkered down below Lou's pillow, wiggling his butt to dig his rear feet in, readying himself for an attack.

"They're just paper," Madison reminded Lou. "What could they do?"

Suddenly Razor pounced. The mouse turned, running as fast as its little legs could go, right toward Madison and up her shirt. Turning her head and closing her eyes, Madison screeched loudly as she fell over backward. The mouse exited through the neck of her shirt and ran down her arm, Razor was hot on its tail, trampling right across Madison's face.

Lou tried to get out of the way as the paper mouse darted around the tent, looking for a place to hide. Its choice at the moment was Lou. Adding to Madison's shrieks, Lou let out a few herself as the mouse and cat raced around her with Razor jumping on her back.

Like a twister, the two paper drawings buzzed around the tent, causing chaos that eventually had the girls darting from their cozy little hut. Swiftly, they ran up to the house.

Running through the back door, the two girls rambled out a chorus of over-excited tales of what just took place in the tent. Madison's mother was not in a good mood.

"Okay, calm down. One at a time. What happened?"

"Madison's stone is magical," Lou yelled out.

"Yeah, Mom, you have to see this!"

"We said a magical charm, and all Madison's drawings came to life!"

"My picture of Razor is alive, Mom!"

Ida rolled her eyes. "Girls, girls, girls. Your pictures are not alive."

"Yes, they are, Mrs. Kleigh. There's this mouse... and Razor... and they're chasing each other around the tent right now!"

"Come on, Mom. I'll show you."

Madison grabbed her mother's hand and pulled her from the couch. She went along reluctantly.

"Over here, Mom. You'll see what we're talking about." The three of them marched across the yard, each girl pulling on one of Ida's arms, dragging her down to the tent as she stumbled behind.

Inside the house, Jim stepped out of the bathroom. "Hello? Where'd everybody go?"

The girls quickly yanked the tent flap back, and Ida looked inside. Everything was quiet. She was not amused.

"Madison, your cat picture is not running around the tent."

Madison and Lou looked inside. The cutout of the mouse and the cutout of Razor lay flat across the sleeping bags as lifeless as the paper they were drawn on.

"But, Mom, you should have been here. Razor really was running around the tent."

"Madison, I'm not in the mood for these games tonight. I had a long day. Now go to sleep."

"But, Mom, the stone. All I have to do is blow on it, watch." Madison reached into the tent and grabbed the onyx stone.

"Madison, I'm tired."

"Just watch," she said, then blew on the stone. Nothing happened.

"I'm waiting, Madison," her mother said with her hands on her hips.

She blew again, but the stone did not glow.

Her mother put out her hand. "Okay, I've had enough. Give me the stone."

Madison's face dropped. "But why?"

"I'm not going to argue with you. Give me the stone."

"But, Mom," Madison whined.

"Now!"

With protest, Madison grunted and handed over the stone.

"Now go to sleep," her mother said sternly and carried her stone with the little blue box off to the house.

Madison dropped to her sleeping bag with a serious pout on her face.

Lou pursed her lips. "Sorry about your stone, Maddy." She looked around the tent and picked up the onyx stone from Madison's rock collection. "At least you still have this one."

"That one doesn't bring things to life," Madison said in a huff.

Lou turned the stone over in her hands, noticing the chip on one side. "There's a chip in this stone too?"

"No," Madison said, suddenly becoming interested in the rock.

"This one has a chip in it," Lou repeated.

Madison snatched it from her as a big smile dissolved the pout on her face. She laughed.

"What?" Lou asked.

"I was wondering why it didn't glow." She looked up at Lou. "Mom took the wrong stone."

12

The Pact

"**O**kay, here's the deal," Madison said with a serious look on her face. "We can't let anybody know we still have the stone, especially my Mom."

Lou nodded.

"If nobody knows we have it, nobody can take it away. Got it?"

"Got it," Lou agreed.

"We have to promise each other," Madison continued.

"I promise," Lou said.

"That's not good enough."

"Okay, I promise, cross my heart..." Lou made a crisscross motion across her shirt with her finger. "Hope to die, stick a needle in my eye."

Madison sat back and stared at Lou.

"Now you do it," Lou said.

"I don't know," Madison contemplated. "I don't think that's enough."

She stood up on her knees. "Pinky swear," she said, holding out her pinky. Lou wrapped her pinky around her friend's, and they each promised not to tell.

"How's that?" Lou asked.

"Do you have to ask?"

"What do you mean?"

"If you have to ask, then it wasn't good enough. It has to be something so obvious that we won't ever wonder if anybody will break the promise." Madison flopped onto her back and stared up at the roof of the tent, deep in thought.

Lou reached over and opened Madison's drawing pad. "We could write it down, like a contract."

"No, that's boring." Madison lay there, thinking. "I got it!" Madison exclaimed as she sat up. "We each write down something bad that will happen if we break the promise. You write something bad that will happen to me, and I'll write something bad that will happen to you. Just don't write something that will cause either of us to die, though. Write something like, I'll fail eighth grade. Okay?"

Lou nodded in agreement.

Madison tore two squares of paper from her drawing pad, and they each began to think.

"I don't know what to write," Lou said.

"Just write anything. Make it bad, but not too bad. But don't tell me what you write. We can't know each other's curse, or it won't come true."

Lou thought for a while, then began to write. Madison did the same. When they were finished, without looking at what Lou wrote, Madison placed the two papers face-to-face and folded them tightly together. "Now, we have to bury them in the yard."

"What for?"

"You'll see."

Outside the tent, Madison found a stick and used it to dig a small hole nearby. She placed the folded up papers in it and covered them with dirt. "Now," she said as she patted the ground down. "If either one of us breaks the oath, the bad thing that we wrote down will come true." She reached out with an open palm. "Now, get me the stone."

Lou reached into the tent, grabbed the onyx stone, and placed it in Madison's hand.

Madison lifted the stone to her lips and blew. It glowed bright blue. She shook the rock vigorously until blue rays began stemming out from the chipped area, then promptly dropped it onto the fresh patch of dirt. Waves of blue flowed over the ground for a few seconds, then the stone went dark.

"Good, that seals our agreement." Madison retrieved the stone and sat back, admiring her creativity. The girls were about to return to their tent when movement under the soil caught their attention. Bewildered, they inched forward, staring at the bare ground when suddenly a green chute burst through the dirt.

Lou jumped back, and Madison gasped. Their eyes widened in disbelief as the girls watched a plant grow instantly out of the ground. A bud appeared at the top of the stalk, bursting out a yellow flower. Leaves sprouted from the sides, and the girls watched in amazement as a chrysalis formed under one of them. It grew to its full size in seconds then split open. A butterfly emerged from the cocoon, spreading its bright blue wings with orange circles outlined in black.

Madison couldn't believe her eyes. She dodged into the tent and grabbed her sketchbook, flipping through the pages until she came to the butterfly she had drawn before her party started.

"Look, Lou," she called out, unable to contain her excitement. "That's the same butterfly I drew this morning." Madison shoved the drawing pad at her friend.

"What kind is it?"

"That's just it," Madison said. "It doesn't exist. I made it up!"

Bewildered beyond their imaginations, the girls stared at the plant as the butterfly flew off.

"Did we just make a new kind of insect?" Lou asked as it disappeared into the trees.

"I don't know. I think so."

The girls sat and pondered the possibilities of the stone for quite some time.

Suddenly Madison looked over at Lou and shook her arm to get her attention. "Lou, I know what the stone's purpose is."

"What's that?"

"It creates life."

"I can see that," Lou said, as she glanced to where the butterfly flew off.

"No, you don't understand," Madison said as she grabbed a flashlight. "Razor."

"Yeah, we know. It brings him to life."

"No, not the paper Razor." Madison gazed into Lou's eyes. "The real Razor."

Suddenly Lou was scared. "Maddy, I don't think—"

Madison was jogging to the front yard before Lou could finish her thought.

"Maddy," Lou called out, but she wasn't listening. Lou jumped to her feet and ran after her.

Madison ran down the road and up the long dirt driveway with her flashlight beam leading the way. Lou ran behind her the whole time. Finally, her flashlight found the stone that marked Razor's shallow grave, and Madison stopped short. She stood there, catching her breath as she clenched the onyx stone in her hand. Lou ran up behind her.

"Madison, don't." Lou's calm voice of reason flowed.

Madison began to lift the stone to her lips.

"Don't," Lou said again as she grabbed Madison's arm. "Some things were meant to be."

Madison slowly lowered her hand. A tear trickled down her cheek.

"We don't know what will happen, Maddy. He might be walking around but still be dead, like a zombie. Or maybe plants will grow, and tiny insect cats with wings will come out of them. We don't know what the stone is capable of doing."

Deep down inside, Madison knew Lou was right.

"Well," Madison said, turning to Lou. "I intend to find out just what this stone can do." She looked down at the ground. "Tomorrow, we'll test it on something else."

13

Putting it to the Test

"What do you girls have planned for today?" Madison's mother asked as she set the pancakes on the table.

"We're going exploring in the woods."

"Well, just be careful," her mother said. "And stay away from that old house at the end of the road. I've told you before, I don't want you going in there."

"Why?"

"Because I said so, that's why. It could be dangerous. The roof could cave in on you or something," Madison's mother answered.

"It seems pretty safe to me."

Her mother gave her a stern look.

"We'll stay out of the house, Mrs. Kleigh," Lou spoke up.

Madison gave Lou a sly smile, and Lou smiled back.

Once outside in the back yard, Madison and Lou examined the flower that the butterfly had hatched from.

"It's still alive," Lou said.

"Why shouldn't it be?"

"Well, Razor doesn't stay alive."

Madison pulled the drawing of Razor out of her backpack along with the onyx stone. "It's probably because he isn't supposed to be alive. The plant grew into a real flower. It's not a drawing like Razor. It can survive on its own without the stone's power, but Razor isn't actually alive, so once the energy wears off, he goes back to being just a drawing."

Lou nodded.

"Ready for this?" Madison asked as she squatted on the ground.

Lou took a step back. "Ready."

"First, we blow on the stone." Madison lifted the stone to her lips and blew. Immediately the stone began to glow bright blue.

"Second, we give it a shake."

"Wait!" Lou interrupted. "What about the rhyme?"

"What rhyme?"

"You know," Lou chirped. "Stone so dark without the light..."

Madison frowned. "I don't think that actually did anything." She continued shaking the stone, and it immediately began to spit and sputter around the chip.

"Then we drop it onto the object," she said quickly before her hands could become irradiated. The stone plopped down onto the paper cutout of Razor, and rays of blue energy engulfed the drawing. Razor's eyes blinked awake, and he stood to his feet, still glowing blue around his edges. The stone faded to black as it dropped to the ground.

"I think you're getting the hang of it," Lou said, noticing how smooth things went this time. But Razor wasn't so sure. He shied away when Madison reached out to touch him, hopping out of her reach.

Madison stood, and Razor ran across the lawn about ten yards away, then turned and watched.

"How are we going to keep him from running off?" Lou asked. "What if he runs into the woods?"

"Then we'll just wait for the stone's power to wear off and go get him, I guess."

"If we can find him."

Madison held out the stone. "I have an idea." She blew on it, then held it up, letting its light shine across the lawn.

Lou looked back at the house. "Someone's going to notice."

"We have to take that chance," Madison said as she held out the stone for Razor to see. Mesmerized by the light, Razor was captivated.

"It's working," Lou said, watching Razor slowly walk back toward the stone.

Madison got down on her knees. "Come on, boy, it's okay."

Cautiously, Razor walked up to her and sat down. The blue light reflected off his face as he gazed into the orb. Closing his eyes, he lifted his head high and began to glow as if he were absorbing the stone's energy. Madison and Lou looked on in amazement.

"It's like he knows this is his life force," Madison said. While the stone had Razor mesmerized, she reached out with her other hand and stroked him on his side. Razor reacted by rubbing his face against her hand. As the light slowly died out, he continued to rub against Madison and eventually jumped up onto her arm. She giggled.

"He's heavy," she said. "Like a real cat."

"He wasn't heavy when he jumped on me the other day," Lou said.

"He must get lighter as the energy wears off, and he goes back to being just a paper drawing."

Razor crawled up her arm and cuddled up to her neck. Madison scrunched her shoulders and laughed. "That tickles!"

"Okay, so now what?" Lou was getting impatient. She wanted to put the stone to use somehow.

"Let's go back to that old house," Madison suggested. "We can test it on the things inside."

Lou agreed, and the two girls headed to the street with Razor following behind. Madison kept looking back to be sure her paper cat didn't run off. She held the stone out, and Razor followed. He padded along behind the girls as they trotted down the sidewalk.

"Aren't you afraid someone might see?" Lou asked.

"I don't care."

"But our agreement."

"We agreed not to tell anybody about the stone. That has nothing to do with Razor."

"I think it does, being that the stone is what brings him to life."

"Nobody cares. Look!" Madison said, pointing to an older woman hobbling out to get her paper. "There's Mrs. Jacobs." Madison waved. "Hi, Mrs. Jacobs."

"Hi, Madison," the woman answered back. Looking at Razor, she asked, "Did you get a new cat?"

The girls giggled as they trotted on past, not answering. Madison leaned over and whispered to Lou, "Watch, she won't even figure it out."

The woman stared at the creature walking behind the girls. "What *is* that?"

Laughing, they jogged off with Razor tailing behind.

Confused, Mrs. Jacob shook her head, blowing it off as if it were some sort of gag the girls were pulling on her.

"See, I told you so," Madison said. "She doesn't even care."

At the end of the street, they turned onto the dirt road where Lou and Madison hopped over a mud puddle. Curious as to what Razor would do, they turned to watch.

"His feet are just paper," Lou said. "What happens if they get wet?"

"I think the power of the stone will protect him."

"The power of the stone?" Lou said with a patronizing tone. "What do you think? The stone gives you superpowers?"

Madison shrugged her shoulders.

Razor stopped at the water's edge and stared at his reflection as the girls looked on. Reaching out with his paw, he tapped the surface of the puddle. A circle of ripples formed, expanding outward. Inside the ring, Razor's reflection disappeared as the water surface turned solid black.

The girls stood and watched in amazement. Razor looked up at them, then strode across the top of the puddle. Each footstep formed a solid black circle that the paper cat was able to walk on without getting wet. The girls were dumbfounded.

Madison took the stone from her pocket and stared at it. "What are you?" she asked in awe. She stretched her hand out over the puddle and set the stone on top of the water surface. It didn't sink. A solid black disk formed under it as the molecules in the water bonded together, creating a surface tension as strong as steel.

Madison looked up at Lou, who was unable to speak. Her mouth hung open, and her eyes were wide. Razor sat by the puddle, licking his paws. "I wonder what else it can do?" Madison said.

Once over their shock, the girls continued on their way to the old house.

"Do you think it could bring a tree back to life?" Lou asked as she stepped up to a dead elm tree.

"Let's find out," Madison answered with the stone in her hand and ready to go. She blew on it until it glowed blue and was just about to shake it up when Lou reached out and stopped her. Lou noticed Razor staring with sad-looking eyes as if he didn't want them to continue.

"What's wrong?" Madison asked.

"Look at Razor."

"What about him?"

"I don't know," she answered as the stone slowly dimmed. "He seems sad."

Madison craned her neck to get a better look. "He looks fine to me."

"Okay, if you say so."

Madison blew again, and the stone shone brightly. She shook it up and dropped it at the base of the tree. The stone snapped and sputtered near the chip, and random blue rays of light illuminated the roots. The girls stepped back to where Razor was sitting. Lou thought he looked worried.

At first, nothing happened, but then the tree started snapping. Flakes of bark dropped to the ground as the branches vibrated. Suddenly it began to split open, and fresh branches emerged. The old bark cracked and crumbled to the ground as new bark took over. Leaves sprouted from the branches as the tree renewed itself. In a matter of minutes, the tree was full of life, thick with branches and leaves.

"Wow!" is all Madison could say as they watched the tree come back to life before their eyes.

Lou picked up the stone and examined it closely. "Do you think that would have happened if you tried it on Razor? I mean the real Razor?" she asked. "Like, a whole new cat would burst out of his body?"

"Or a tree," Madison answered. "I guess it's good that I didn't try it on him."

Lou swallowed hard as she handed the stone to Madison. Her eyes were wide. "This is a very special stone. You better keep it safe," she said, remembering the note that came with it.

Madison nodded.

"I wonder how the tree died before." Lou pondered. She looked at Madison. "Do you think it'll just die again in the same way? Are we really helping it?"

Madison shrugged, "I don't know. Maybe we should try using the stone on something that's not a living thing."

"Like what?"

Madison took off toward the house. "Follow me."

"Maddy, we told your Mom we wouldn't go into that house," Lou protested.

"Maybe you did, but I didn't."

Lou grumbled under her breath. "Come on, Razor," she called out and ambled after her friend.

Inside the house, Madison was picking up old junk and tossing it back to the floor. "No, nope, not good enough, not a chance," she commented with each object. Razor meandered through the junk as if he were looking for something himself.

"What are you looking for?" Lou asked.

"I don't know. I'll know when I find it." Madison tramped on into one of the bedrooms.

"Just don't go into the backroom," Lou called out.

"Found it!" Madison yelled.

Lou popped her head into the doorway and saw Madison standing in the middle of the room, holding up an old baby doll. "No way!"

A big devious grin spread across Madison's face as she nodded. "Yes, way."

She tossed the doll to the floor and took the stone from her pocket.

Lou glanced at Razor. He wasn't acting the same as he had when they healed the tree. He seemed as if he didn't care. "Okay, go ahead," Lou said, taking her cue from the paper cat who appeared to have some insight into the stone's ability.

Madison blew on the stone, shook it, and dropped it on top of the doll. It spat and sputtered, illuminating the toy with rays of blue light, then went dark. Madison watched in anticipation, but nothing happened.

"Nuts," Madison said in disappointment. She picked up the stone. The dolls dress still glowed slightly but went dark after a few seconds. "Not even a flower."

"I guess it doesn't work on non-living things," Lou speculated.

Madison gestured to Razor. "Duh, he's paper," she said sarcastically.

"Yeah, but you made him. He came from your mind, and we already know that the stone is somehow connected to our minds."

"How do we know that?"

"Remember? The butterfly."

Madison looked around the room. She picked up an old soda can, then glanced about for something more. Inside an old box, she found a collection of pencils and pens. Grabbing up a thick marker, she jammed it into the top of the can. "There, I made something."

"I don't think that's going to count," Lou said.

"Oh, now the stone's an art critic?"

Lou groaned and walked back to the door. "I'm going out to get some fresh air. It stinks in here."

Madison tossed the can away and ran through the junk to catch up with Lou.

"Maybe it works on Razor because he is actually part of you," Lou said. "You know… because you created him from your heart."

Madison shrugged, then looked back to see what Razor was doing. Lou did the same, but the cat was gone.

"Where's Razor?" Lou asked. The girls looked around, but he was nowhere to be seen.

"Here, boy," Madison made a cat call sound, "*Pss, pss, pss.*"

"What are you doing?" Lou asked.

"Calling Razor."

"He's not a real cat, you know. He doesn't know what *pss, pss, pss,* means."

"Yes, he does. I call him that way all the time."

Lou smirked as she rolled her eyes.

They wandered back into the hallway, looking into each room. Opposite the bedroom was a small office where the girls found Razor sitting on an old fashion secretary desk.

"Come on, Razor, let's go home," Madison called, but the paper cat didn't move. Madison walked around a turned over rolling chair. "What's wrong, boy? Did you find something?"

"Why did he come in here?" Lou asked.

"Beats me," Madison answered as she pawed through papers on the desk. She found some old coupons and a stationary pad. There were a few pens scattered around that looked like they would never write again.

Lou stepped up beside her friend and picked up an old cigar box. When she did, the bottom dropped out, and loose change fell, bouncing off the desk and onto the floor. "Money!" she yelled and grabbed for the falling coins. Madison and Lou scrambled to pick up several dollars in quarters, dimes, nickels, and pennies.

"Some went in here," Lou said, reaching for a drawer that was open slightly. She pulled it out and dug around inside for the rest of the change.

"Here, take this," she said to Madison, lifting an old photo album out of her way so that she could retrieve more coins.

Madison took the book and examined it. Her eyes widened as she flipped the cover open. "It's a scrapbook of the Apollo missions."

"What?" Lou asked.

"The Apollo moon landings and stuff," Madison clarified. She flipped the chair back onto its legs and sat down with the book across her lap. "Wow! This is incredible."

Lou looked on as she stuffed her pockets. "What's so incredible about it?"

"It's the actual newspapers from that time," she said as she thumbed through the pages. "And look," she pointed to a piece of scrap paper. "There's a handwritten note here."

Lou stepped in closer. "What does it say?"

Madison read the note out loud.

September 12th, 1959: Russia sent Luna 2 to purposely crash into the moon. It landed near the Sea of Tranquility. Since then, Russia and the US raced to be the first to go back.

July 13, 1969: Russia launched Luna 15 in an attempt to beat the US to the Luna 2 crash site.

July 16, 1969: The US launched Apollo 11 with three astronauts on board. Their destination was the Sea of Tranquility.

July 24, 1969: Apollo 11 landed on the moon at the Sea of Tranquility before Luna 15 could land, but they missed the mark.

July 24, 1969: The Russian automated spacecraft, Luna 15, malfunctioned and crashed on the moon near the Sea of Tranquility.

September 12, 1970: Russia launched Luna 16, which successfully landed on the moon and returned with objects it collected.

"What's it mean?" Lou asked.

"I don't know, but I'm taking this home with me."

"Uh, Maddy." Lou pointed to her lap.

"What?" Madison said, glancing down to where Lou was pointing.

"Ew!" she screeched and jumped to her feet, sending the book crashing to the floor. She frantically brushed a dozen or so silverfish off her pants. The girls ran back through the house, leaving the scrapbook behind.

Lou followed Madison out the back door. "That was gross," Madison said, still wiping her hands on her pants. She glanced back to check for Razor, who decided to follow along this time. They strolled through the overgrown backyard and sat down on an old stone wall watching Razor chase after a grasshopper.

"I guess you don't want the scrapbook anymore," Lou said facetiously.

"Ha-ha, very funny."

"So, now what do you want to do?"

Madison began to speak when the distinct sound of an air rifle being pumped grabbed her attention. Madison glared into the woods. "It's Harold and his bullies."

"We should get out of here," Lou suggested.

"No, I want to see what they're up to." Madison made her way through the underbrush, crouching down low. She crawled up to the top of a small hill and hid behind a fallen tree trunk. Cautiously, she lifted her head to see over. After a few seconds, she motioned for Lou to join her.

Lou clucked her tongue, "Here we go again, Razor." The paper cat followed Lou up the hill.

"They're over there shooting at birds," Madison said as she pointed into the woods.

"I see them. What are you going to do?"

Madison turned around and leaned back against the tree, pulling her pack across her lap. "We need to teach those boys a lesson."

"How? Make an army of paper animals and attack them?"

Madison smiled big.

"No, I was just kidding," Lou said. "You're not actually going to—"

"I'm not kidding," Madison cut her off as she pulled her sketchbook from her backpack.

"You're crazy, Maddy. How are you going to get your drawings to obey you? Even Razor tried to run away after you brought him to life."

"We'll try it on one drawing," Madison said as she flipped to a picture of a bird. It was bright pink with white and orange wings. There was a crown of tiny blue and green feathers covering its head. "We'll teach the stone that the boys are evil."

"How?"

"Watch and learn," Madison said as she began cutting out the bird from the paper. "We'll see just how much the stone is connected to my mind."

Lou shook her head. "What kind of bird is that anyhow?" Lou asked.

"I don't know, I made it up."

Lou noticed that Madison had drawn both wings spread out as if it were in flight. "If you didn't draw the bird flying, would it be able to fly when it came to life?"

"Probably not," Madison answered. "It'll just hop on the ground, I guess."

On the other side of the log, the boys yelled in glee that they had shot another bird. Lou looked over the fallen tree and saw them laughing. It disgusted her more than the paper army idea. When she turned around, Madison was already dropping the glowing stone onto her bird cutout. Blue energy rays flowed through the paper, and before Lou could protest, the bird stood to its feet. Madison grabbed the creature before it could fly off and lifted it up over the log.

"Ready?" she asked.

"Ready."

"Let's see what happens when they shoot at this bird," she said as she hurled the bird into the air toward the boys. Even Razor hopped up onto the log to see what was going to happen.

The bird flew around the trees and landed in the bushes just a few yards from where the boys were shooting.

"Do you think they saw it?" Lou asked.

"I think so, look." Madison pointed in the direction of the boys. "Harold's raising his gun."

14

Paper Allies

Harold saw a large pink bird land in the bushes nearby and scurried over, keeping low, trying not to frighten it. He lifted his gun and pulled the trigger. The bird jerked as the BB penetrated its paper body, but didn't fly away. He pumped up his air rifle and loaded another BB into the chamber. Taking aim, he fired again.

The other boys joined in, pelting the bird with multiple steel pellets. "Hold, it!" he shouted. Chad let out one last shot. "Stop!" Harold said as he pushed the barrel of Chad's gun to the ground. "Something's wrong."

Harold pushed his way through the thickets until he came up close to the bird. "It's paper!" he shouted. Annoyed, he reached down and snatched the drawing from the bushes. "It's just a picture." He looked around the woods. "Madison!" he growled.

Chad and Bryant scanned the trees for the girls. Finally, they saw them stand and run away. "Should we go after them?"

Harold stood up straight. "We will. But, first, I want to get some target practice in," Harold said, glaring through the brush as the girls disappeared over the hill. He set the bird up in the tree and joined his gang. The three of them pumped up their guns and fired at the bird. Each time a BB penetrated the paper, the hole glowed blue. The bird's eye beamed at the boys, watching their every move. They had no idea of the life force that was at work in the drawing. Pieces of paper ripped off and fluttered through the air as the guns tore the bird apart. Finally, it fell from its perch and drifted to the forest floor.

Satisfied, Harold backed off, and the boys walked through the woods in the direction the girls had run. The bird watched as they disappeared into the trees, then closed its eye. Just before going dormant, rays of blue energy flowed from its paper body across the ground. Several tiny blue flowers instantly grew up from the litter of dead leaves.

Madison and Lou left the woods and hiked across an old field when they finally came to the stream. Madison sat down on the bank to check her paper cat.

"Do you think Razor needs to be charged up?" Lou asked. "He's been alive for a long time."

Madison looked at her and laughed. "I think that's the weirdest thing you've ever said," she chuckled as she pulled the stone from her pocket.

"That's what happens when I hang around *you* all the time. I begin talking weird."

Madison held up the stone and blew on it.

"Hey! Let me do it this time," Lou demanded.

"No, it's my stone."

"Come on, it's my turn," Lou insisted.

Madison ignored her and held the stone up for Razor. Lou quickly snatched it from her hand.

"Lou!" Madison yelled, reaching for the glowing orb.

Lou held her back with one hand, keeping the stone away. "It's my turn!" she cried.

"No, it's not. It's my stone, *Louise,*"she said with a condescending tone. "I decide whose turn it is."

"You've used it every time so far. Give me a chance."

Madison jumped on Lou, pulling on her shirt. Lou turned over and used her body weight to fling Madison off. Madison pulled again on her arm, and the stone shook in her hand, causing it to activate and send out waves of energy.

Noticing the rock was sparking, Lou let it go, and it fell onto Madison's shoulder. It rolled down her arm, sending out blue rays of energy as it bounced along. Madison shrieked. Lou jumped to her feet to get out of its way, but fell backward, almost landing on top of Razor.

Madison stood up quickly, and the stone dropped to the ground, rolling down the bank, spewing out blue rays of energy as it went. She held out her arm as the two girls gawked, wondering what was going to happen next. Suddenly several flowers sprouted from her shirt. She quickly brushed them off before they could take root. "Ew!" she shrieked in disgust.

Lou laughed.

"Give me the stone," Madison said, holding out her hand.

"I don't have it."

Madison looked around the ground, kicking at the tall grass. "Where did it go?"

"I didn't see, I was too busy getting away from it."

Madison's eyes followed a thin line of newly grown flowers and ferns leading down the bank to the stream. Horror filled her face. "It's in the creek!" The stone had bounced out a few feet and was sitting on top of the water.

Madison didn't waste any time scrambling down the riverbank. While reaching for the stone, her foot slipped into the water and drenched her shoe. Annoyed with the whole situation, she snatched up her stone and clambered back up the bank, grumbling the entire way. "It's okay, I have it," she said, "Give me a hand."

Madison reached up to grab Lou's hand when she noticed Harold and his gang running across the field.

"Oh, no," Madison said, her voice showing her irritation.

"What now?"

"Turn around," she growled.

Lou looked behind her and panicked.

"Back to the stream," Madison yelled. "We have to get across somehow."

"I'm not going in there," Lou complained. "There could be alligators in that water."

Madison glared at her. "We'll use the stone."

"How?"

"Like Razor did."

Madison scrambled back down the bank. "The water surface turns solid where ever the stone touches, right?"

"Yeah, but how are you—"

"There they are," Harold called out. Madison gasped, jerking her head around toward the field. The three boys were closing in on them fast.

Madison held the stone to her lips and blew on it. Once it was glowing, she flung it hard, spinning it as it left her fingers. It bounced and rolled across the top of the water, coming to rest near the shore on the other side. There, the stone floated, holding its position against the current. At each spot on the water surface where the stone had touched, circles of ripples slowly made their way out, forming a string of rings to where the stone now rested. Inside the rings, the water had become pitch black except where the sun gleamed off them, reflecting bright colors of the rainbow like a streak of oil.

Madison took one more look behind her. The boys were already at the top of the bank. Panicking, she took one shaky step out onto the first black circle made by the stone. The surface of the water held her weight. Holding her arms out to each side for balance, she stepped across to each dark circle, slowly making it across the stream. Lou followed behind. Razor walked across the water on his own. At the last ring, Madison hopped onto the other shore, turning around quickly to retrieve her stone. By then, Harold and his gang had made it to the stream.

The boys tried to cross the same way the girls had. However, the solid surface of the rings faded, and their feet sank to the bottom. With their shoes already wet, going in further seemed like no big deal. "Come on, guys, it's not very deep," Harold said, and the three of them began to wade across the creek.

Madison pulled her sketchpad from her backpack and began flipping through pages of pictures she had drawn.

"What are you doing?" Lou fretted as she glanced back to the boys. "We don't have time..."

Madison ignored her. She flipped past birds, cats, spiders, snakes, and fish until she reached a page with an alligator. Looking up, she saw that the boys were almost halfway across the stream and nodded with approval. It will be the alligator, she thought. She tore the page from the sketchpad and began to cut the image out. Glancing up from time to time, she cut through the paper, hurrying to finish before the boys made it across. The current was strong and the bottom slippery, causing them to stumble, slowing their progress, but they kept moving forward.

Finally, the alligator was free from the page. Madison stood up tall and bold at the edge of the stream—as tall as a thirteen-year-old girl could. "Let's see you get past this!" she called out as she dipped the paper alligator into the water.

The three boys looked at her, confused as to what she meant. Then their eyes widened as the paper alligator began to swim toward them. "That thing's alive!" one of them yelled.

"It's only paper, ignore it," Harold ordered his friends. Being the leader of their group, the others obeyed him and continued forward as the alligator approached. Harold pumped his gun, aimed it at the paper creature, and pulled the trigger. Water sprayed into the air as the BB hit, and the alligator went under. Only bubbles escaped to the surface. "Ha!" he bellowed. "Is that the best you can do?"

Lou looked on in disbelief. "I thought that was going to be more effective," she said.

However, Madison's confidence in the stone was much higher. "Wait for it..." is all she said.

At that moment, directly in front of the bully kid, the alligator leaped into the air, gnashing its teeth and striking with its tail. Harold put up his hands to block the advancing gator, but its paper-thin body cut into his skin. "Paper cuts!" he yelled. "He's giving me paper cuts!"

In mid-air, the gator spun itself like a propeller, sending tiny beads of hardened water spraying in all directions. On the shore, Madison and Lou ducked behind a tree avoiding the pellets as they pelted the ground.

"Get back," Harold yelled as the tiny BBs blasted them. The three bullies splashed through the water.

The girls laughed as the boys scrambled back across the stream with the paper alligator hot on their trail.

From the other side, the boys yelled back, "That's the last time, Madison, that we're going to put up with you meddling in our business. Next time we see you,

you're dead meat!" Chad and Bryant took aim at her with their BB guns.

Madison scooped up Razor and slid him down inside her backpack, then pulled it up over her shoulders. She began the ascent to the top of the riverbank behind Lou, but before she got out of range, she felt the impact of two BBs on the back of her pack. The girls crested the hill and ran across the field away from the boys and their guns.

"How did you know the alligator would chase them?" Lou puffed as she kept pace with Madison.

"I didn't. I just thought that if the stone knew what I was thinking about the butterfly, it would know what I was thinking about the boys."

"So, why didn't the paper alligator make the surface of the water turn solid like Razor did?" Lou asked.

"I don't know." Madison stopped running and turned to Lou. "The stone didn't come with an instruction manual, you know."

When the girls had traveled far enough to feel safe, they scurried behind a bush and knelt in the shade, catching their breath. Madison glanced back in the direction of the stream as she pulled off her pack. "Those boys won't dare try to cross now."

Madison flopped to the ground in exhaustion. "My heart's still pounding."

"Mine too," Lou said, breathing hard.

Razor's paper head popped out from under the backpack. "I'm sorry, Razor. I forgot you were in there." Madison held the flap up so he could step out. Razor slunk from the pack and turned to examine his tail. There were two small holes where BBs had penetrated his drawn paper body.

"Oh, no, you're injured," Madison said, with empathy in her voice. "I'm going to have to draw you a new tail." She laughed. "Just don't drink any water. You'll probably leak."

Lou laughed with her.

Razor squinted his eyes in disapproval as if he understood the comment, but didn't like it.

15

Dinner for Four

Ida ran back and forth, preparing herself to go out for dinner. "Are you just going to sit there watching TV, or are you going to get ready?" she grumbled at Madison as she buttoned her blouse.

"What's there to do? We're just going to eat," Madison whined.

"Could you at least wash your face and put on a clean shirt?"

Madison snorted as she got off her chair and sauntered up the stairs.

The television rambled on as Ida got ready.

"After twelve months of cutting and hauling, the jungle-like growth in Korolyov has finally come to a stand-still," the anchorman on the television announced. "Scientists are still baffled as to the exact cause of the uncontrolled growth, saying it most likely was part of an experiment to feed astronauts during long space flights. Peter Oxlin doesn't agree."

"They want to terraform Mars," the old maintenance man said.

Ida shook her head. "Terraform Mars? Really? I think your brain's been terraformed, old man," she said as she reached to switch the television off.

"You see, they found this stone—" The television went dark.

"Are you done, Madison?" Ida called up the stairs. I'm walking out the door."

"Coming, Mom," Madison yelled as she ran down.

- - -

The sound of silverware could be heard clanking together in the kitchen as soft music played in the background. Other than some dim mood lamps, a candle on the table was the only lighting.

"This is nice," Ida said, breaking the awkward silence. "Thank you for taking us out tonight, Lauro."

"My pleasure. I told you I was going to keep my eye on you two while Michael was away."

"And you've been doing a great job of it," Ida said.

"So, how is your summer going?" Dr. Alazar asked Madison.

"Good."

The three of them sat at their table, making small talk as they waited for the waiter to bring the meals they had ordered. It was a classy restaurant with a menu to match. Madison noticed right away that there were no dollar signs next to the prices. There weren't even any .99s after every price like she always saw in other places. It was just a thirty-five or a forty-one. At first, she had thought the numbers were meal designations. Her mother had laughed when she had asked for a thirty-two. "No, Maddy. That's the price," she had said. Madison blushed.

"Will you please hold still?" her mother said as Madison rocked back and forth in her chair with her legs swinging.

"I'm bored."

"You brought your drawing pad, didn't you?" her mother asked.

"Yes."

"Well, then draw something."

Madison pulled her backpack onto her lap. She pulled out her sketchbook and reached for her pencil case, but it had opened up and spilled out into the bottom of her pack. "Great," she grunted.

"What's wrong?" her mother asked.

"It's so dark in here I can't see anything. Can I dump out my bag onto the floor?"

"No! For crying out loud, Madison, you're in a restaurant. Act civilized for a change."

Madison scowled. Reaching into her backpack, she pulled out a handful of pencils, but the color she wanted was not in the bunch. She dug in again and found her onyx stone. Then an idea struck her.

She glanced up at her mother, who was now holding a conversation with Dr. Alazar, not paying attention to what Madison was doing. She snatched up the stone, keeping it inside her bag, and blew on it. It began to glow, illuminating everything inside. She saw all the items more clearly, including the picture of Razor, which was in a dormant state at the moment.

Madison grabbed the colors she wanted then dropped the pack onto the floor. It wasn't until blue rays flowed out and around the edges of the bag that she realized she had set her backpack down a little too hard.

The stone had been jarred just enough to excite it into action. Moments later, Razor popped his head out. Madison reached down to close the flap as quickly as she could, but the cat was out of the bag. She gasped.

"What now?" her mother asked in an annoyed tone.

"Um..." Madison looked around. Razor was making his way across the restaurant. "I have to go to the bathroom."

"Did you lose something?" the woman asked as Madison tiptoed past, glaring under their table, whispering her cat's name.

"Oh, um... My little brother," Madison lied. "Have you seen him?"

"Heavens, no. How old is he? Would you like me to call the manager?"

"No, he always does this. I'll find him."

Madison went on to the next table. "Razor!" she whispered.

From table to table, she went until she finally got a glimpse of the little cretin. Madison dashed across the restaurant and crawled under a table full of silverware and cloth napkins. She almost had him in her hands, but he escaped through a narrow opening and bolted across the floor right in front of a waitress.

Everybody jumped when the woman let out a scream and dropped her platter of dirty dishes onto the floor.

Two bussers ran to help her pick up the mess.

"There's a cat in here!" she squeaked out.

Patrons began rising to their feet. "A cat? In a restaurant?"

"Please, ladies and gentlemen," the manager said as he rushed over to prevent a panic. "I assure you, there are no animals in the restaurant." He smiled, remaining very calm in front of the guests. "Please return to your seats."

Turning to one of the workers, his face went serious. "Find that animal and get rid of it, now!" he growled. "I don't care how you do it."

Madison remained hidden under the table, a vantage point that allowed her to see across the floor at the cat's level. It also hid her from her mother, who was looking around the room, wondering what all the commotion was.

Ida was relieved to know that her daughter was in the bathroom and couldn't possibly have anything to do with whatever was happening on the other side of the restaurant. Still, an uneasiness set into her stomach since she wasn't able to actually see what Madison was doing.

"Excuse me," she said to Dr. Alazar. "I need to check on Madison."

He nodded.

From under the table, Madison watched her mother head off to the bathrooms. She didn't have much time before her mother would discover that Madison wasn't where she said she would be. The place was dark, but one side of her cat was solid white since she had only drawn on one side. That was something Madison had been thinking about remedying, but for now, she was glad for it. Anything white would be easier to see in the dark, and then... there he was. A few tables over, her cat sat licking his paw. "Gotcha," Madison whispered to herself.

She blew on the stone, not realizing how bright it would be in a dark room. Blue light beamed from under the table and lit up the floor. Razor was mesmerized and couldn't help being attracted to the glowing orb. He pranced across the floor in the direction of the glow, somehow managing to do so without drawing attention to himself.

Because the light was a pleasing blue glow, and down low, the guests must have passed it off as part of the ambiance of the place. However, anybody working there would have known that something was amiss, and one of the bussers bent over to take a look under the table. He lifted up the cover, and Razor jumped out.

The paper cat hopped up onto the man's shoulder and jumped across to one of the tables, sending a spoonful of spaghetti into a chubby woman's face. He bolted from one table to another, dashing across a grilled porterhouse steak, crashing through a pile of crab legs, and hopping across someone's chicken piccata.

Patrons screamed and hollered, children laughed, and the manager was furious. Madison ran through the restaurant holding out her glowing stone, hoping to catch Razor's attention. The paper cat leaped onto a service cart, sending it whirling between the tables just before crashing into the side of a grand piano. Dishes and silverware flew through the air. Razor slid across the piano keys creating a beautiful glissando before plunging into the server board and falling to the floor. Knives and forks fell all around him, nearly tearing through his paper-thin body. The experience was so terrifying that he was glad when Madison appeared around the corner and snatched him up. Immediately, he went dormant in her hands.

The manager stormed around the piano and glared at Madison. "Did you see a cat run through here?" he asked.

Madison nodded and pointed to the kitchen.

"What's that?" he barked, pointing at the picture she was holding in her hands.

"It's just something I drew."

The manager grumbled and huffed off to the kitchen with several employees following after him.

Madison made her way back to her own table and slid into her chair.

Dr. Alazar was gazing off across the restaurant, trying to make out what all the commotion was.

"What's going on?" Madison asked.

"I don't know. Something about a cat running across the tables."

"Oh? That's strange. I wonder who would bring a live cat into a restaurant?" she said as she wiped spaghetti sauce off her drawing.

"What's that?" Dr. Alazar asked.

"It's just something I drew," Madison answered him the same way she had responded to the manager. "His tail got wrinkled," she said as she flattened it with her hand.

"Madison, put that away," her mother scolded as she came back from the bathrooms.

"You said I could draw."

"Yes, but anything other than a cat."

Madison tucked Razor back into her bag and zipped it up.

"So, Lauro," Ida went on. "What do you do these days, now that you're retired from the German Space Center?"

"Well," Dr. Alazar shifted in his seat. "Nobody actually retires from the DLR. I do some traveling for them. I'm an investigator."

Madison's eyes widened. "Are you a spy?"

"Madison!" her mother shot her a glance with eyes of daggers.

Dr. Alazar laughed. "A legitimate one, I suppose, in a way. I work with both our governments in matters of top secret."

"Can you tell us any secrets?" She couldn't contain her excitement.

Ida grunted. "Really, Madison?"

"It's okay," Dr. Alazar said in a calm, cool voice. "I don't mind at all." Leaning over his plate, he continued. "What kind of secrets would you like to know?" he whispered with enthusiasm.

"Well," Madison thought. "Is it possible for somebody to bring a stone home from one of the space missions?"

"That would be stealing. Our governments own those stones."

"But is it possible?"

"There are a lot of samples from the moon that have gone missing. Yes, I suppose it's possible."

"Have you ever brought a stone home with you?"

Her mother rolled her eyes.

Dr. Alazar laughed. "I have no need for a stone from space. Besides, I've never been to the moon. Why are you so interested in space stones?"

"I was just wondering," Madison answered, looking down at her backpack where her onyx stone was stashed.

"She's wanted a stone from the moon since she was five, the first time her father went up into space." Ida interrupted. She smiled at her daughter. "You'll have to become an astronaut and go get one yourself."

Madison smiled back. "Maybe, I will."

"With your determination, I don't doubt it," her mother said.

16

Breaking the Promise

The chain-link fence that enclosed the soccer field rattled as Madison dragged a stick along it. It was too early to meet Lou for soccer practice, so she wasted time walking slowly. Razor bounced along behind her. Being outside in the open, a confrontation with Harold's gang was the last thing she expected.

"Going someplace?" Harold asked in a gruff voice as he stepped out from behind the fence. Trying to avoid a conflict, Madison stumbled backward into the field. Razor trotted around her.

"Look!" Bryant yelled out. "It's alive!" he said, pointing at the paper cat.

"Okay, Madison. How are you doing it?" Harold demanded. He stood at least a foot taller than Madison, and he knew how to use his height to intimidate others.

Madison didn't answer. She slowly reached into her pocket and wrapped her fingers around her stone.

"Boys," Harold said coldly. "Destroy it."

"No!" Madison yelled out, but Bryant and Chad ignored her. Both of them reached down and picked up rocks to throw.

"Run, Razor, run!" Madison cried.

Razor looked up. He didn't understand Madison's words, but he knew danger, and when a rock whizzed past his head, he ran. Grass flew as his little paper legs dug into the ground for traction. He ducked just in time to avoid a stone aimed at his head, and flipped over when another one slammed into his tail. He jumped to his feet immediately and ran off.

Madison was terrified. In desperation, she pulled the onyx stone from her pocket and blew on it, hoping it would help her in some way. It glowed bright blue in her hand.

"What's that?" Harold asked in a demanding tone as he reached out to grab it. Madison stepped away, pulling the stone from his reach.

"Give it to me," the boy ordered.

"No. It's mine," she said, turning to run.

Harold reached out and grabbed her by her backpack, holding her so she couldn't leave.

"Let go," Madison grunted while squirming to escape.

"Not until you give me that thing you have."

Madison pulled hard, pushing against the ground with her feet.

"Get back here, you little creep," Harold hissed.

Madison felt her backpack come loose from her shoulder as she pulled herself away from the bully. Unable to get ahold of the girl, Harold grasped the pack as it slid from her arm, knocking the onyx stone to the ground.

The boys jumped back as waves of light scattered across the grass, illuminating it in blue. Instantly weeds and vines grew from the soil, reaching up as they twisted their way to the sky, creating a barrier between them and their victim. Madison bent down and retrieved the stone as quickly as she could, then ran off after Razor.

Harold picked a leaf off one of the plants and rubbed it between his fingers.

"Is it real?" Bryant asked.

"It's real," Harold said as he flung it to the ground. "How did she?... we should go after her." Chad cut him off, getting ready to run.

"No, let her go." Harold looked around. Some of the other kids were watching now. The struggle had caught their attention. "Too many people here. Put your rocks down. She'll be back. We have something of hers now," he said, looking at the backpack. "Let's get out of here." The boys ran off into the woods taking Madison's pack with them.

···

Madison sat on the top of the light blue benches feeling depressed. Razor crawled up alongside her. Blue arcs of energy were snapping across his wrinkled tail. She bent down to examine it closer and found that the tip had almost ripped completely off.

"I'm sorry, boy," she empathized with him. "It's this or hide away at home every day. It's a dangerous world. We could sit inside on the couch and watch TV all day, or we can be out here living it. I'd rather take the chance, wouldn't you?"

Razor tipped his head, looking up at Madison as if he was saying he agreed.

"Lou will be here soon," she said, worried about what her friend might say.

With her elbows on her knees, she rested her head in her hands and watched as the grounds maintenance crew examined the vines and weeds now growing along the fence. One of them was carrying a Weed-Wacker. She wished she could hear what they were saying.

"Care to explain yourself?" Lou asked as she stepped around the bleachers, gesturing to the patch of vines.

"Hi Lou," Madison said with a downhearted tone in her voice.

"What were you thinking?"

Madison sat up straight. "It was Harold and his goons," she whined, arguing in her defense. "They took my backpack."

"They got the stone?" Lou gasped.

"No, I have it in my pocket."

"See, this is what I'm talking about," Lou grumbled. "If that stone had been in your pack, they would have it now. And who knows what they would use it for."

"Well, they didn't get it."

Lou leaned against the benches. "What's up with Razor's tail?" she asked, noticing that it was shorting out.

"Harold's minions threw rocks at him," Madison answered.

"Oh, poor guy," she said in a motherly tone as she bent down to pet her paper friend. "Why is it all wrinkled?"

"Oh, that happened at the restaurant last night," Madison answered before she remembered she didn't want Lou to know about that.

"Restaurant? What happened at the restaurant?"

Madison moaned. "It was nothing. Just a little slip, that's all."

"What do you mean, *a little slip?*"

"Nobody saw. Well, they saw, but they thought it was a real cat. It was dark."

"Saw what?" Lou pressed.

Madison grunted. "He got out and ran across the tables."

"What?" Lou was getting hysterical. "Madison! You're breaking our promise."

"I can't help it. Everybody keeps forcing it on me."

"For now on, you need to leave that stone home, always."

Madison went back to pouting with her head in her hands. "What about Razor?" she asked, trying to make excuses to keep the stone with her at all times. "We can't let him just go back to being a paper drawing."

"Okay, we'll use it only to keep Razor alive, but it must be done at home. Got it?"

Madison nodded.

Lou sat down next to Madison, and the two of them pondered to themselves for a while.

Breaking the silence, Lou giggled. "What did they say at the restaurant?"

"The manager was furious. All the people were running around, freaking out." she laughed.

"Where was your Mom?" Lou asked.

"In the bathroom. She missed it all," Madison chuckled. "Not even Dr. Alazar knew what was happening."

"Dr. Alazar?"

"Yes, the German space guy who was assigned to our family during the launch."

"He's still coming around?"

"Yeah, he checks in on us from time to time."

"Huh," Lou said aloud as she drifted deep into thought.

"Is something wrong?" Madison asked.

"No, it's just that your family is weird. I guess you have to be to fly all the way to Mars for no reason."

"What do you mean, *no reason?*" Madison snapped.

"What's he going to Mars for anyhow?" Lou asked.

"To explore! The same thing we do every day in the woods."

"What do you think they're going to find on Mars?"

"I don't know. More rocks?"

"Why? We don't have enough rocks here on Earth for Harold's gang to throw at Razor?" Lou said sarcastically.

Madison pushed her away, "Shut up."

Razor glanced at his tail, which was sparking off blue rays of energy around the new damage. Not only was the tip hanging loose, but there were also BB holes, and it was wrinkled up pretty bad. He tried to flex it out, but it just crackled with blue energy.

"If I had my backpack, I could tape it up," Madison said.

"What do you have inside that thing anyway, an entire office supply store?" Lou asked.

"Don't poke fun at me. It's a good thing I have all that stuff," Madison answered. "You never know what you're going to need when you have a paper cat following you around."

"You know, you're so lucky, Maddy," Lou continued. "You get to have a paper cat that's alive. Do you think your Dad could get me one of those space stones too?"

"No, he wasn't supposed to bring this one home. He could get in big trouble if someone finds out, and besides, he doesn't know it has powers. And we're not going to tell him either. You got that?"

"Yeah, yeah, I got it. What are you going to do about your backpack?"

"Go and get it back, I guess," Madison said as she examined Razor's tail.

17

Monsters and Dragons

Edwin Gordon was an eccentric millionaire, or at least that's what he wanted everybody to believe. His mansion was in desperate need of maintenance, but it was too much work for the man to do himself. He lived there with his son, Harold. His ex-wife had run off, taking half his money with her and draining away much of what was left in legal battles. He could barely afford to keep his large house in good repair.

Edwin sported a neatly trimmed mustache and beard, which had turned white on his chin, giving it the appearance of a goatee. He was balding on the top of his head but had plenty of dark curly hair above his ears. He answered the massive oak carved front door in his evening jacket, smoking his pipe. A pair of thin-wire glasses framed his narrow gray-blue eyes.

"Yes, may I help you?" he asked, looking at Ida.

Madison's mother tapped her on the shoulder and gestured to Edwin.

"Um," Madison stammered. "Harold has my bookbag."

Edwin laughed. "So, he does. Must have borrowed it from you, eh?"

"Not really..." Madison started to say.

"Come in, come in," the man said, holding the door wide open.

As Madison and her mother stepped into the house, they were immediately captivated by the charm of the old place.

Edwin led them into a large foyer with knotty pine floors. A red carpet with intricate designs lined the room. Madison stared up at the beautiful chandelier hanging from the cathedral ceiling. She had been in elegant houses before, but none were as charming as this old place. A staircase with ornate spindles and a beautiful banister curved around to the upper floor balcony which encircled the foyer..

"Sorry for the mess, my housekeeper quit on me a few years back," he laughed. "And Harold, well, let's just say he was used to having a housekeeper." He led the two into the library just off to the right of the main foyer. Madison stared at the thousands of books which probably hadn't been removed from their shelves in a hundred years, she thought.

"I'll get Harold," Edwin said as he left the room. "Make yourselves comfortable."

Madison walked over to an old floor globe set inside a wooden cradle. She spun the world watching the continents whirl past. Bookshelves went from the floor to the ceiling. There was a spiral staircase in the corner leading to a walkway that encircled the room, providing access to the higher shelves. More crystal chandeliers hung from the ceiling. There was so much to see, Madison couldn't sit down and wait. She wanted more than anything to have a chance to explore this fantastic world.

"Do you like it, Madison?" her mother asked.

"I love it," she exclaimed, standing in awe of the place.

"You have to have a lot of money to afford something like this," her mother said.

Madison turned slowly, taking it all in until she came to the far corner of the room when she let out a squeal.

"What's wrong?"

Madison didn't answer, she just pointed to the corner.

"Oh, my," her mother said, getting up from the couch. "What is it?"

"It's a dragon!"

The two of them walked over to the eight-foot-tall monster with two-inch fangs. Horns jutted out from its head and jaw. Its claws looked like they could ravage any living creature. Even the fierce grizzlies of the North wouldn't stand a chance in a fight with this behemoth.

"I see you found my sculpture," Edwin said as he returned to the room carrying Madison's backpack.

"Sculpture?" Madison asked. "It looks so real."

"Yes, watch this." Edwin picked up a remote control and pushed a few buttons. The dragon came to life, letting out a snarl as it waved its head back and forth. Its arms moved in and out, extending its claws.

Madison jumped back. "I wouldn't want to meet a living one like him."

Edwin laughed. "There isn't such a thing—not anymore. But I can make real what isn't real. That's what I do." He handed Ida a business card. Edwin Gordon, sculptor of Monsters and Dragons."

He passed Madison's pack to her. "Thank you for letting Harold borrow it."

"I didn't let him borrow it," she snarled. "He took it from me."

"Madison, we're guests, watch it," her mother warned.

Edwin took a puff on his pipe. "Teasing you, is he?"

"Yes," she said. "Only it's much worse than that."

Edwin laughed. "He must like you."

"He shot at me with his BB gun."

That only amused Edwin even more. "When I wanted to get a girl's attention in school, I used spitballs," he said.

"I don't think he wants to get my attention," Madison scowled.

"Don't pay him any mind. He doesn't mean anything by it. He just doesn't express himself very well. Always getting in trouble for that, he is." Edwin went on. "The school's always calling me. I tell them you have to know how to handle him. Don't treat him like a sissy. He won't respect you for that."

"I don't treat him like a sissy. I tell him how it is," Madison said with her spunky attitude.

"I can see why he likes you."

That made Madison angry. "He doesn't like me," she said with sass in her voice.

Edwin laughed. Turning to Ida, he asked, "Would you like to see the rest of my work?"

"I don't know," she said. "I really should be—"

"Nonsense, it's just right through here," Edwin said as he set out across the room.

Ida followed hesitantly.

Edwin led them through a doorway on the far side of the library. It was a small door compared to the others in the house, tucked under the walkway that encircled the room.

Annoying as this guy was, Madison was also curious about what he had created and followed behind.

Inside the next room, Edwin showed off his realistic sculptures of creatures that could have been the subject of any child's nightmare. There were beasts with long fangs and red eyes that stood on two legs, dragons of all shapes and sizes, monster gorillas, snakes with arms, and underwater creatures that would make you afraid to step into your bathtub.

The art was creepy, yet very intriguing. It was so fascinating that Madison had forgotten all about the onyx stone in her pocket. She hadn't thought about it at all until her mother spoke up.

"I would hate to see any of these things come to life."

Madison's throat tightened. She realized now more than ever how important it was for her to keep her stone hidden. She couldn't begin to think of what could have happened if Harold had gotten hold of it.

Edwin led them around the room and introduced every creature, much to Ida's dismay. "This is my Hydra," he said as he pointed to a dragon with three heads.

Madison stared into the eyes of one of them. "Why does it have three heads?" she asked.

"Hydras are water serpents with multiple heads. If you cut one off, it grows two more in its place."

Madison cringed. "I hope I never run into one of these things in real life."

"This one is a drake," Edwin said as he pointed to the next sculpture. "It's a common dragon with four limbs and crawls around like a lizard, dragging its belly and tail on the ground. Goliath in the other room is a Drake."

Ida stepped slowly behind Edwin as she gawked at the lifelike work.

"Over here is an African dragon. It's more like a snake than a dragon. It doesn't have any arms or legs, but it is swift and strong. It can crush a man in seconds," Edwin continued.

"Why do you like dragons so much?" Ida asked.

"They fascinate me. Look at them. They are actually very beautiful and powerful. Look at the colors in the cockatrice over here. Notice the glistening green and blue skin and the deep reds in the wings and tail."

"I can understand why medieval men were so enthralled by them," Ida commented as she touched the large bird-like bill of the cockatrice.

"They killed them all off," Edwin said. "They were terrified of them."

"Who wouldn't be?" Madison added.

"I wouldn't be," Edwin said as he stroked the amphitere's head. "I don't think they would have all been evil. Some may even have been vegetarians. Eastern dragons were said to possess great wisdom, and oriental dragons were guardians that helped people."

"You don't believe these things actually existed, do you?"

"There are a lot of fictional tales about dragons, but fables are often born from truth."

"What's this one?" Madison asked as she examined a beautiful creature with a horse head and long mane flowing down the back of its neck.

"That's a lindworm. They like to swallow their prey whole."

"What did they eat?"

"People," Edwin said with a smile.

Madison swallowed hard. "It looks like a horse with a dragon body." Madison stared at its over-sized eyes. They looked like burning coals.

"This one is a wurm," Edwin continued. "It had no legs, but was extremely fast and exhaled noxious fumes. They could grow several hundred feet long or more."

Ida picked at the dragon's horns that protruded from its head and jaw bone. She looked up into its mouth, noticing the hundreds of sharp teeth.

"Of course, these are all much smaller models of their actual sizes. These monsters were quite large. My largest sculpture, besides Goliath in the library, is Caphira, over here." He walked to a giant dragon standing in the corner on two sturdy rear legs. Instead of arms, it had wings that spanned out at least fifteen feet.

"Pretty impressive, huh?" Edwin said with a proud grin. "She's a wyvern dragon with wings like a bat and a long tongue." Edwin went on. "She looks big, but her wings and legs fold up against her body." He stood and admired his creation for a minute before moving on.

"Over here are four dragonnets. They are very similar to the western dragon, except they are much smaller. They can be as small as a kitten or as big as a lion, and they hunt in packs like other smaller animals do."

Madison couldn't help imagining Edwin's dragons coming to life and attacking, now that she knew it was a distinct possibility with the onyx stone. "Mom, can we go home now?" she asked in a shaky voice.

Ida nodded. "Thanks for the tour. It was fascinating."

"My pleasure," Edwin said and led them back into the library.

Madison eyed the dark behemoth in the corner as the three of them walked by.

Edwin continued leading them through the library and into the front foyer. "Are you coming next week?" he asked.

Ida gave him a puzzled look. "I'm sorry?"

"To the convention center."

Ida shook her head, having no idea what he was talking about.

"They're having an art show featuring the top artists in the country. Malcolm Toka is going to be there, and Janet Velasquez, with her modern classics. They're even going to have the famous violin player, what's her name?" Edwin snapped his fingers, trying to remember. "Jackie Gyllenskog," he said, pointing to Ida.

"I've heard of her," Madison interjected.

"I don't know, I'll check my calendar," Ida said, not sounding very enthusiastic about the whole thing.

"The media's going to be there. They're doing a story on the artists. My dragons have been chosen as the centerpiece for the show." He gestured with his pipe to the library. "I wanted to bring ol' Goliath in there, but he's too large. He won't fit inside my van. I'm bringing Caphira instead. She's going to be set up in the lobby over the fountain in front of the main stairs. You should come. You'll love it."

Ida smiled. "I'm sure. If I'm not busy," she said as Edwin escorted them to the front door.

He grabbed a piece of paper from a table in the foyer. "Here's information on the show, the dates and times are right here," Edwin pointed to the page as he handed it to Ida.

"Thank you," she said, handing the sheet to Madison.

Edwin watched from the doorway as the two of them walked down the walkway to their car. "See you next week," he called out.

Ida smiled back at him and nodded.

Madison folded the paper up and put in in her pocket.

The two of them drove off, neither of them able to shake the images they had just seen from their minds.

"Mom."

"Yes, Madison."

"I don't want to go to that art show."

"Neither do I," Ida chuckled.

18

Intruder Alert

The front door of the Kleigh's residence was partially ajar when Dr. Alazar pulled up. He could see the hallway light on inside, but Ida's car was not there.

"Interesting," he said out loud as he pulled off to the curb. He decided not to park in the driveway.

Dr. Alazar hustled up to the door and slipped inside as stealthily as he could. He found drawers opened and dumped out as if someone had been looking for something, although he did not suspect a burglar looking for valuables. This was Michael Kleigh's home, and Dr. Alazar was very aware of what that meant. He cautiously sneaked around the house. Though he was in good physical condition, he wasn't as young as he used to be and may not come out on the good end of a fight.

Upstairs he heard a thud and someone walking around. He picked up a heavy giraffe sculpture carved from snakewood and crept up the stairs. Inside one of the bedrooms, a man was rummaging through the closets and drawers. Dr. Alazar hid behind the bathroom door, planning his next move.

A frontal assault would be a bad idea, he thought. The man may be armed. He could call the police, but they would ask too many questions. He didn't like questions. He could call NASA, but they weren't equipped for such things. They would just tell him to call the local police. He stood there in the darkness, wondering what to do when suddenly the man was standing in front of him, looking down at something in his hand.

Dr. Alazar recognized him right away, but he knew this would be a dangerous time for the two of them to meet. He had to react fast, which is precisely what he did. Without thinking, he brought the giraffe down on the back of the man's neck. He tumbled over and rolled down the stairs, creating a hideous crashing sound. Halfway down the stairs, the man lay in a heap.

"Now, let's see what you had in your hand," Dr. Alazar said, looking down from the top of the stairs, knowing the man couldn't answer. He scanned the hallway floor until he spotted a dark object lying near the front door.

Hopping over the unconscious man, Dr. Alazar scooted down the stairs and reached for the object. At that moment, Ida stepped into the house.

"What's going on here?" Ida snapped.

Dr. Alazar put out his hands to try to calm her down. "Don't be angry, Ida. I caught a burglar."

"A burglar?" Ida gasped. Her eyes darted around the room. "Where?"

"I want to see," Madison spoke up as she craned her neck to see into the house. .

"Go back to the car, Maddy," her mother said with a stressed voice.

"But, Mom," Madison whined.

"I mean it, now. Go to the car."

Madison reluctantly went and stood in the driveway.

"Did you call the police?" Ida asked, turning back to Dr. Alazar. As he paused to think of an excuse for not calling, Ida made her way into the house to get a look. "Jim!" she shrieked.

"You know him?"

"He's not a burglar, he's my... a friend." Ida rushed to the stairs and felt him for a pulse. "What did you do?" Dr. Alazar stammered. "I-I was coming to see you and found the door open." He looked around. "Look at this place. It looks like he's been through every drawer in the house."

Ida ran to the kitchen and returned with a damp cloth. "He probably lost something."

"Yeah," Dr. Alazar said. "I wonder what that could have been." He glanced over at Ida. Jim was coming to. "I would check him for weapons before you did that."

"Weapons? Why on earth would he have a weapon?"

"Where did you meet this guy?" Alazar asked.

"What does that have to do with anything?" she asked with an irritated tone, throwing his question back at him.

"A lot, actually."

"If you must know, he was with the catering company on the day of the launch. He found my wallet and returned it to me the next day."

"Uh-huh. Found, huh?"

"I'm not sure I like the tone of your voice," Ida said, stepping down from the stairs. She reached out suddenly and grabbed Dr. Alazar's hand. "What's this?"

"Oh, I found that on the floor by the door."

Ida looked up at Dr. Alazar. "That's Madison's stone. What are you doing with Madison's stone?" she asked with a suspicious tone in her voice.

"Look, I tried to tell you, I came to see you..." He gestured to the door. "The door was open, I came in and found someone going through your things." Shrugging his shoulders, he continued. "I didn't know he was a friend. I knocked him down the stairs with your... your..." He pointed to the broken sculpture on the floor. "Your giraffe thing. I'm sorry. I thought he was robbing you." He gestured back and forth. "Look around. The place has been ransacked. I think he was looking for this," Dr. Alazar said, holding up the stone.

"Why would he want a stone?" She held out her palm for Dr. Alazar to give it to her.

"I don't know," he said, rubbing his thumb over the rock. "Where did it come from? It's perfectly smooth, not a mark on it."

"What?"

"There are no defects on it anywhere."

"Let me see that."

Dr. Alazar handed Ida the stone, and she looked it over carefully.

"Is there something wrong?" he asked.

"Oh, it's nothing," Ida answered. "It's just that I need to have a little talk with my daughter."

Jim began to moan.

"Now we'll get some real answers," she said, turning to her friend. "Jim, can you hear me?"

The man looked up at her, then over at Alazar.

"Jim, it's me, Ida. Are you okay?"

He stared at Ida like he didn't know what to say.

She held up the stone. "What did you want with this?" she asked.

Jim pushed himself up along the wall and stepped down the stairs slowly. When he got to the bottom, he bolted out the door as fast as he could.

Madison watched as he ran down the driveway toward his car, which he had parked a little way down the road. A few seconds later, there was a sound of tires squealing. All three of them stood there, wondering what had just happened.

"I told you so," Dr. Alazar said.

An hour later, several police officers roamed through Ida's home. She sat at the table with Madison and Dr. Alazar, answering questions.

A few minutes later, Officer Matos stepped into the kitchen. "We checked out the address you gave us. It's an empty apartment. We found a mattress on the floor and some takeout food cartons. That was all."

"I don't believe this," Ida said. "He set me up."

The officer held out the stone. "Are you sure this is what he was looking for?"

Ida looked at Madison. Madison shrugged her shoulders. "No, I'm not sure. We found it on the floor. It could have rolled there when he was going through our things."

"Well," the officer handed the stone back to her. "If you notice anything, or think of anything else, don't hesitate to call us."

Dr. Alazar stayed and helped Ida and Madison clean up the house. It was late when he finally said his goodbyes. "Don't be afraid to call me any time, even at two in the morning."

Ida nodded. "Thank you, Lauro, for everything. I'm sorry..."

"Sorry for what?" he asked.

"Sorry for, you know, for earlier."

"Don't worry about it. After all. It's my job, right?"

Ida smiled as she closed the door, making sure it was locked tight.

19

Time Out

"Did you bring it?" Lou asked.

"I thought we weren't going to use it anymore," Madison said.

"I know, I know, but this is different."

"In what way?"

"We have to win this game. We're playing against Chad's team, and I want to show him up," Lou said.

"But how is the stone going to help our team win the game?"

"Good luck!" Lou said with excitement.

"Good luck?" Madison glowered.

"Come on. You want to beat him just as bad as I do, and you know it. All I want is to keep it in my pocket during the game. What harm can that do?"

"Why don't I just keep it in *my* pocket?"

"Because I'm our team's best player. I always get the most goals," Lou boasted.

Madison couldn't say anything about that. She knew Lou was right. Madison couldn't hit the broad side of a barn with the ball. "Okay, but don't lose it."

Lou squealed with glee as Madison set the stone in her hands.

"I mean it, Lou," Madison repeated. "Don't lose it."

The score was twelve to eight, and the girls' team was winning. The other kids cheered as Lou scored another point. She was playing better than she had ever played before. "See, I told you so, the stone is bringing me good luck," she said as she slapped hands with Madison.

Although Madison was happy their team was winning, she wasn't so sure that the stone had anything to do with it. Lou was just good at playing soccer. Actually, she was good at any sport.

Lou was playing stopper when the opposing team outsmarted the defensive midfielder with an inside scissor kick, then headed straight for Lou. *Would he use the same maneuver on her?* she wondered. Probably not. She prepared herself for something new.

Two players from the opposing team were running up on each side, so she was sure he was going to pass the ball—but to which one, she wondered? Figuring he would make that decision based on her move, she decided to surprise him with a scissor move of her own. She ran to the left, keeping her weight on her other foot, then spun around, jumping fast to the right, faking him out. She stopped his pass and stole the ball, dribbling straight on down the field and kicking it into the goal, right past Chad.

Playing goalie for the other team, Chad's face grew red with fury. "What are you, anyway, a boy or a girl?" he asked in a derogatory manner.

"What's it to you?" Lou spat back.

"Definitely a girl," he said.

Lou could feel the anger boiling inside. With her good-luck charm stashed safely in her pocket, her confidence swelled so much that she took a big chance and charged Chad. She tackled him to the ground, beating on him with her hands. Chad threw her off and tried to get her in an arm lock, but she threw her legs around and tripped him up. The two of them tumbled to the ground again. Neither one of them heard the coach blowing his whistle.

"Fight! Fight!" someone yelled, and both teams went running over to watch.

Lou rolled over to get away from him, but he kept with her, grabbing at her legs to flip her back over. She went down head over heels but managed to swing back around and get him in a headlock. By that time, the coach had managed to push himself through the group and grabbed Chad by his collar, pulling him off Lou.

"I said, stop!" he yelled at the top of his lungs.

Lou stood up. Pieces of grass were in her hair, and her shirt was stained green. Chad wasn't in any better shape. His face was scratched and sweaty. "She fights like a girl too," he said bitterly.

"Both of you," the coach continued in a grouchy tone. "To the benches, now!" he said, pushing Chad away. "You," he said, motioning to Lou, "That bench," he pointed again to the opposite side of the field. Lou scowled at Chad, then stormed off to the benches.

"Ten minutes for both of you," the coach yelled. "Everybody else, positions. Let's go, look alive!"

Madison jogged over to Lou on the bench.

"What are you doing?" she growled. "You don't have to sit out."

"Well, if you don't play, I don't play. Besides, there are only a few minutes left anyhow."

Lou grumbled. "I hate that kid."

"If we're both not playing, we might as well go home now," Madison suggested.

The two girls sauntered down the sidewalk, rehashing the fight.

"Man, you tore him up," Madison said.

"I heard his back crack when I tackled him," Lou laughed. "At least I think it was his back."

"Did you see how flustered he was?"

"Yea, he's a wimp. But did you see how well I was playing?" Lou exclaimed. "I was on top of the world," she said as she spun around. "The stone really does bring you good luck."

"Yeah, about that..." Madison held out her palm. "Hand it over."

Lou reached into her pocket. A sudden look of terror flooded her face.

"What's wrong?" Madison asked.

"The stone..." Lou cried. "It's gone."

"What?" Madison yelled. "I told you not to lose it."

"It must have fallen out of my pocket when we were fighting."

The girls spun around and gazed back toward the park. "Let's go!" Madison screeched, and the two of them ran as fast as they could back to the fields.

The game had ended, and parents were picking their kids up as Madison and Lou walked around the goal where the fight had taken place.

"Do you see it?" Madison asked, worried that her stone may be lost for good.

"No, it's not here."

"Keep looking."

They walked back and forth, kicking at the grass.

"Madison," Lou called.

"What?" she answered without taking her eyes off the ground.

"Madison, look." Lou grabbed her arm.

Madison looked in the direction Lou was pointing. Chad was standing on the sidewalk waiting for his ride, looking at something in his hand. It was hard to see from their distance, but it looked like a dark object. "The stone," Madison moaned.

Chad glanced up at the girls, then shoved the object into his pocket.

"Come on!" Madison shouted, and the two of them ran toward the boy. A red BMW pulled up, and he jumped inside before the girls made it across the field. The car pulled away before they reached the sidewalk. Madison stopped running, dropping her hands to her side in defeat. She could see Chad's devilish smirk through the window as the car rounded a turn.

"It's no use. They're gone," Madison whined.

"We can go to his house," Lou suggested.

"Do you know where Chad lives?"

Lou looked down at the ground. "No."

"Besides, it's just a small stone," Madison lamented. "He'll just lie about it. And how will we convince his parents that the stone is valuable? They'll just get one from the back yard and say *here, go have fun with your rock,*" she mocked in a condescending tone.

"Then what are we going to do?" Lou asked.

Madison had no idea. "I wish my Dad were here."

Madison's mother was waiting for her when she walked into the house.

"We need to talk," she said sternly.

"About what?" Madison asked.

Her mother held out the stone.

Madison's heart raced with excitement. "You found it?" she screeched and ran toward her mother.

"This is not the one we got in the mail, is it?" she asked.

Madison deflated quicker than an untied balloon. "Oh," she said as she slowly turned away.

"Oh?" her mother repeated, looking for an explanation.

Madison sighed as she dropped into the armchair.

"What are you trying to pull?" her mother stood before her like an attorney interrogating a witness. "Did you think I wouldn't notice?"

"It was an accident," Madison said in defense. "I didn't mean to give you the wrong stone."

"So, where is the real one?"

Madison's cheeks puffed as she blew out through her lips. "It's gone," she finally said. "Harold and his gang took it."

Her mother sat on the couch, resting her forehead in her hand as she shook her head. "Madison, when will you ever learn?"

"It wasn't my fault," she whined.

Her mother's mouth dropped. "Wasn't your fault? Why didn't you leave it in the box like you were told?"

"You don't understand, Mom. That stone has special powers. It brought Razor to life."

"Madison, Madison, Madison." Her mother sighed in frustration. Standing up, she crossed the room, then turned back to her daughter.

"Well, it's gone now," she said, dropping her hands to her side. "No more worrying about the stone. It's over. Now, maybe we can get back to our normal lives."

Madison gripped the arms of her chair and stared at her mother. The finality of the situation suddenly hit her hard, sending strong emotions through her body. She pushed herself up and ran up the stairs to her room, doing her best to hold back the tears.

Before going to sleep, Madison sat her picture of Razor at the foot of her bed, where he liked to curl up at night. The energy from the stone had worn off hours ago.

"I'm so sorry, Razor," she said, stroking the paper. "I was so stupid letting Lou use the stone. If I ever get it back, I'll never let anybody touch it again." She crawled into her bed and reached to pull the chain on the lamp. "Goodnight, buddy," she said just before shutting off the light.

Ida pushed the bedroom door open slightly and peered in. Light from the hallway cut across Madison's bed. She had already fallen asleep. Her mother noticed the cat picture lying across the covers next to her pillow. Ida shook her head and sighed. She was concerned that Madison's worry over her father was the root of her obsession with the stone.

20

Recruiting Help

"Thanks for meeting me, Lauro," Ida said as Dr. Alazar took a seat in the booth. It was late, and there wasn't much activity in the diner.

"My pleasure," Dr. Alazar said. "What can I do for you?"

"It's Madison. She's distraught. I'm afraid that her father's mission is taking its toll on her," Ida explained.

"How can I help?"

"You know that stone we thought Jim was after the other day?"

"Yes?"

"Madison thinks... She believes..." Ida sighed. She felt silly putting it into words. "Well, it means a lot to her and..."

Dr. Alazar nodded. "Go on."

"There's a group of boys in the neighborhood that pick on her. They took the stone from her today."

"The same stone I saw?"

Ida's face went blank. She couldn't help thinking there was something special about the stone that came in the mail. Something she needed to keep to herself.

"What's wrong?" Dr. Alazar asked.

Ida shook it her head. "It's nothing. It's one just like it. Madison switched them. It's a long story. Would you mind helping to get it back? I'm not sure how to get the boys to admit they have it."

Dr. Alazar leaned back in his seat, deep in thought.

"Can I get you something?" the waitress asked as she pulled her pencil and pad from her smock.

Ida looked up. "Just a coffee, black." She smiled.

"I'll have the same, cream and sugar on the side," Dr. Alazar added.

The waitress spun on her heel and headed for the counter.

"Do you know where these boys live?"

Ida dug through her purse and pulled out a note. Here's his address. It's in the next development just a short way down Marigold Avenue. His name is Chad Baggett. If he doesn't have it, I can get you the addresses of the other two boys. I know the one lives in that big mansion off of Marigold, near the creek.

Dr. Alazar took the note. "I'll see what I can do."

The waitress brought their coffee. Dr. Alazar emptied a sugar pack and two plastic creamer tubs into his cup. "Where did this stone come from?" he asked.

"It came in the mail on her birthday," Ida answered.

"Who sent it? Maybe they can send another one."

"That's a mystery," Ida said, fumbling with her cup. "There was no return address on the package."

"Very interesting," he said as he lifted his cup to his mouth. He sipped his coffee, then set his cup back down. "Very interesting," he repeated.

21

Fellowship of the Stone

"Okay, what's the big important message that you couldn't tell me over the phone," Harold barked as he barged into the back door of Chad Baggett's house. Bryant was right behind him.

"Remember the other day when you ridiculed me for signing up for soccer?" Chad asked.

Harold shrugged.

"Well, it wasn't a waste of time after all," Chad continued.

"What are you talking about, loser?"

Bryant had begun rummaging through the cupboards in Chad's kitchen. He slammed the cabinet door behind him. "Don't you have anything good to eat around here?"

"Hey! Knock it off. I'm trying to tell you guys something," Chad grumbled.

"Well, I'm hungry," Bryant said, pulling a bag of potato chips from the cupboard. "Where are your parents anyway?" he asked as he stuffed his face full of chips."

"They're out," Chad growled. "Put those down."

"Not until I'm done," Bryant growled back.

"Give me that," Harold demanded, as he snatched the bag from Bryant. Several chips flew out across the floor.

"Watch it! My mother just cleaned the house. She'll go berserk on me if I get one thing out of place."

Harold tossed the bag onto the table. "So, what about soccer?"

"We had a game yesterday, and guess who was there?"

"Do I care?" Harold asked, pretending not to be interested.

"You would if you knew what I have," Chad taunted.

"Just tell me before I get sick," he said, pulling a chair around backward and straddling it.

Suddenly a rubber band flew through the air and stung Harold in the ear.

"You scum bag!" he yelled as he jumped up from the chair. He grabbed Bryant, pushing him onto the couch as he wrapped one arm around his neck, getting him into a headlock.

"I give, I give." Bryant barely choked out the words as his face turned bright red. Harold pushed him away. "Pansy," he scoffed.

"Will you two knock it off?" Chad yelled.

"What did you call us here for, you dork?"

Chad grabbed the stone out of his pocket and plunked it onto the table.

Harold's eyes widened. "Why didn't you say you had this?"

"I was trying to," Chad griped.

Harold let out a maniacal laugh as he picked up the stone and studied it. "Have you figured out how to make it work?"

"No, I can't get it to do anything."

"How long have you had this?" Bryant asked.

"Since yesterday," Chad answered.

Harold's eyes shot toward Chad like daggers. "You weren't going to tell us, were you?"

"I was going to."

"Yeah, after you couldn't figure it out. You needed our help, dweeb. That just cost you the stone."

"Just help me to get it working, Harold," Chad whined.

Harold shook the stone—hard.

"Already tried that," Chad said in a sing-song.

Harold smirked, then tried rubbing it.

"Tried that too," Chad groaned.

Harold glared at him. "What else did you try?"

Heating it up... putting in the freezer... dropping it on the ground... rolling it around... nothing worked."

"Did you try singing it a lullaby?"

Chad scowled at him. "No, I didn't sing it a lullaby," he said, mocking the older boy.

Harold sat back in the chair and thought. He tossed the stone up in the air and caught it.

"What about water?" Bryant asked. "Did you get it wet?"

Chad's eyes lit up. "No! I didn't try that."

The three of them ran to the sink and turned on the faucet. They watched with anticipation as Harold slowly pushed the stone under the running water. They watched in amazement as the water beaded up into tiny black hardened pellets as soon it touched the stone.

Chad reached his hand under the orb and caught the beads as they dropped. "They're hard, like black BBs," he said, puzzled.

"What in the world?" Harold mumbled, pulling the stone from under the water and examining it up close. "What is this thing?" he wondered out loud.

Reaching into the sink, Harold scooped up some of the pellets. He glanced up at the other boys with the look of pure bewilderment. The pellets rolled around in his hand as he studied them up close, pushing them with his thumb. As he stared into his hand, the pellets slowly melted back into water. He dumped the water back onto the stone, and once again, it beaded up into hardened balls.

The boys stood there, dumbfounded, when a loud knock startled them back to reality. Chad jumped and glanced at the front door. "Someone's here."

Dr. Alazar held up his ID when Chad opened the door. "I'm from the NASA investigation team. I'm working with the FBI investigating the disappearance of an experimental stone that was stolen from our laboratories. You wouldn't happen to know anything about it, would you?"

"Uh, no. I-I don't know what you're talking about," Chad stammered.

"Are your parents at home?"

"No, they're out right now. Maybe you can come back later."

"Are you Chad Baggett?"

Chad began to sweat, concerned that this man knew his name. "I, um—"

"What's going on here?" Harold said as he pushed Chad away from the door.

Dr. Alazar took a deep breath. "I was telling your friend that we are investigating the disappearance of an experimental stone—"

"Mister, we don't have any stone here, okay?" Harold said and began to close the door.

"We have you on the park's video camera," Dr. Alazar said in desperation.

Harold stopped. "Not me, you don't. Look at it again for that Madison Kleigh girl."

"We already talked to her. She told us that someone living here took the stone. Would that be you?"

"There's no stone here, he said as he resumed closing the door."

"Your fingerprints will be on the stone, Harold Gordon. We *will* get it back, and we *will* know you had it." Dr. Alazar took a guess that it was Harold he was talking to. The boy fit the description Ida had given him.

Harold finished closing the door and locked it. He ran to the kitchen. "Quick, give me the stone," he demanded.

"Why?" Chad asked.

"You have your greasy fingerprints all over it." He grabbed the stone and exhaled deeply to fog it up so he could wipe it clean, and it began to glow bright blue. Surprised by the unexpected reaction, Harold instinctively dropped it to the floor. The sudden jar activated the stone, and it began to spark and sputter at the chipped end until blue rays of energy flowed out over the floor.

"What the..." Harold whispered as he watched the light show.

"This is the same thing that happened when Madison dropped it on the ground the other day," Bryant reminded them. "Then weeds grew up five feet tall."

"That's not going to happen now, is it?" Chad asked. "We're indoors, right? There's no dirt."

"We're talking about *your* house, right?" Harold chimed in. "It's not exactly clean, you know. I don't care what your mother says."

Suddenly green shoots began to creep up from the floor. They twisted and mingled with each other as they grew through the kitchen chair and up the table leg.

"Get back," Harold barked, and the boys took refuge in the living room as the thorny vines spread out across the kitchen. They had slithered through the cupboard doors, across the counters, around the coffee maker, and over the refrigerator before they finally stopped growing.

"My Mom's going to pitch a fit!" Chad grumbled.

Outside, Dr. Alazar got into his car. He could see he wasn't going to get anywhere with the boys. He would have to speak with the parents, he thought. Perhaps they would have more sense and not want to risk trouble with the law—if they cared about such things. He put his car in gear and drove off, passing an old, white Pontiac parked against the curb.

Inside the car, Jim ducked down so he wouldn't be seen. In his hands, he caressed a .45 revolver.

22

A Lost Cause

Harold was bored. He sat on an old rickety chair inside the abandoned house, tossing pieces of broken tile at the windows. Vines and thorns had sprung up all around the place. A crude stick figure of a cat was scratched into an old board.

"Hey, dweebs! Is that all you can do with that thing? Grow weeds? Our gardener could do better than that," he complained.

"I don't get it. Madison's paper cat was alive," Chad said as he knelt on the floor, examining a fern.

"You were seeing things," Harold grunted. "It was on a string."

"We've been here for hours, Chad," Bryant complained. "It doesn't do anything but make weeds grow."

"It made water turn to stone," Chad said in an attempt to regain their interest.

"I'm hungry," Bryant moaned. "Let's go get a slice."

"Do you have any money?" Harold asked.

"No, you?"

"If I did, I wouldn't buy you any pizza, that's for sure."

Bryant glanced at the stone as Chad rolled it back and forth between his knees. "Maybe we can make weeds grow up in everybody's lawn, then charge for chopping them down."

Harold frowned at him. "*You* can, but I'm not going to cut any weeds. I had enough of that in Chad's kitchen this morning. I'll go home and have my father order a pizza."

"Yeah, let's get out of here," Bryant agreed as his stomach growled.

The three of them meandered through the woods until they were back on the road. Reaching Chad's house, they pushed their way through the back door.

"Guys," Chad froze after walking into his living room. "I think we've been robbed."

Harold and Bryant stepped into the room and glanced around. The place was a mess. Every drawer and cabinet had been emptied out onto the floor. It looked worse than the abandoned house they had just left.

"I'm outa here," Harold said as he headed for the back door. "I don't want to be around when your Mom gets home."

"But wait," Chad grabbed his arm before he could step outside. "You have to stay and help me explain this to my mother."

"No, that's your problem," Harold said as he grabbed the stone out of Chad's hand. "I'll take that."

"Hey, I found it!" Chad protested.

"Yeah, and now you lost it," Harold said as he walked out the door.

Bryant ran to catch up. "Can you order enough pizza for me, too?"

"Get lost, dweeb." Harold answered as they walked past a white Pontiac that was parked along the curb.

A few streets over, Bryant walked into his own house. "What's for dinner?" he called out as he closed the door behind him. He never noticed the white Pontiac creep up to the curb across the street and slowly come to a stop.

Jim waited for the family to leave for the pizza restaurant, then pulled on his gloves.

Chad's mother was hysterical as she paced back and forth, her cell phone pressed to her ear. "I don't know, I just got home and found my house a wreck!" she shouted at the officer on the other end of the phone. "Just get here as soon as you can," she barked and pressed the hang-up button.

She sat on her couch and rubbed her forehead. "I need a drink," she groaned.

Back at the Gordon mansion, Harold stepped into the dragon hall. He pulled the onyx stone from his pocket and circled slowly around the room.

"Now for the real test," he said in a low, devious voice. "How about you, Mr. dragon with three heads. Would you like to become living art?"

Harold blew on the stone and waited for it to glow blue. His face lit up as he glared into the stone's light. Lifting the rock slowly, he hesitated as second thoughts flowed through his mind, but he shook them off and banged the stone against his other hand. Sparks spat from the chipped area, and Harold gently rolled it under the dragon's feet. He stepped back and watched the show.

Blue rays of energy flowed up the hydra's legs and across its entire body. Just before the glow faded, the three-foot-tall model blinked its eyes on all three of its heads.

Harold gasped. "It must be only art that can come alive. Something hand made."

The dragon stood up straight and looked around until its eyes fixed on the boy.

Harold stumbled backward. "Good dragon," he said with a shaky voice. With a thud, the creature hopped from the display bench to the floor and advanced toward Harold. It hissed as its three heads bobbed to and fro.

Keeping his distance, Harold shuffled backward until he bumped up against the doorframe. The dragon continued advancing, hissing and snapping its teeth. With his back against the wall, Harold quickly slid through the doorway and made a hasty retreat into the library.

The dragon followed close behind, hissing as it lumbered across the room. Using all six of its eyes, it surveyed its surroundings. Harold ran through the library, across the foyer, and into the family room where he threw open a closet door. Board games and electronic toys spilled to the floor as he rummaged through the shelves, hoping to find a net or something to trap the creature.

Unfortunately, there was nothing that could help, so he grabbed the only item he could use as a weapon, an old baseball bat. Harold picked it up and held it firmly in his hands.

"This will have to do," he mumbled and swiftly swung the door closed. To his surprise, the hydra was standing on the other side. Harold jumped back against the wall as the beast snapped at him. Remembering the bat, he lifted it high and swung. The creature ducked out of the way and backed off.

"Get away," Harold yelled as he swung the bat again and again. The nimble creature avoided each stroke as it retreated, getting a few good snaps in here and there, missing the boy's body by mere inches. Harold turned and ran to the hallway. As fast as he could, he pulled the door open to the lower level and jumped inside.

The dragon was on him immediately, getting two of its heads inside the doorway before Harold had a chance to pull it closed. He dodged down the stairs, skipping two steps at a time. The dragon, however, being unaccustomed to stairs and having a limited mindset of attacking its victim, miscalculated the steps and tumbled over.

Harold leaped out of the way as the dragon plunged to the bottom of the staircase. Disoriented from the fall, the beast fumbled around to regain its orientation. Harold took advantage of the situation and climbed back up the stairs as quickly as he could.

It didn't take long for the dragon to get back to its feet, and it was at Harold's heels the whole way. At the top of the stairs, Harold grabbed the doorknob and slammed it closed. There was a loud crash on the door as the dragon plowed into it. Fortunately for Harold, the beast didn't have enough force to break through. Harold leaned back against the door as he slid down to the floor. He could hear the dragon snorting on the other side.

"Okay, Madison," he said out loud. "I understand how your stone works now." He glanced back at the lower level door. "And why you chose a paper cat."

23

Just a Dragon

Edwin Gordon unloaded his dragon sculpture at the Atmore Convention Center. He had hoped someone would be there to help him, but all the volunteers were already working with other artists as they set up their exhibits. He continued on his own, lugging the beast into the building on a wheeled cart.

The building was an old theater house built in the 1800s. The slanted floor and seating were removed when it was converted into a Grange hall sometime in the '50s.

Before the center opened, exhibitors hustled about, setting up tables, hanging art, and running extension cords. Edwin could ignore their stares as he set up his dragon exhibit, but not their mumbling. He desperately wanted to hear their comments, especially those of Janet Velasquez, the famous impressionist, one of the best in the modern art community. He imagined her gawking at his work, jealous that he was the best in the show. Edwin tidied up as quickly as he could before Ms. Velasquez chanced to walk past.

There was also the media he intended to impress. He had already dropped a screwdriver into the fountain and ruined half a roll of gaffer's tape because he couldn't keep his mind on his work. He kept glancing up to see if any members of the press had stepped through the front doors.

"Where is that boy?" Edwin complained to himself, blaming his blunders on his lack of help. An hour into the day and Harold was a no show. "He was supposed to be here long ago," Edwin grumbled on.

The dragon stood about six feet tall, with its neck stretched out over the fountain. Edwin repositioned the large planters in the foyer to create a jungle-like environment. He also placed two smaller dragonnets, one on each side of the larger beast. Finally, he had a large banner to hang across the foyer, welcoming guests.

There were about fifteen minutes left before the doors opened to the public, and Edwin was still busy hanging the banner. With no help, holding it in place while tying off the anchor ropes was a monumental task. As he struggled on the ladder, he could hear the comments from another exhibitor behind him.

"How gruesome," the voice said in disgust. "That's going to cause a massive disturbance in the feng shui of the show. I hope its negative energy doesn't reach my booth," the voice continued.

"Feng shui is nothing but a load of phony hocus pocus," Edwin spat out as he knotted the last rope in place. "The best way to make people remember you is to shock your name into their brain," he said as he turned to face his protester. When he realized whom he had been talking to, the name Janet Velasquez became permanently engraved into his mind.

"Ms. Velasquez!" he croaked out as the ladder shook beneath his feet. "I-I didn't know it was you."

"You would have shown more respect if you had known?" she asked as she looked up at the dragon and grunted. "No amount of respect from you could overpower the negative influence of this monstrosity.

How could you respect me when you obviously have no respect for the health and tranquility of the environment?"

Edwin couldn't move. He couldn't even step down from the ladder, let alone say something in return.

"Your banner's crooked," Ms. Velasquez said and walked away.

Edwin was crushed. He stepped down and sat on the side of the fountain, listening to the water rain into the pool. Glancing up, he noticed that Ms. Velasquez had been telling the truth. His banner hung lower on one side, but he didn't care anymore.

The coordinator opened the doors and announced that the fifteenth annual Atmore Art Show was now open. People began to flood the foyer and admire the entrance display. The comments from the public were much more encouraging than those from the other exhibitors, which helped to lift Edwin's spirits. However, his mood was still somewhat bitter since Harold hadn't shown up to help.

"No way!" one patron wearing a tee shirt with a yellow smiley face on the front exclaimed. "This is awesome. Dude! Why weren't you at Comic-Con?"

"This is not a comic," Edwin barked back. "This is real art."

"Well, excuse me," he said as he backed away. He took one more look at the sculpture before turning toward the stairs. "By the way, your banner's crooked. Still pretty cool, though." In seconds he was gone.

A five-year-old boy hid behind his mother as they walked past. The presence of a real-looking dragon didn't sit too well with him. Many more guests admired the work of Edwin Gordon. Some were freaked out, some were awed, but the real test was still to come. He was sure he'd please the media when they came in. And it wasn't long before a woman, and a man with a professional video camera on his shoulder, walked through the front door.

Ms. Lisa Erickson, a well-known reporter for WKHJ-TV4, stepped in front of the fountain and readied herself for an introduction clip. Edwin stepped up as she adjusted her lavaliere.

"What do you think?" he asked, gesturing toward his dragon.

"Are you the artist?" she asked coldly. She appeared to be a little hostile, but Edwin figured it was due to the pressures of being a reporter.

"Yes, I am," Edwin said proudly.

Mrs. Erickson looked over her shoulder. "It's a perfect backdrop for my intro," she said. "Would you mind if I ask you a few questions on camera?"

"Not at all," Edwin responded. Finally, he was going to get the attention he deserved, he thought as he fixed his hair.

"What's your name?"

"Gordon. Edwin Gordon," he answered.

The cameraman signaled Ms. Erickson, and she began. "Hello, I'm Lisa Erickson, and I'm standing in the foyer of the Atmore Convention Center with artist Edwin Gordon." She stepped off to the side as she continued to speak. "Behind me, dozens of exhibitors will be displaying their work today inside this beautiful historic building." She waved her hand, gesturing to the broad stairway and hall behind her.

"These artists represent humanity's best works of art designed to hang on your wall and sit on your fireplace mantel. They are the heartbeat of our culture. This building has been chosen as a setting to display their work because of its historical background and intricate architecture and design. But as people roam the halls, taking in the beautiful work of the artists here today, they have no idea of the dragons lurking in the dark, preparing to destroy the very thing that brought us all here today.

"The Skyner Corporation owns this building, this irreplaceable historical marker, and they are planning on destroying it. There are plans in the works as we speak to tear down this beautiful piece of art, and to replace it with a larger, modern building."

She stepped up alongside Edwin and asked, "Mr. Gordon, how do you feel about destroying the Mona Lisa in favor of a new, more modern painting?"

Edwin's jaw dropped. He'd never been sideswiped so hard before in his life. "I... uh..." he turned and pointed to his dragon. "I... uh..."

"Speechless!" Lisa Erickson said as she turned to the camera. "That's exactly how I was when I first heard the news. And so should you." She turned back to Edwin.

"What do you plan on doing to help prevent this tragedy from befalling your local town?"

Edwin rubbed the back of his neck. "I really hadn't thought about it."

Ms. Erickson nodded. "Well, maybe you should start." She turned back to the camera. "All of us should be thinking about preserving the precious art that surrounds us. Lisa Erickson, WKHJ news." She smiled until the cameraman tipped the camera down and nodded, then her frown returned.

Edwin stood there, staring. He couldn't think of anything to say.

"Oh, thank you. You were perfect," Lisa said as she packed up her things. Just before she left, she looked up at the display. "Your banner's crooked," she said, then headed out the door.

Frustration and depression flowed over Edwin, causing his head to spin. He sat down and watched the visitors come and go. At least they stopped to admire his work from time to time. More than an hour into the show, two women approached the front doors. Both were dressed in business attire, and one of them held a professional camera. Edwin was sure they were writers for an art magazine. The one with the camera started taking shots of the entry display as soon as she stepped into the foyer. The other woman walked straight over to Edwin. His heart skipped a beat. *Finally*, he thought as he stood to greet her.

Edwin reached out to shake her hand. "Edwin Gordon," he said. Her face dropped, and she pulled a handkerchief from her purse, holding it so her hand wouldn't touch his skin.

"Uh," he said, feeling a little spurned. "Are you with one of the art magazines?" he asked, shaking her hand carefully.

"Art World," she answered. "Clara Shay. Are you the artist?"

"Yes," he said proudly. "It's animatronic. I can activate it by remote control."

She turned to the dragon and shrugged. "Did you get a shot, Alecia?"

"Sure did," her photographer answered. "But the banner's crooked."

Edwin cringed.

Clara thanked him, and the two women went off.

Edwin watched them crest the top of the stairs, wondering what could possibly be more intriguing than his dragon. Finally, he stood and went up himself.

The main hall was filled with displays from one corner of the room to the next. Some artists had tables set up, others had foldout walls where they hung paintings. Artwork of all types filled the center. Looking around, Edwin saw Clara and Alecia interviewing one of the artists along the West wall. He stepped up to hear what they were saying.

"Where do you get your inspiration?" Clara asked.

"I get my inspiration from the energy that flows from all living things," the artist answered.

Edwin wanted to be sick.

Clara walked over to one of the paintings. "This one is especially enlightening," she said. "I'd have to say it's my favorite. It has so much feeling." She waved over her photographer. "Alecia," she called out. "Get a shot of me with Mikaela near this painting." Alecia held the camera to her eye as the two women smiled. She clicked the shutter release, and the flash fired.

Edwin waited until the artist engaged another guest, then studied the painting for himself. It was a splatter painting where the artist throws paint at the canvas.

"What do you think of it?" Clara asked, approaching from behind, catching Edwin off guard.

"It's just a bunch of paint splatters," Edwin said honestly.

"But how does it make you feel?"

"Like I want to blow my nose because I just sneezed with a mouthful of spaghetti sauce."

Clara laughed. "You don't understand real art, do you?"

"What's there to understand? This painting took her what? All of five minutes to create. My dragon took months of painstaking work. I had to understand electronics, welding, computer programming, molding, sculpting, to name just a few of the skills involved. That represents years of work and studying." He pointed at the painting. "This thing? How long does it take to learn how to fling a paintbrush?"

"That's why I can't write up your work as art. Your work lacks spirit. You can't become an artist by reading books. Look at this, for example." Clara led Edwin to a painting with large yellow splotches over a blue background. Tiny green sprinkles filled the blotches. "Do you see the use of color here, the way she tells the story of life emerging from the sun? Look at the title of the painting."

Edwin bent over and read the fine print aloud, "Creation."

Clara went on, "This painting is alive without motors and gadgets. Can you say that about *your* work, Mr. Gordon?"

"Maybe not. But I don't need to put a label on my work to know that it's a dragon."

Clara smirked. "Then what is there to write about? There's nothing more to say. It's just a dragon."

The columnist and her photographer moved on, leaving Edwin to wallow in his own pity.

24

Not Just a Dragon

Edwin sat on the bench near his dragon exhibit in the front foyer of the Atmore Convention Center. He watched patrons come and go, each one stopping to admire his creation. Clara's words, *it's just a dragon*, kept spinning around in his head.

No, he thought. He was not going to accept that. It was not just a dragon. But Clara was correct about one thing. It wasn't alive. Edwin watched its head sway back and forth on its electric servo motors. As much as he tried to, he couldn't make it feel alive. It was fake through and through, and that would never change— not without a miracle.

The front door swung open and Harold came running in. Out of breath, he leaned on the bench and bent over, breathing hard.

"What did you do, run all the way?" his father asked.

"Yes," he gasped between breaths. "I have something to tell you. You're not going to believe this."

Edwin turned back toward the dragon. "Shut it. I don't want to hear your excuses."

"Excuses?" Harold asked.

Edwin gestured to the dragon. "Helping out! Ten a.m., remember?"

Harold looked up at the electronic sculpture. "You said *if I wanted to*. I didn't want to."

"I said that to be nice. I didn't really mean for you to not show up," his father complained.

"That's not important now," Harold tried to explain. "You need to hear what I have to say."

Edwin shrugged.

Harold pulled the stone from his pocket. "Look what I have."

His father leaned over to take a look. "It's a rock," he glowered.

"This is no ordinary rock."

Edwin looked at him like he had gone mad. "Okay, what kind of rock is it?"

Harold smiled. "It's a life-giving stone."

"A what?" his father asked, his voice full of skepticism.

"It makes things come alive."

Edwin's head dropped forward as he let out a puff of air. "Not you, too," he groaned.

"What do you mean, *me too?*"

"Everybody's been talking about art that's full of life and positive energy all morning. Frankly, I'm getting pretty sick of it, if you don't mind my saying so." He held his arms up to the dragon. "Apparently, my art has no life in it."

Harold smiled. "Do you want it to?"

"What are you talking about, Harold?"

He reached out with the stone, but his father waved it away and went to get the ladder. "Here, help me make this banner even."

"Dad, you're not listening."

His father continued to pull the ladder over.

"You know your small hydra dragon with the three heads?" His father kept working. "Well, I brought it to life. I had to lock it in the lower level of the house."

Edwin immediately stopped what he was doing. "You were messing with my artwork?"

"I had to, Dad. I needed to see what the stone could do," Harold answered.

"If you got one scale out of place, so help me, Harold, one single scale, I'll have your head," his father threatened.

"It's fine, Dad, will you forget about that for one moment and look at this?"

"Enough about your rock!" Edwin bellowed. "I need your help here. I'm becoming the laughing stock of the convention center."

"What do you think I'm trying to do? But you're not listening," Harold yelled. "Just watch for one minute." He blew on the stone, and it began to glow bright blue.

"Harold," Edwin screamed. "I don't care about a stupid rock. Get up that ladder and help me fix the banner."

"Dad, no!" Harold yelled back. "Forget the banner. This is going to make us rich if you'd just pay attention."

Edwin grabbed the stone from Harold's hand. "It's just a stupid rock," he yelled as he threw it toward the fountain, intending for it to land in the water. But as soon as the stone hit, the surface hardened like steel and it bounced off, flying up into the dragon's mouth. The stone sparked and sputtered, emitting blue rays of energy that radiated across the entire dragon.

"No! Not the big one . . . Dad, what have you done?"

Edwin stood with his mouth open as the dragon came to life. Its eyes blinked and the metal in its neck screeched when the monster swayed its head in ways it was not designed to move. It's bulky tail twitched, knocking over the potted plants Edwin had placed around the mechanical behemoth. Alarmed by the unbridled movement, people walking through the lobby stopped and stared. Edwin and Harold staggered backward as the dragon lifted its feet. It raised its head and thundered out a wicked roar.

"Now this is really cool!" the man with the yellow smiley face shirt came running back down the stairs. "Better than anything they had at Comic-Con."

The dragon whipped its tail around, clobbering the man, sending him sliding across the floor. "I take it back, Comic-Con was better," he said, straining to talk. He got up and limped across the foyer, holding his stomach.

Edwin couldn't believe what he was seeing. "This is impossible," he grunted as the dragon stepped closer. "Okay, I believe you, now shut it down."

"I can't, Dad."

"What do you mean, you can't," Edwin yelled without taking his eyes off the dragon.

"I don't know how to. I only know how to make it come alive."

"The remote!" Edwin cried out. "Maybe we can still control it," he said as he grabbed up the device. He forced the joystick up and down, left and right, but it had no effect on the animal who had his eye on the boy.

Harold cowered against the wall as the dragon lunged forward to get a closer look. With the creature so near, he could see his own reflection in the animal's glassy eye. Mesmerized by the dragon's stare, he watched as the image of himself morphed into a pink paper bird, which suddenly began to break apart. It was playing back a memory of the day Harold had shot up Madison's drawing with his BB gun. *How is this possible?* Harold thought. The dragon reared back and let out a terrible cry.

Suddenly somebody grabbed Harold's arm and pulled him away. "Let's get out of here," his father said, and together they ran up the stairs.

"Where did you get that stone?" Edwin gasped as they ran.

"The Kleigh girl," he answered.

"The astronaut?"

"Yes, his daughter had it."

"Are you telling me that stone came from outer space?" Edwin bellowed.

"I think so. Where else would something like that come from?"

On the main floor, people were already gathering along the terrace railing overlooking the front foyer.

"Is it a show?" one beefy man asked, hurrying to get the best view.

Edwin glanced down, hoping the dragon was unable to climb stairs. He was wrong. The wooden planks snapped and cracked as the dragon's metal claws tore into them, pulling the beast effortlessly up after Harold and his father.

"This way," Edwin shouted and led Harold to the booth with the splatter paintings. The dragon stopped at the top of the stairs and let out another loud screech. Harold turned to watch. He was amazed that nobody was running away. They all had their cell phones out, recording the creature.

"Amazing," Harold said out loud. "He's not hurting anybody. They all think this is a show." Suddenly the dragon's eye found him.

"Time to go," his father said, grabbing his arm again. "What is it with you and this dragon? He seems bent on getting even with you or something."

"I may have ticked him off without realizing it, Dad," Harold answered as they weaved through the art. "Do you know a way out of this place?"

They ducked behind a wall of paintings. "I saw an exit sign in the back," Edwin puffed. "I need to rest a minute, though."

It was then the screams started, and there was a horrible crashing sound. "I knew that was coming," Edwin said.

From the sound of art being crushed behind them, it was obvious the dragon was in hot pursuit, but then everything got strangely quiet.

"What do you think is going on?" Edwin asked.

Harold could hear heavy breathing and a sound like a clicking insect. He peered around the corner, right into the dragon's face. Quickly, he grabbed the painting with the green specks and thrust it at the beast, whose head burst right through it.

"What did you think that was going to accomplish?" his father asked as the two of them dashed off. "It doesn't matter. I hated that painting anyhow." The dragon crashed through a wall of photographs sending scenes of Venice flying through the air.

At that moment, several gunshots rang out, and the dragon screamed again.

"I think the police are here," Harold said as they screeched to a halt.

"Quick," his father said as he grabbed his son's arm. "Let's get out of here while they're keeping the dragon busy."

"Wait, Dad. What if the stone's still in its mouth?"

"So what," he said anxiously. "Let's move!"

"But what if one of those bullets hits the stone? If that thing has the power to bring things to life, who knows what would happen if it gets split apart. It could be like an atom bomb or something."

Edwin looked hard at his son. Inside, he knew Harold was right. "What do you suggest?"

"I don't know," Harold answered. "But we have to do something."

Edwin thought for a moment. "The lower level, you say?" he asked.

"What about the lower level?"

"You said that you locked my hydra dragon in the lower level of the house."

"Yes, I did," Harold answered.

"How did you trick it into going down there?" Edwin asked as they made their way to the back of the building. "I ran down the stairs," Harold puffed, "and when the dragon came after me, he misjudged the drop of each step and fell to the bottom. I jumped over him and ran back up, slamming the door." He shook his head. "I only had a few seconds before the thing was back on its feet."

Edwin stood up straight. He could hear crashing on the other side of the art wall, but it was too high to see over. The distinct sounds of radio chatter echoed across the center. The police were moving in.

Harold swallowed hard. "Do you think they have a lower level here?"

"The front foyer," Edwin said excitedly. "We'll lead it to the stairs that go down to the front foyer."

Edwin led his son silently through the art displays. "What are you planning?" Harold asked.

"We're going to show the dragon where we are," his father whispered. "Then, it will chase us."

"How are we going to do that, sneaking around?"

"We don't want the police to escort us out of here before we get that chance."

"But how is the dragon going to know—"

Harold didn't have time to finish his sentence when they once again came face to face with the beast. The dragon flicked its tail, sending an entire wall of hanging brass sculptures into the air. Behind the wall, the police were poised with their guns aimed.

"Hold your fire," the captain yelled to his men. "We have people in here."

The captain yelled to Edwin and Harold, but they were already running as fast as they could, returning to the front of the convention center. The dragon was right behind them.

"Hello, Ms. Erickson," Edwin called out as he ran past the news reporter who had returned to the show as soon as she got wind of the disturbance. Her cameraman had his camera on his shoulder and his eye to the viewfinder, capturing everything. He didn't even flinch when the dragon came crashing through the end exhibit sending paintings flying above its head.

Edwin and Harold flew down the steps, skipping three at a time. The dragon stormed around the corner of the aisle, losing its traction on the polished wood planks. With its legs flailing, its heavy body slammed to the floor as it slid toward the stairs.

The dragon did its best to slow its tremendous momentum, but it was moving too fast. It became airborne off the top of the stairs and crashed several steps below, its weight bending and twisting its metal interior frame. Its skin ripped apart as it crashed again onto the lower steps when parts of its body tore loose, spiraling across the front foyer.

The dragon finally tumbled into the fountain where it came to rest, dropping the stone from its mouth. Blue waves of energy flowed over the beast as it glowed a faint blue before it finally went dark. Water rained down from the fountain over the dragon's mangled body. The stone rolled across the floor, coming to rest at Harold's feet. He warily reached down and picked it up.

Anger flared in the eyes of the other exhibitors. At that moment, all Edwin wanted was to run out the front doors, but he knew that was not an option. Edwin finally got what he wanted: attention from the media. Far more attention than he had ever hoped for.

25

Edwin Makes the News

"**A** runaway art exhibit destroyed the fifteenth annual Atmore Art Show today, causing the Skyner Corporation to shut down the show permanently. At least fifty-thousand dollars of paintings, sculptures, and other valuable art were destroyed when sculptor Edwin Gordon's mechanical dragon went amuck," Lisa Erickson's voice boomed from the television speakers.

Dr. Alazar put down his drink and leaned forward in his chair to get a better look. He couldn't believe what he was seeing.

"It was alive!" one of the guests said as he stared into the camera with wide eyes. "They say it was a mechanical dragon, but that thing did not behave like it was mechanical. I'm telling you, it was alive."

The television cut to scenes that Ms. Erickson's cameraman had recorded earlier of the dragon running through the art exhibits. Dr. Alazar was astonished as he watched the dragon tear through one-of-a-kind paintings. It was apparent, this was no ordinary exhibit. Alazar became even more interested when the TV cut to an image of Harold Gordon running from his father's dragon. "There's no stone here, huh?" he mumbled to himself.

"You say you spoke with Edwin Gordon shortly before his mechanical dragon went on the rampage," Ms. Erickson said as she interviewed Clara Shay.

The columnist nodded.

"And what was your impression of him?"

"Angry. A deep down inside anger," Clara answered.

Lisa continued, "Police are investigating the incident that took place earlier today. They are especially interested in what Edwin Gordon has to say about his so-called mechanical dragon, as are we all. This is Lisa Erickson for WKHJ news."

Dr. Alazar sat back in his chair. "Time to pay the Gordon mansion a little visit," he said to himself.

26

Life without Razor

Ida smacked at a mosquito that landed on her arm. "How can you stand it out here?" she asked Madison as she knelt to look into the tent.

"It's fun, Mom. Nobody can tell us what to do or when to go to bed when we're out here." She pointed into the sky. "And at night, we can look up and see real stars."

"Well, you mind Mrs. Ferrer while you're here. I don't care if you are outside. Understand?"

"Yes, Mom."

"You too, Louise. Mind your mother," Ida instructed.

"I will, Mrs. Kleigh."

Ida gave her daughter a kiss on the forehead. "I'll be back in time to watch the landing with you." She headed to the car, stepping awkwardly on an uneven part of the lawn. "Ouch!" she complained as her high-heel turned over, twisting her ankle.

Madison watched her mother leave, then slid back onto her sleeping bag.

"Your mother hates the outdoors, doesn't she?" Lou said.

"Yep." Madison answered. "That's why I like it!"

"What do you want to do now?" Lou asked.

"I don't know," Madison whined as she turned over onto her back. She held her picture of Razor up over her head and rocked him back and forth, pretending he was walking through the air.

"This sucks," Lou said as she dropped down onto her own sleeping bag. "It was so much more fun with the stone."

"Yeah," Madison agreed. "We should just go to Harold's house and demand it back."

"How do you know Harold has it?"

"Duh, he's Harold," Madison groaned. "He controls that gang. Do you really think he'd let one of his minions have it?" Without waiting for an answer, Madison got up and stepped out of the tent.

Lou sat up. "You're going now? What about the Mars landing?" she asked, pointing to the house.

"We'll be back in plenty of time."

Lou shrugged her shoulders. "Okay, let's go."

"Do you really think we should?" Madison asked.

"What can it hurt?"

"Okay."

The girls hustled down the road toward the old mansion.

27

Is Anybody Home?

The large Oak door echoed as Madison banged the huge metal knocker.

"Do you think this is a doorbell?" Lou pointed to a narrow, white button mounted on the doorframe.

"Let's find out," Madison said as she pushed it several times. "Did you hear anything?"

Lou shook her head. "I don't think it's working."

Madison pushed it several more times in rapid succession.

"Don't." Lou smacked her hand away. "What if we just can't hear it out here?"

The girls waited for a while, but nobody came to answer the door.

"Do you think they're out?" Lou asked.

"How should I know?" Madison said in her snotty tone. "Wait a minute," she said as she pulled a flyer out of her pocket. It was the one Edwin had given her when they visited him to retrieve her backpack. "The art show," she said.

"What art show?" Lou asked.

Mr. Gordon is displaying his dragons at an art show in town today."

"Dragons?" Lou said.

"Maybe we can wait for them," Madison said as she sat down on the front stairs.

Lou joined her. "What about dragons?"

Madison pulled her knees up against her chest and poked at the mortar between the stones. "He makes these mechanical dragons. See?" she said as she handed Lou the flyer.

"Cool." Lou looked at the photos on the paper. "Uh, Maddy," she groaned.

"What?"

Lou tapped on the flyer. "The show doesn't end until nine o'clock tonight."

"Let me see that," Madison said as she grabbed the paper away from her friend. "What time is it now?"

"I don't know, look at your phone."

"I forgot to charge it last night. The battery's dead."

Lou huffed as she pulled her smartphone from her pocket and tapped the display. "It's almost five-thirty."

"That's like, hours from now," Madison whined.

The girls sat, watching ants crawl around the stone steps.

Lou finally stood to her feet. "This is boring. Let's do something."

"What do you want to do?" Madison asked.

"Let's walk around the house."

The two girls wandered around, following the enormous stones that made up the foundation of the old mansion. "This place is huge," Madison said, looking up the side of the three-story house.

"Look at this," Lou yelled as she scampered over to a glass building that jutted out the back of the house. She put her face to the window, cupping her hands around her eyes to block out the sun.

Madison did the same. "It's a swimming pool."

"Cool," Lou exclaimed. "An indoor pool." Through the glass, the girls could see an open door on the other side of the room.

"Come on. Let's go in."

They ran around and cautiously stepped through the door into the pool house.

"Eww," Lou said as she peered into the green water. "That's disgusting."

The girls ambled alongside the neglected pool. "Why would anybody let such a fantastic place get so dirty?" she wondered out loud.

"This place hasn't been cleaned in years," Madison said.

Suddenly Lou shrieked and jumped back.

Madison's heart was in her throat, pounding. "What?"

Lou had her hand on her chest. "A frog jumped," she said.

Madison smacked her. "You scared me to death because of a stupid frog?"

The girls laughed together until something caught Madison's eye. She slowly walked to a back entrance to the house.

"Where are you going?"

"Look, Lou." Madison pushed on the door, and it swung in. "It's open."

28

A Dead Giveaway

"This house is huge," Lou said as the girls tiptoed past the changing rooms into a great room with a large fireplace and pure white plush couches. "How will we ever find the stone in this place?"

"That's easy," Madison answered. "All we have to do is find Harold's room. I'm sure it's not much bigger than any other normal bedroom."

"How will we know which room is Harold's?"

"It'll be the messiest and smelliest room in the house. I guarantee it," Madison said as she crossed the room quickly and quietly. Lou stayed close behind.

On the other side of the great room, the girls passed through the rear foyer into the kitchen. Pots and pans were scattered across the floor.

"What happened here?" Lou asked. "It looks like Harold and his father had a big fight over breakfast."

Madison reached down and picked up a large knife. "Wow," she said. "Sometimes, I fight with my Mom, but never this bad." She put the knife back, and the girls continued to sneak through the house.

"Where are the bedrooms?" Lou asked.

"Probably upstairs," Madison answered.

"Where are the stairs?" Lou asked again.

"What do I look like? The butler?" Madison asked in a loud whisper.

They continued through the kitchen and into the family room. There were a series of couches and armchairs sitting around another fireplace with a large screen TV mounted on one of the walls. Several shelves encompassed the room filled with DVDs and video games. An entertainment center housed several video systems and players.

"Wow. Harold's so lucky. Why is he so mean if he has so much?" Lou asked.

"Because having things doesn't make you happy," Madison answered.

"It would make me happy," Lou countered.

Madison rolled her eyes. "This way," she commanded.

"Do you know where you're going?" Lou asked.

"I'm looking for stairs," Madison answered.

Leaving the family room, they stepped into a hallway leading in multiple directions.

"Which way? Lou asked.

"There," Madison pointed into a service area for the kitchen. On the way, they passed a door that Lou decided to open.

"What are you doing?" Madison asked.

"I'm checking this door."

"Stairs won't be behind a door."

"Well, *you* haven't found any yet, have you?" Lou asked as she pulled it open.

Trying her best to stifle her scream, she pushed backward into Madison until both girls tumbled to the floor. Lou kicked her feet, trying to stand back up as Madison blocked her flailing arms from smacking her in the face.

"What's wrong with you?" Madison cried, trying her best to be quiet, but having a hard time controlling her volume. Finally, she was able to push Lou off and see what it was that had scared her friend half to death. Madison found herself staring into the eyes of a three-headed dragon and began to panic until she realized that it was not moving.

"It's a model," Madison said, no longer trying to be quiet.

Lou leaned back against the wall and whimpered. "It's not real?"

"No," Madison answered. "From now on, let me open any doors. I know what the dragons look like."

Lou nodded.

Madison closed the door, and then reached out to help Lou to her feet. With the dragon safely tucked away in the stairwell, the girls continued their journey around the house.

"Come on," Madison urged. "We'll find some other stairs. Besides, I doubt his bedroom would be down there."

They moved through the service area into a large dining room where a massive oak table had been knocked over onto its side. Madison felt her foot kick something when she walked into the room, and an apple rolled across the floor. Along with a crystal bowl and candle holders, more apples, grapes, and oranges littered the room. Lou was beginning to get scared.

"Maybe we should go home, Maddy," she suggested. "My Mom's going to wonder where we are. Besides, we're supposed to be watching the Mars landing tonight."

"No, we've come this far, we might as well keep going. We need to get that stone back. Don't worry, we'll make it back in time. The landing isn't for two more hours. Besides, I thought you liked exploring."

"Well, I do when it doesn't include dragons."

"We'll be fine once we get the stone back, then nobody else will have the power to bring the dragons to life."

"Bring them to life?" Lou asked, her voice shaking with worry as she glanced at the scratches on the wall.

"Don't worry," Madison insisted.

"But, there's something you need to know," Lou continued.

"What's that?"

"Remember that day when we made the promise that we wouldn't tell anybody about the stone?"

"Yeah," Madison said.

"And we wrote down something bad that would happen if we broke the promise?" Lou went on.

"Yeah,"

"Well, I wrote that you would get eaten by a dragon."

"What?" Madison blurted out. "I said not to write anything that had something to do with death."

Lou moaned. "I thought it was such an impossible thing that it could never happen."

Madison grunted, "Never underestimate the power of stupidity."

"I'm sorry," Lou whined.

"I'm not going back." Madison insisted. "Not until I have that stone."

Lou stayed close behind her friend as they made their way along the wall. Madison reached up and ran her hand across a set of deep scratches in the paneling.

"What did you stop for?" Lou asked.

"Nothing," Madison said, not wanting to frighten her friend anymore.

"You're lying," Lou said as she looked up at the wall. "What is that?"

"I don't know," Madison said, trying to make it seem harmless. "It looks like scratches."

"Scratches from what? A giant grizzly bear?" she squeaked.

"No, not a grizzly bear." Madison turned to face Lou. "A dragon."

Lou's face went pale. "I'm sorry, Maddy. I really didn't think it was possible."

Madison turned and continued through the doorway and into the main foyer.

"I remember this," Madison said. This is the front door where my mother and I came in." She was getting excited now. "The library's in there," she said, pointing into the next room. "And that's the staircase." Madison pointed down the foyer. "Come on, we're almost there," she said as she ran to the bottom of the stairs.

Lou chased after her. Madison jumped onto the first step and began running up. It was a circular staircase that traversed the East wall of the foyer. As Madison climbed higher, she could see more of what was ahead of her until she saw that some clothing had been tossed down the stairs, blocking her path. She stopped short, and Lou almost ran into her.

"What's wrong?" Lou asked.

Madison didn't answer. She had backed up against the wall and was slowly sliding back down to the next step.

"Madison?" Lou asked.

Madison couldn't talk.

Lou turned to examine the pile of clothing, then quickly covered her mouth with two hands, but not before she let out a short screech. She turned quickly to face Madison.

What Madison saw in Lou's eyes was utter shock and terror before she bolted down the stairs. Madison took another look. It wasn't just a pile of clothes. It was Harold Gordon's father, Edwin. His shirt was stained with blood. Madison gasped and ran down after Lou.

Downstairs, Madison found Lou hysterical in the hallway, confused as to which way to go. She grabbed her friend by the shirt and called her name. "Lou, look at me!" she shouted.

Tears were streaming down her face. "I want to go home," she cried as her throat tightened with emotion.

"Wait, Lou. Get ahold of yourself."

Lou pushed Madison away and fell against the wall. "I want to go home now," she said again, through her tears.

Madison stepped back and sighed. "I do, too, Lou. But I can't. I have to get that stone."

"I don't care about that stupid stone. I want to go get my Mom."

"Remember Razor?" Madison asked. "How I was afraid to do anything about him, and now he's dead because of it. Well, I'm not going to let that happen again. I'm getting my stone back."

"Then go and get the stone. But I'm going home."

"Okay," Madison said. "But you can't tell your Mom anything. We'll both be in big trouble if you do. Don't you see? They'll want to know what we were doing in here," Madison begged her. "Okay?"

Lou covered her face with her hands and sobbed.

Madison led Lou to the pool and watched her run around to the other end. Hesitating at the door, she turned briefly and looked back.

"Whatever you do, don't tell your Mom," Madison repeated, and she ran off for home. Madison was now alone.

She knew she was in over her head. She knew she needed help. But she also knew that her mother was not the type to help her out in these crazy situations. Madison needed someone who would understand her. She needed Harold Gordon.

Behind her, somewhere in the house came a loud thud. Madison spun around. Perhaps she wasn't alone after all.

29

Reunited

The old mansion was frightfully spookier now that Lou was gone. Madison noticed that her hands were shaking. And she wasn't thrilled at all about what she had to do next; climb over Edwin Gordon's body.

There must be another staircase in a house this large, she thought, and proceeded to explore the downstairs, heading through the library. She had been in this part of the house with her mother, and she felt she had seen a staircase, but that meant going into the one room she wished to avoid—the dragon room.

Madison could feel her heart pounding in her ears as she tiptoed through the library, but she was determined. As she moved about, she noticed a new sound and stopped in her tracks. There was something alive in the room with her.

She listened carefully. It was whimpering. The sound was definitely human and didn't seem threatening. She turned to look but saw no one.

Inching her way through the room, Madison followed the noise. As she got closer, the sound dissipated until she couldn't hear it any longer. She slowly crawled up onto a reading chair and peered over its back.

The chair suddenly flipped up into the air, throwing Madison backward. She screamed in pain as it came crashing down on top of her. As she struggled to wiggle out from under the heavy piece of furniture, she could see a dark figure in the corner. It was a man with a club, ready to strike.

Madison panicked, kicking frantically to free herself from the weight of the chair as the man came at her. She screamed again, covering her face with her hands, and froze. Nothing happened. She slowly moved her hands away from her face and glanced around.

The man had dropped against the wall and slid to a sitting position.

"Harold?" Madison called out, but he did not respond. Pushing with all her strength, she freed herself from the overturned chair and crawled up to the once-proud bully.

"You scared me half to death!" Madison blurted out, but he did not acknowledge her. "Harold, what's wrong?"

He finally looked into her face. "Madison? What are *you* doing here?"

"I came to get my stone back."

Harold laughed, but there was no joy in his voice. It was a hopeless laugh. "You want the stone? Take it." He reached into his pocket and pulled out the onyx stone. Madison's eyes lit up. It was finally over. Now she could go home.

Harold's expression hardened as Madison took possession of the stone. "Good luck getting out of here alive with it."

30

Trapped

"Why don't we call for help?" Madison asked. "Be my guest," Harold gestured to the phone on the desk.

Madison ran to it and picked it up. "There's no dial tone," she said, holding the receiver in her hand.

Harold chuckled. "He thought of everything, didn't he? What about your cell phone?" he asked.

"Battery's dead," Madison groaned as she hung up the phone. "I didn't charge it today. What about yours?"

"*What about mine,* she asks," Harold moaned as he dropped his head back and looked up at the ceiling. "What about mine?" he repeated. He pulled his phone out of his pocket and let it drop to the floor. Madison could see that it had been smashed.

"Look, I'll just go out the front door and get help, okay."

Harold glanced over at her. "You don't get it, little girl?" he blurted. "You're trapped in here."

Madison shot him a confused look. "How? I walked in with no problem. I can walk out the same way. Lou did."

Harold laughed a pitiful laugh. "We may have checked in, but we can't check out!"

Madison stared at him like he was insane.

"He let her go," Harold bellowed.

"Who?"

"… and I doubt you'll get the same treatment."

"Who let her go?"

Harold let his head drop as if he had no strength. He let out a grumbled laugh. "Who else?"

Madison was beginning to get annoyed. "You're not making any sense."

"Him!" he growled as he pointed to the corner of the room.

Madison turned to look, and what she saw caused her heart to pound. The corner of the room was empty. The huge dragon Edwin had called Goliath was gone.

With a jerk, Madison turned back to Harold. Her eyes shot through him like daggers. "What did you do?"

Harold laughed. "I had to do it."

"Is that how… Did it… Your father?" Madison stammered.

Harold's laughter faded into a low moan.

"Why would you…" Madison didn't know how to ask the question.

"Not me…" Harold muttered. "Not me."

Madison stepped away from the bully. "You killed your own father?"

Harold lunged forward and yelled in anger. "I did no such thing!" He fell on his face and began sobbing. "I did no such thing," he repeated.

Madison turned and walked toward the door.

"He won't let you go," Harold called out. "Not with the stone."

Madison turned back. "Then, I'll leave it here," she said and sat the black rock on the desk.

Harold rolled over and laughed.

Madison gave him a look. "You're crazy, Harold," she said and turned to leave.

"He knows!" Harold yelled out.

Madison paused. "Knows what?" she asked.

"Everything," Harold groaned. "Everything the stone sees, that is." He pushed himself up into a sitting position. "When you see him, look into his eye." He laughed with an eerie tone. "You'll see what I'm talking about."

Madison stared at Harold.

"Go," he shouted. "Take your stone and get out of here."

Madison grunted, then reached across the desk, grabbed her stone, and slipped it into her pocket. She stepped to the doorway and peered out into the foyer. "I don't see anything," she said, turning back to Harold.

"He's everywhere. Look closer... In the shadows... He's watching you."

Madison looked into every corner of the room. There was no dragon. She glanced over at the front door. It was a mere twenty-five feet away. "I can make it," she mumbled to herself.

She counted to three, took a deep breath, and then dodged out of the room. She walked as quickly as she could, looking straight ahead. The door was close. She was going to make it, she thought.

Suddenly there was a terrifying roar, and the shadow under the balcony grew as the dragon spread its wings and crawled out across the front door. Madison shrieked as she scurried backward, falling to the floor. The dragon slithered forward, silent as the night, and crawled right up to Madison. She gasped for breath as she scooted backward, but the dragon crept even closer.

Remembering how the glow from the stone calmed Razor, she pulled it from her pocket, fumbling with it as she blew. The stone glowed a bright blue, stopping the dragon in its tracks. It held perfectly still, staring at the rock. Madison's hand shook as she held it out.

She cautiously pushed herself up against the wall until she was standing on her feet again.

Her reflection glistened in the dragon's eye as it stood there, absorbing the energy from the stone. Slowly, her image began to morph, but she didn't plan on sticking around to see the outcome. Backing away slowly, she turned and made a mad dash into the library, throwing herself behind the overturned chair.

Harold let out a wicked laugh as Madison caught her breath. "Well, what did you see?"

"He was under the balcony. You could have warned me about the balcony," Madison grumbled.

Harold laughed even harder. "I told you. He's everywhere. Now what did you see?"

"What do you mean? I saw the dragon."

"His eye. Did you look into his eye?" Harold growled.

"Yes. No... a little," Madison yelped.

"Did you see anything?"

"I saw myself," Madison said.

"And then what?"

"It started to change, but I ran. I didn't see what it was changing into."

Harold groaned. "You're not a perfect person, Madison. There's something about you, and the stone knows what that is. You'll find out sooner or later." Harold rolled over and propped himself up against the wall.

"Why doesn't the dragon come in here?" She asked.

"Because," Harold answered.

"That's not a reason."

"Because *I'm* in here, that's why," Harold growled.

"I don't get it. If it wants to kill you, then all it has to do is come in here," Madison said as she pondered their bizarre situation.

Harold threw his arms into the air. "Because I'm the king of the dragons," he exclaimed, dropping back against the wall. Harold continued with a chuckle, "He won't kill the king. Not this king. He needs me."

Madison glanced over at the doorway to the foyer. "It's guarding the door," she mumbled.

"No," Harold said as his eyes grew large. "He's guarding the stone."

Madison stared at Harold, unsure how much of what he was saying was true. "So, then all we have to do is wait for the stone's power to wear off. He'll become a simple sculpture again, and we'll just walk out."

Harold shook his head.

"Why not?" Madison asked.

"Because we can't, okay? That's all you need to know," Harold grumbled.

"Well, no matter what you say, the power of the stone will wear off, and then I'm going home," Madison said, feeling pretty sure of herself.

"No, not going to happen."

Madison snorted. "Yes, it will."

The two of them sat waiting. Across the library, an old grandfather clock ticked, breaking through the ghostly silence.

"What are you doing here, anyway?" Madison asked. "You're supposed to be at the art show."

"They closed it early."

"Oh, why?"

"On account of the dragon."

Madison jerked her head and looked at him. "You made the dragon come alive at the show?"

Harold grumbled.

Madison began to giggle. "I'll bet that went over big," she laughed.

Harold chuckled as a tiny flame of happiness ignited inside him. "It got everybody's attention," he said. But that fire was quickly extinguished as he continued. "And then we came home."

Madison looked over at Harold. "What happened when you came home?"

Harold didn't answer.

The silence was suddenly broken by a beeping sound. Harold pulled a stopwatch from his pocket. "It's time." He said.

"Time for what?" Madison asked.

Harold reached out his palm. "Give me the stone."

"Why?"

"Just give it to me, okay?"

Madison was suspicious but handed it over.

Harold crawled to the doorway to the foyer and blew on the stone. He got down low and extended his arm out, keeping himself out of sight the best he could. The dragon climbed down from the shadows and basked in the glow of the stone.

"What are you doing?" Madison asked as she crawled up behind him. "You're recharging him."

"Get back," Harold hissed, keeping his voice down.

Madison didn't understand until a shot rang out, and pieces of wood splintered off the door frame inches above Harold's head. Rearing up on its hind legs, the dragon let out a deafening screech. The two of them ran back to the hidden corner of the library.

Harold breathed hard. "I don't know how many bullets he has left. I keep hoping this is the last."

"Who's shooting at us?" Madison asked.

"I don't know," Harold answered. "He surprised us when we came home from the show. Or should I say, we surprised him? I think he was looking for the stone."

"Why do you think that?"

"Because he hasn't left. There are other ways to get out of the house, you know."

"So, your plan is to keep the dragon alive until he runs out of bullets?"

"Do you have a better idea?"

"You said there are other ways out of the house, right?"

"Yeah, and then he shoots us from the windows upstairs and takes the stone from our dead hands."

Madison thought. "He could have shot Lou when she ran home."

"I know. I'm glad he didn't. Do you think she'll bring help?" Harold asked as a bit of hope blazed through.

Madison's face glazed over like a mask as she answered his question. "I made her promise not to tell anybody."

31

The Sting

Madison pulled her sketchpad from her book bag.

"Do you carry that thing with you wherever you go?" Harold grumbled.

"Yes. Yes, I do," Madison answered as she flipped to a blank page. She stretched across the plush carpeting and began to draw.

Harold crawled over and draped himself across the over-turned chair. "What are you drawing?" he asked.

Madison spun around, dragging her sketchbook with her. "Sorry, I'm not going to tell. It's my turn to be the crazy one."

"Crazy?" Harold asked. "You haven't seen crazy yet."

Madison ignored him and kept drawing. After a while, she began cutting her drawings out and folding them over.

"Is that a mosquito?" Harold asked.

"Nope," she answered sharply.

"Dragonfly?"

"Wrong again," Madison said as she continued to work.

After she had made several of the things, Harold realized what she was up to. "It's not going to work," he said.

"What's not going to work?"

"It's only paper. The stinger won't actually do anything. Annoying, yes, but it won't stop the guy upstairs."

"All we need is a diversion," Madison said.

"You'll need thousands of them."

"Then, I'll make thousands of them."

Harold huffed out a growl.

"Well, at least I'm trying," Madison hissed. "All you're doing is sitting around. If all this does is poke at that guy and annoy him, then something useful came from it."

Harold smiled. "Did you say poke?" he asked.

"Yeah, why?"

"Wait just a minute." Harold ran across the room to the desk, pulled a small plastic box from the drawer, and then darted back.

Madison's eyes grew as she opened the case. "Straight pins!" she yelped. Looking up at Harold, she asked. "Why do you keep straight pins in your library?"

"Don't ask," Harold said as he rolled his eyes.

Madison stared at him.

"Okay, my Mom used to make dresses in here," Harold barked.

"Why is that such a big deal that you didn't want to tell me?"

"I'll get some tape," Harold said, ignoring Madison's question.

"Come on, tell me," she prodded.

Harold grunted. "See that stool over there?" he asked, pointing across the library.

"Yeah," Madison answered.

"My mother would make me stand on it and put the dresses on while she sewed and measured them."

Madison couldn't help picturing Harold standing on the stool wearing a dress, and she laughed out loud.

"It's not funny," Harold yelled. "I had to stand there for hours while she measured and cut. And if I moved, she would poke me with one of the pins. I hated it."

Unable to control her giggling, Madison tried to sound more sympathetic toward Harold's unpleasant past. "No wonder you became a bully," she said.

"A what?" Harold grimaced as if he couldn't believe she could think that of him.

"A bully. You know, always picking on everybody and shooting little animals."

"I'm not a bully. I just give everybody what they deserve. Everybody else is afraid to fight back. Not me."

Madison couldn't believe her ears. This kid regularly picked on the younger, weaker children and shot innocent creatures with his BB gun, but didn't think of himself as a bully. She shook it from her mind and went back to her drawing.

"What are these things you're making, anyhow?" Harold asked.

"Yellow Jackets."

Harold smiled. "You know, for having such a bleak outlook on bullies, you're well on your way to becoming one yourself. You made weeds grow in the soccer field, broke into my house, you're sending yellow jackets after some guy upstairs, and you're completely obsessed with that stone. Does your mother know where you are right now?"

Madison growled. "I'm not a bully! Now tape those pins on to their butts."

"Right," Harold said in an incredulous tone and began taping the *stingers* onto the bees.

Madison could see a gleam of joy in Harold's eyes as he worked with the pins. "Better than making dresses?"

"I'll say," Harold answered.

"I'll keep drawing. You cut them out," Madison said, and the two of them worked together, making as many paper yellow jackets as they could before the dragon lost its energy charge. Madison bit her tongue as she gripped her pencil firmly in her hand, drawing many bees on one sheet. Harold took the pages that were finished and cut out the drawings, freeing them from the paper.

"How did your father get so rich anyhow?" Madison asked as she worked.

"That's just it," Harold grumbled. "He didn't. It was my grandfather and my great-grandfather who made all the money. My father just spent it all after they passed away. Now there's nothing left for *me*. Not after my mother took most of it."

"You can go to college, right?"

"No, I'm not good at school."

"Then why don't you work with your mother?"

"She makes dresses remember? Can you imagine me making dresses?"

The thought of Harold standing on the stool in a dress returned, and she had to stifle another chuckle. "A lot of men design clothing for a living, and they make good money doing it."

"I am not going to make dresses. Now drop it."

"Okay," Madison squeaked as she shrugged her shoulders. "It's your life."

Harold glowered at her.

After working for a good half-hour, the two of them had filled a cardboard box with little paper bees.

Madison shook the box, settling the yellow jackets down so that they all fit inside. "Do you think that will be enough?"

"It'll have to be," he said as he glanced at his stopwatch. We only have a few minutes. Got the rock?"

Madison nodded as she pulled the onyx stone from her pocket. She blew on it, and it began to glow. "Ready?" she asked.

Harold lifted the flaps over and closed the box up. "Ready," he said, swallowing hard.

Madison shook the stone until it began to spit and sputtered blue sparks. She quickly dropped it on top of the box, and the two of them stepped back to watch the show. The entire carton of bees glowed as blue energy waves flowed over it. After a few moments, the stone went dark.

"Did it work?" Harold asked.

Madison put her ear to the box. "I'm not sure."

Harold lowered his head to listen. "I hear something."

"There is definitely movement in there." Madison laughed.

"Do you think it's enough? I mean, they don't seem very threatening."

"I don't know," Madison answered.

"Let's find out," Harold said as he picked up the box and gave it a little shake. "Oh yeah," he said with a laugh. "They're moving now."

"Shake it more," Madison suggested.

Harold held the box firm with one hand on the top, holding the flaps down, and one hand on the bottom. Smiling big, he gave the box a good hard shake.

"Not that much!" Madison screeched.

The box trembled in Harold's hands as the creatures inside fought to get free. "They're angry now," he exclaimed with a devious laugh. Suddenly something came piercing through the side.

"Whoa!" Madison shrieked. "Was that a pin?"

Harold looked around the box as another pin came poking through the cardboard, jolting the entire carton. "We have to get this thing out of here quick," he said, but before he could get very far, another pin came through the cardboard, this time under his hand.

"Ouch!" he yelped as he pulled his hand away, almost dropping the box.

"Watch it," Madison screeched, covering her mouth with her hands.

Harold couldn't wait any longer. He made a mad dash for the doorway before another pin could stab his hand.

The foyer was dead quiet when Harold bolted out of the library, catching both the dragon and the man hiding on the balcony by surprise.

"I have something for you," Harold yelled as he threw the box as hard as he could onto the upper level. The box struck the doorframe of the room where the gunman had taken refuge and sprung open, spewing its contents. One shot rang out from his gun before he was overtaken by a swarm of angry yellow jackets with straight pins for stingers.

Harold spun around and fell to the floor as the bullet skimmed his left shoulder. Grabbing his arm, he cried out in pain. In seconds, the dragon was on the floor and headed right for him.

Madison came barreling out of the library, intercepting the beast with her onyx stone glowing. Hungry for energy, the dragon stood still, absorbing the orb's power.

"Go, get out of here," Harold yelled as he caressed his arm. Cries of pain flowed down from upstairs as the man fought off the bees.

"What about you?" Madison asked.

"This is my house. I'm not leaving."

"But you'll be killed," she cried. The stone began to dim.

"I know of a good place to hide. They'll never find me," Harold said. "Now go, before the stone stops glowing."

Not wanting to leave Harold behind, Madison hesitated, slowly stepping backward toward the rear foyer. She glanced up the stairway where his father's body lay.

"Go!" Harold yelled again just before disappearing into the dining room. The dragon began to stir.

Madison slipped the stone into her pocket and turned to run. The changing rooms for the pool were on the other side of the great room. Taking deep breaths, she made her way through, but before she could reach the exit, the dragon crashed through the Ballroom backdoor, blocking her escape. Madison screamed. As quick as she could, she pulled out the stone and blew on it, holding it up to calm the beast. After several seconds, she turned and ran the other way.

Inside the kitchen, Madison stood with her back against the wall, trying not to breathe hard. She gingerly turned her head to peer around the corner. The dragon was nowhere in sight. Just a few feet away was the breakfast room and on the other side, another outside door. Madison closed her eyes for a couple seconds, took a few deep breaths, and flung herself around the wall—finding herself face-to-face with the gunman.

"Going someplace?" he asked in a harsh voice.

"Jim," Madison gasped.

32

Static

Brad Hankins waited anxiously onboard the Excalibur as the landing craft descended to the surface of Mars. The lander had entered the blackout zone when radio signals were unable to penetrate the plasma envelope caused by superheated atmospheric molecules. He watched the clock without blinking.

"Four minutes to reestablishing communication," he reported back to Earth." Mission control would not hear the message for another fifteen minutes. Because of the delay, the landing had to be directed from the orbiting craft. A bead of sweat dripped from Hankin's forehead as he waited.

"One minute to communication link."

Suddenly a staticky voice came through the headset. "This... pilot... man... you read... calib..."

"Lander, please repeat, you're transmission is still garbled," Hankins answered.

"This is pilot Francis Beckman, do you read?" the voice came again.

"I read you loud and clear. What's your status?"

"We are about to detach the parachutes and start our power breaking in three... two... one... chutes away."

"Roger, lander, I have you on radar. You're looking good." Hankins watched his screen from the orbiter, checking the craft's altitude and speed.

"Mars lander to Excalibur. We have the landing site on our screens," Michael Kleigh announced over the radio. A flat area without any rocks lay a few miles ahead.

"Roger, lander. You're a go to continue power descend," Brad Hankins' voice came back.

"Radar flight looks good," Hankins continued. "Six thousand feet."

"Delta-H is minus six-thousand, eight-hundred," Kleigh confirmed as he studied the readouts. The dashboard on the tiny capsule lit up with LED lamps and digital readouts along with multiple computer screens.

"You're looking good," the voice rang back.

"Five thousand feet, seven-hundred per second," Kleigh announced.

"Four minutes to touch-down," Hankins said. "Hang tight down there."

"Main engines on full," Kleigh relayed into the mic.

"I'm feeling a bit of a rumble here," Beckman said as his seat began to vibrate. "This didn't happen in the test flights. How's it look on your end, Kleigh?"

"We have an alarm." Kleigh tapped the indicator on the console.

"Repeat, lander. You say you have an alarm?" Hankins asked. "What kind of alarm?"

"Gimbal control alarm."

"We're pitching," Beckman called out as he reached up to throw a few toggles. "Switching to auxiliary control."

The craft's gimbal control, which helped stabilize the ship during touchdown, had malfunctioned.

"Are you able to manually correct your attitude?" Hankins asked. The tension was evident in his voice.

"That's a negative," Beckman answered. "I can use the port thrusters, but we're going to drift from our landing site."

Michael Kleigh could feel his heart begin to pound. He remembered how he had felt the day his father had been killed during his second mission into space. The fuel cell on the main booster had split open and exploded. For weeks he had asked when his Dad was coming home until he had finally realized that day would never come. He remembered how much it had hurt. It made him think about his own daughter, Madison.

"Can we abort?" he asked.

Beckman looked at him. They knew from their training that once they entered the atmosphere, they wouldn't be able to abort until the craft came to a complete stop. That meant they had to land without the correcting boosters.

"Are you okay?" Beckman asked.

Kleigh nodded. His training taught him not to panic in any situation and to keep a level head so he could think clearly.

He checked the readouts. "Four-thousand feet, five-hundred per second. Pitch, ten degrees."

"You're going in too fast. Can you increase your burn?" Hankins buzzed over the radio.

"Negative, not without flipping us over," Beckman answered.

"I have an idea," Kleigh called out. "We'll burn the port thrusters at a forty-five-degree pitch. That should prevent us from going over with the heavier burn."

"Are you sure it'll work?"

"We have no choice. It's either that or we crash."

"Go," Hankins yelled over the radio.

"Go," Beckman said.

"Roger."

Beckman slowly increased the burn as Kleigh punched a code into the council and swung the port thruster attitude lever. The ship groaned as it tipped abruptly, then gradually stabilized. Kleigh watched the gauges and manually adjusted the thrust, keeping the pitch as close to zero as possible.

"There's no telling where we're going to come down," Beckman said. "Excalibur, you'll have to watch your radar for us. We're too busy down here to monitor it."

"Roger, lander, I have you. You're drifting to a large crater to the East."

"One-thousand feet, two-hundred per," Kleigh announced.

"Letting up on the burn," Beckman said into his radio.

Hankins watched the radar. "Can you hold it for a few more seconds? You're almost clear of the crater."

"Speed at one-fifty fps. We can't go much slower without stalling."

"You're almost clear of the crater."

"This thing's beginning to hop around like a jackrabbit down here. Without full gimbal mobility, we have no control at these slower speeds."

"Six hundred more feet to clear the crater," Hankins called out.

"Pitching, five percent, letting off the throttle now to correct," Beckman said.

"Five-hundred feet, one-fifteen per, I have no more range on the thruster. We're coming in."

"Three-hundred more feet to clear the crater."

"One-hundred, fifty-per," Kleigh called out.

"Engaging auto landing procedure, now," Beckman said.

Now it was time to panic. Kleigh and Beckman heard Hankins shouting into the radio, "The lander is in the crater, I repeat, the lander is in the crater. You don't have a level landing site."

Without full gimbal control, the rocket would simply turn around and crash full thrust into the planet. There was nothing to do but to keep descending.

Kleigh and Beckman felt the rocket touch down, and immediately, it began to lean.

"We're going over," Beckman yelled.

At that moment, Kleigh got an idea, but there was no time to discuss it with his crew members. He jumped up and pushed the maneuvering thruster control to full, tipping the craft in the opposite direction.

"Good thinking, Kleigh," Beckman said as the rocket fell toward the crater wall instead of over into it. The two men braced themselves as they watched the Mars landscape spin past the front windows.

"Hold on to your butt," Beckman called out. "This thing doesn't have any airbags."

It felt like an eternity for the rocket to fall over against the crater wall, but the ship eventually slammed into the rocky side, sending anything loose inside the capsule flying through the air. The ship slid several feet and rolled slightly before coming to rest against a huge boulder. The first thing Kleigh noticed was the sound of rushing air.

"We have a hull breach," he yelled as he released his harness and dropped down into the capsule. Pulling himself across the control panel, he reached up for the compartment where four spacesuits were stored, two per astronaut. He pulled it open, and the outfits crashed to his feet. As he grabbed his own, he tossed one to Beckman, who was still fastened in his seat.

"Beckman," he yelled out, but there was no response. "Damn!" he shouted and stumbled back over to the cockpit. Beckman was unresponsive. Feeling for a pulse, Kleigh could see blood trickling from his fellow astronaut's nose.

"Are you guys okay down there?" Hankins' voice buzzed through the radio.

"We're venting atmosphere and Beckman's unconscious. He must have hit his head," Kleigh bellowed as he pulled on his suit.

"Get yourself secured first, then go help Beckman," Hankins ordered.

"Copy that," Kleigh said as he fumbled with his outfit. He left his helmet and gloves off so he could work Beckman into his suit. With gravity one third that of Earth's, it wasn't a difficult task to free Beckman from his harness and lower him down. Kleigh worked as quickly as he could to get him into his pressure suit.

By the time he was able to snap his own helmet into place, the air had become so thin it was difficult to breathe. He switched on the oxygen and sat back to rest.

They had survived the crash. Now they would have to endure the planet.

Michael Kleigh assessed the damage from outside the craft. The hull was gouged but appeared to have survived intact. To fly it out of the crater meant repairing the malfunctioning gimbal and standing the rocket up straight. An impossible task for two astronauts with only four hours of air and no heavy equipment.

"Lander to Excalibur," Kleigh spoke into his helmet radio.

"Go ahead, Kleigh," Hankins answered.

"She's not going to fly us out of here. Not without a miracle."

The radio went silent. Both men knew how this mission had to end. The orbiter was designed to fly back and set down on Earth via parachute. It would not be able to land in Mars' thin atmosphere, so a rescue was out of the question.

"Michael, I can't leave you here."

"You're going to have to," Kleigh answered as he stared into the Martian sky. "Give my best to Madison."

Fifteen minutes later, the radio signals reached mission control where everybody listened to the last ten minutes as the Mars mission ended in disaster. They were aghast when the astronaut's voices came through the speakers. Reporters reluctantly trudged back to their computers and relayed the news.

The nation was in shock. NASA's mission coordinator, Ryan Newberry, sent one simple message back to astronaut Michael Kleigh, "Complete your mission." Nobody questioned him about what he meant.

33

After the Beep

"Where is that girl?" Ida hissed as she listened on the phone.

"Hi, it's me, Maddy. I can't answer now, leave a message."

She waited for the tone, then began. "Madison, it's your Mom, I need you to come back to Lou's house ASAP. There's been an accident," she said into the phone, then pressed the hang-up icon.

Lou rocked back and forth in her living room with a worried look on her face. They were all supposed to meet to watch the landing at Lou's house, but Madison never showed up.

"You say she went over to Harold's house to get her stone?"

Lou nodded.

"Where is Lauro when you need him?" Ida complained. "He's practically in my back pocket every other time, and when the most important day comes, he's nowhere to be found."

"That's why I live alone now," Lou's mother said.

"Thank you for everything, Karen, but I have to leave. I'll drive over and get Madison.

"Would you like me to go with you?" Karen asked.

"It won't do any good. We're going to head straight to Kennedy Space Center. They will only allow family in."

"Then we'll wait in the car," Karen said as she stood. "It's an hour drive there. You'll need someone to talk to. Madison will need someone to talk to also. Come on, Louise. We're going for a ride."

The three of them left the house and headed for the car.

"Mom, there's something you need to know," Lou said as she slid into the back seat.

"What do I need to know, dear?"

"There's a dragon in Harold's house."

Her mother laughed. "I know about the dragons. Mrs. Kleigh has told me all about them."

"No, Mom," she argued. "The dragon is actually alive."

Karen and Ida exchanged glances.

"I assure you, Louise," Ida said, looking into the rearview mirror. "The dragons are not alive."

"You don't understand," Lou continued in frustration. "The stone brings things to life."

"Louise, that's enough," her mother said sternly.

"They're animated with motors, Louise. They're not alive," Ida said.

Ida glanced at Karen as she pulled out of the driveway. "I'm sorry about that. I didn't realize that Madison's insecurities were affecting Louise too."

"They're best friends," Karen said. "They share everything."

Ida smiled.

"You're in for a big surprise," Lou mumbled under her breath.

34

Reflection

Jim Gawlick was covered in red welts. His hair was a mess, and his clothes were a shamble.

"I've had enough of you, snot-nosed little brat," he scowled as he reached out his palm. "Now, hand it over."

Madison's voice trembled as she stepped backward. "I-I don't know what you're talking about."

Jim advanced as she moved away. "I'm losing my patience," he snarled.

Madison continued walking backward. She stumbled over a pan on the floor and fell back into the service area. The door pushed open as she fell through, then swung back closed.

Jim leaped forward, pushing the door open, but Madison was gone.

"You little Houdini," he mumbled to himself. "Alright, Madison. I'm not in the mood for games," he shouted.

Hiding behind the vanity in a small bathroom, Madison tried her best not to breathe hard. She peered around the sink just in time to see Jim creep by. Light reflected off the .45 pistol he held in his hand. Gasping, she pushed herself further back out of sight.

"I know you're here, little girl. I don't want to hurt you. All I want is the stone, and you can go home."

The floor creaked as he slithered past. "That's what you want, right? To be safe from the dragon?"

Jim's voice faded as he crept into the next room. "You don't want the dragon to get you, now, do you? He's waiting for you," Jim taunted. "A sweet little girl will make a nice snack."

Looking around the little bathroom, Madison realized she was cornered. If Jim came in and turned on the light, she would have no place to run. She stood and stepped silently to the door.

"Do you know why your father was sent to Mars?" Jim asked, knowing that Madison could hear him.

Madison froze. *To be the first man on Mars*, she thought.

"They told you it was to be the first man on Mars, right?"

Madison listened.

"They lied to you, Madison." Jim edged his way slowly through the hallway, looking into every corner. "Your father lied to you. You don't really believe NASA would spend all that money to send a man that far away from his family just for bragging rights, do you?"

That's not true, Madison thought. *My Dad would never lie to me. Would he?*

Madison wanted to run, but Jim's voice told her that he was near. She'd be caught. She noticed a linen closet with a louvered door and carefully pulled it open. Its hinges squealed just a little. She froze.

Madison slipped into the closet and quietly pulled the door closed.

Out in the hallway, Jim stopped. The latch clicked, and Jim turned. A devious smile broke his sour scowl.

"They sent him to get another stone, Madison. One just like the one you have in your hands. Only it won't have a chip that leaks energy."

Jim stepped into a bathroom on the other side of the den. "The European Space Agency's newest orbiting probe discovered it a few years ago. You didn't know that, did you?"

Jim clasped his hand around the doorknob on the linen closet.

"Now the United States has gone to retrieve it. Do you know what that means, Madison Kleigh?"

He turned the knob and pulled the door open fast. "Gotcha!" he yelled, but the closet was empty. He had chosen the wrong bathroom.

"Where are you, little snot rag?" Jim snorted as he made his way back through the service area.

Waving his gun back and forth, he entered into the server room bath and pulled open the linen closet door. Madison was gone, so Jim went back to taunting.

"That means the U.S. will have two stones. Do you think that's fair?" he yelled. "You're a good kid, right? You know it's good to be fair, don't you? Isn't that what you want? We should share the stones. Sharing is a good thing, and you're a good person," Jim continued as he inched his way through the rooms.

"Do you know what will happen if the United States doesn't share its stones with the rest of the world, Madison?"

Madison had pushed open her closet door and sneaked through the service room into the dining room, where she quickly ducked behind the overturned dining room table.

From her hiding place, she heard pots and pans clang across the floor when Jim clumsily stumbled over them. She heard him cuss a few times. Knowing Jim was in the kitchen, she decided to attempt a break for the front door. She jumped up but stopped short at the entrance to the main foyer.

Scanning the shadows, she could just make out the outline of the dragon, clinging to the crown molding above the door. Its eye opened and stared back at her. Madison growled under her breath and ducked back into the den, retaking her hiding place behind the oak table.

"There's going to be war, Madison." Jim stepped quietly forward. "Everybody wants that stone, and people are going to die trying to get it... Lots of people," he continued to taunt. "You can prevent that. All you have to do is give me your stone. You'll be saving a lot of lives." He pulled back the drapes with the barrel of his gun. "Isn't that what you want?"

"Your father will bring back the stone from Mars, and it will be fair. What do you think of that? It's good to share, right? You don't want to see people die, do you?" Jim kept talking as he stepped into the dining room.

"Do you know what the stone is, Madison?" Jim asked as he crept through the room. "You may have seen it bring objects to life, but that's just a side effect," Jim said as he stepped around the tipped-over table. "Did you ever wonder how life began on Earth, where all the trees and plants and animals came from?"

Lips quivering, Madison held her breath. But then, she suddenly saw his face. With a shriek, she jumped to her feet, backing toward the foyer doorway. Holding his gun on her, Jim blocked the exit to the kitchen. He reached out with his other hand. "Now hand it over, and nobody will get hurt," he said with a malicious smile.

Madison shook her head as she backed into the foyer. Jim stepped forward, following her. "Now, now, you don't want anything bad to happen, do you?"

Madison continued to back across the foyer.

"You know, your father is going to be in a lot of trouble when he gets home," he continued to taunt.

Madison stared at him.

"It's illegal to bring any samples home from the space missions. Your father will go to jail for a very long time. But, if you hand the stone over," Jim shrugged. "Who has to know?"

Madison took another step back toward the library.

"But if you don't, I'll expose him," he said, raising his eyebrows. "Now what do you say?" Jim wiggled his fingers as he held his palm open.

She thought about her father. *What if he did send her the stone?* she wondered. He *would* be in a lot of trouble. She fumbled with the rock in her hands.

Jim waved his gun. "Do you see this thing in my hand? I don't need you to be alive to get the stone."

Madison's hands shook as she lifted the black onyx to him.

Jim reached out and grabbed it as quickly as he could. He held it up close to his face to get a good look at it. This one had the chip. It wasn't the phony one he had found in her house the other day.

"My father's not a liar," Madison cried out. "He *is* going to be the first man on Mars. And he didn't have to tell me about bringing back a stone."

"Holding important information from someone is the same thing as lying," Jim argued.

"If that's the case, then I'm a liar too," Madison said as she glanced into the shadows from the corner of her eye.

Jim continued to admire the stone. "My country owes you a debt of gratitude,' he said as he raised his pistol. "Too bad, you'll never receive it." Jim cocked the gun. "You know far too much, little girl."

Madison watched. In the shadows above the front door, the dragon opened his eyes. Like a mirror, its eye reflected what it saw. The reflection of Jim slowly morphed into Edwin's body, lying on the stairs. The colossal creature moved like a ghost. Before Jim knew what was happening, the dragon was upon him. He screeched like a schoolgirl as the monster took him into its jaws and ran swiftly into the great room. The stone dropped to the floor and rolled to Madison's feet.

"Like father, like daughter," Madison huffed as she picked up the stone.

35

A Bully Knows

With Jim out of the way and the dragon busy, the front door was free and clear. Madison could finally go home. She ran to the door and pulled it open, surprised to see Dr. Alazar standing on the front stoop.

"Dr. Alazar?" Madison shrilled. "I'm so glad you're here," she said as she ran and hugged him.

"Are you okay?" he asked. "Did you get your stone back?"

"Yes, I have it," she said as she reached her hand into her pocket to retrieve it.

Dr. Alazar reached out for the stone.

Suddenly a thought came to her. "Harold," she blurted out. "He's still in there." She turned and ran back into the house.

"Madison," Dr. Alazar called out. "Wait," but Madison had already disappeared into the dining room.

Inside the house, Madison called for Harold, but he didn't answer. She stood in the dining room, not knowing where to look, but the gears of her mind were turning, and an idea came. She pulled off her backpack and lifted the drawing of Razor out of the pouch.

Dr. Alazar cautiously stepped into the front foyer. He immediately took note of the deep scratches down the inside of the door and along the ceiling. Much of the plaster on the walls had been pulled away, and pieces lay scattered along the floor. He had seen the news footage from the convention center and knew of the dragon and what it was capable of doing.

"Madison," he called out.

"In here," she answered as she shook the glowing onyx stone.

Dr. Alazar stepped inside the dining room just in time to see the blue energy waves engulf the paper drawing. He was amazed to see the cat stand up on its own volition.

"Quick, Razor. Go find Harold," Madison said to the cat, and he darted off.

"That's the stone?" he asked.

"Yes," Madison said. "Am I going to have to give it back?"

"I'm afraid so, Madison. It's not yours. It belongs to the U.S. government."

"But, Dr. Alazar, Razor... He can't stay alive without the stone."

"I can't help that, Madison. It was never meant for you to have in the first place. Now give it here," he said, reaching out his palm.

Madison stepped up to place it in his hand.

"Don't give it to him, Madison," a voice rang out from behind her. She turned to see Harold and Razor standing in the service area doorway.

"Why?" Madison asked.

Harold locked eyes with Dr. Alazar.

"Trust me, Maddy. A bully knows when he meets another bully."

"But this is Dr. Alazar," Madison said, gesturing to the man. "He's been helping us."

"He's been *watching* you," Harold said harshly.

"But NASA assigned him to our family. He's a veteran astronaut," Madison said in defense of her friend.

"He *was* an astronaut. Not anymore," Harold said as he lifted his bat.

"I'd be careful if I were you, boy. I'm far more dangerous than you could imagine," Dr. Alazar said. His warm, friendly demeanor melted away to one much more sinister. "I can make people disappear with a simple phone call."

"Dr. Alazar?" Madison said, turning slowly to the man. She couldn't believe what she was hearing.

"You should never have meddled in my business in the first place, Madison. *You* were not on my list," Dr. Alazar said, shaking his head. "Such a shame."

"What do you mean, *your* business? Aren't you going to turn the stone over to NASA?"

Dr. Alazar laughed with a nefarious tone, "I think not. My government has been wanting to get their hands on that little marvel." He held out his palm and nodded toward the stone.

Madison was frightened. She didn't know what to do.

"Harold?" she squeaked.

"Razor," Harold said. The paper cat looked up at him. "Go get the dragon." Razor glanced over at Dr. Alazar then bolted out the door.

"You shouldn't have done that, Harold. I have no beef with you."

"Maybe not," Harold answered. "But, I have one with you."

"What did I ever do to make you so venomous toward me?"

"You killed my father!" Harold blurted out.

"No," Madison cried. "That was Jim. Dr. Alazar wasn't here then. I just let him in."

"Yes," Harold continued, "but he hired Jim."

Madison gasped and jerked around to look at Dr. Alazar.

The man laughed. "You're a bright kid. I could use someone like you on my payroll."

"What's the matter? Too chicken to do your own dirty work?" Harold shot back.

"I don't do things that way. Too messy. My way is so much neater."

"And what way is that?"

"I make accidents happen," Alazar said. "That way, it can't be traced back to me."

"What kind of accidents?" Harold asked.

"Oh, I don't know." Alazar threw out his hands. "Perhaps a cut line on a critical part of a spacecraft about to land on Mars."

"What did you do?" Madison yelled. Her fear suddenly turned to anger as she jumped up. "What did you do to my Dad's ship?" she shrieked, grabbing onto Dr. Alazar's shirt. She pounded on his chest with the stone in her hand, getting in a few good whacks before he was able to grab her arms. She tried her best to hold onto the rock, but Alazar was able to wrench it easily from her hand.

He examined the stone, rubbing the chipped area with his thumb. "You know, Madison, you had me going there for a while. When your mother showed me the stone you had received in the mail, and it didn't have a chip in it, I knew it couldn't be the right one. I was about to leave and look somewhere else when I realized you had switched them."

"It's not yours," Madison screeched. "Give it back." Attempting to snatch the stone, she grabbed onto his arm.

Dr. Alazar pushed her away, and she fell behind the overturned oak table.

Harold bolted forward with his baseball bat, ready to strike. Acting on reflex, Alazar put up his arm to block the blow, forgetting he was still holding the rock. Harold swung as hard as he could, hitting Alazar's hand.

As the bat made contact with the onyx stone, the chip cracked a little more, sending out an incredible burst of energy. A light as bright as the sun burst forth from the rock, radiating the entire room. Harold dropped the bat and covered his eyes as quickly as he could. Pain shot through his head from the intense light. Dr. Alazar was thrown against the wall from the immense energy being emitted from the stone. The heavy oak table slid across the floor with Madison behind it, protected from the light. She stretched her legs out with her feet against the table as it pushed her to the other side of the room.

"What did you do?" Dr. Alazar screamed. "What did you do?" His vision impaired from the bright light, he felt along the floor for the stone, only to find that thick grass and vines were sprouting from the carpet. It was gone.

Harold tried to get up from the floor, but vines and weeds had already grown across his body. He pulled with all his strength, ripping the plants out of the carpeting by their roots. As Harold sat up, he realized the plants were not only springing up from the floor, but they were also rapidly growing from his clothing. In vain, he pulled them out as they sprouted, but they were relentless.

Madison jumped up from behind the table. What she saw was incredible. Everything in the room that the light from the stone had hit was thick with greenery and proliferating at an alarming rate. She rushed over to help Harold pull the unrelenting growth from his clothing.

When Harold saw he was unable to keep up with the rapid growth, he reached down to pull his shirt off. It cracked and crumbled, splitting apart as he pulled it over his head.

Madison gasped. Harold's veins had become bright green and bulged from his skin. Harold looked down at his chest in panic. He arched his back and groaned, obviously in pain.

"Harold," Madison screeched. "What's happening to you?"

Harold stiffened up as his joints fused together. His faced tensed as he winced in pain, trying to force his arms to bend.

Madison grabbed his hand to help him move and noticed that his fingers had begun to grow, shedding off his fingernails. They were twice their normal length and getting longer by the second, turning green as they grew. Leaves began to sprout from his arms and chest.

"What's happening to me?" Harold cried out.

"I-I don't know," Madison stammered. "I think you're turning into a plant."

Harold looked down at his feet. Vines began to burst through his pant legs, and his toes ripped through his shoes as they too grew into long roots.

Madison stood back. There was nothing she could do to help him. His arms and legs began to grow longer. When he was finally able to stand, his arms hit the ceiling. "Harold," Madison screeched, putting her hands over her face. "You're a... You're a... You're a plant," she shrieked.

Remembering Dr. Alazar, she turned to the other wall where he had fallen. She let out a terrible scream.

Dr. Alazar was able to stand. His body had grown like Harold's with extremely long legs, arms, and fingers, but unlike the boy, Alazar was covered with thick bark.

He swung his branch-like arm around and knocked Madison to the floor. "This is all *your* doing," he hollered in a gruff voice.

Tearing up some of the boards, Alazar lifted his foot, which had rooted itself into the floor. As he stepped forward to take another swipe, Madison jumped out of the way and leaped over some vines that had wrapped themselves around the table. Alazar pulled up his other leg and went after her. She bolted out through the service room as Alazar crashed through the oak table, sending splinters of wood and new growth spinning across the room.

The doorway was too small for Alazar's growing body, but that didn't stop him. He burst through the doorframe, sending pieces of woodwork crashing to the floor. Madison ran, but heard Alazar's footsteps close behind her.

Vines were spreading down the hallway and into other rooms, growing at an incredible rate of speed. It wasn't long before parts of the mansion became an impassible jungle. Flowers burst from buds as well as butterflies and other strange insects.

Madison dashed past leaves uncurling, letting loose hordes of buzzing flies. The vines continued to slither along the walls, creeping into every crevice. They grew into the heat vents, the cabinets, and around shelves, knocking their contents to the floor. China slipped from their racks and crashed into pieces as vines grew through the glass cabinets.

Madison ran around the corner and back into the foyer. She raced to the front door and tried to pull it open, but it was jammed full of woody vines. They had grown over almost the entire door. She turned to run, but Alazar had followed her into the foyer.

"Madison," Alazar roared. "There is no escape. You'll die here today."

With no place else to go, Madison jumped over the vines along the floor and ran into the library.

Books tumbled from the shelves as weeds and plants grew out of the walls. The entire house was quickly becoming engulfed in vegetation.

Across the room, the only exit was through the sculpture room. Madison bolted for the door as Alazar burst through the library entrance, splintering the wood molding. She ran around the furniture, but Alazar crashed right through it, sending couch cushions and stuffing flying.

She was about to run through the doorway when one of Edwin's smaller Drake dragons confronted her. Its body dragged the ground, and its tongue flicked much like an overgrown lizard. Very much alive, the beast reared back and snarled. Madison came to a screeching halt. She glanced behind her. Alazar had reached back to strike again. Thinking fast, she ducked down and rolled under his swing.

Missing the girl, Alazar's branch-like arm came down on the Drake and flung it across the room into a shelf of books. Blue rays of energy shot out from the impact, irradiating the area. The dragon's body broke apart and fell to the floor along with dozens of books. Flowers and ferns immediately burst forth from the bookshelf where the creature had hit.

In a crumpled mass on the floor, the dragon returned to its inanimate state, but not before its eye caught a glimpse of the tree that destroyed it. Alazar's reflection glowed in its eye before going dark. Suddenly, dozens of living dragon sculptures swarmed from the room, all of them with the image of Alazar in their eyes. Madison dodged back into the foyer, leaving Alazar to fight the dragons.

A red-tailed cockatrice dragon started the assault, leaping up and grabbing onto Alazar's branch-like arm. Alazar immediately swung his other arm around and brushed the beast off, leaving his back exposed. Pieces of bark went flying, and Alazar screamed as a small version of an amphitere flew up and dug its claws into his back. He reached around, grabbing the beast by its neck. He ripped the creature off, flinging it into another drake that was preparing to make its run.

The attack continued as one of Edwin's wyvern dragons charged, jumping into Alazar's chest. Its bat-like wings beat frantically as the beast lunged for Alazar's face, ripping off a limb that had grown from the man's ear. Alazar roared in pain as he grabbed the dragon and tossed it to the floor along with pieces of bark that were caught in the creature's claws.

The dragon rolled over and limped away as a lindworm with the head of a horse and mane that flowed down its neck grabbed onto Alazar's arm. Its powerful jaw gnashed at the tree man while an African dragon slithered into position, wrapping its snake-like body around his legs. Unable to take a step, Alazar tumbled to the floor, taking advantage of his misfortune by crushing the lindworm on his way down. The creature flashed blue for a few seconds, then went dark.

Alazar grabbed the African dragon and ripped it in two. Blue rays of energy shot out as the creature broke apart in Alazar's steel grip. The cockatrice went back to work, tearing at Alazar's back with its massive beak. Alazar bent forward and reached over his shoulder. The dragon's beak grabbed onto Alazar's limb with a vise-like grip. The tree-man pulled his arm back, bringing the dragon over his head and smashing him onto the floor. Blue energy irradiated the carpeting, and vines sprung up instantly.

Before Alazar could get back on his feet, the legless amphitere came about, grabbing onto his arm. The dragon wrapped its long, thin body around Alazar's waist and pulled. There was a loud cracking sound, and Alazar thundered in pain as the serpent tore the tree-man's limb off.

Alazar struggled with the creature wrapped around his waist and his other arm. Finally, he roared, then puffed out his chest as if he were flexing his pectoral muscles, expanding the size of his body. The amphitere dragon split apart, falling to the ground around the tree-man's legs. Blue rays of energy flowed over its body for a few seconds before going completely dark.

Alazar looked down at the stump where his arm used to be and grimaced. Closing his eyes, he clenched his teeth and tightened his muscles, and a new tree limb burst instantly from his shoulder, spraying splinters of bark into the air. It grew into a full limb in seconds.

A few dragons were still circled around him, ready to pounce. Alazar reached down, plucking a dragonnet and a wurm from the floor and bashed them together, sending broken body parts flying. Standing amidst a dozen trashed dragons, Alazar looked around, surveying his situation. A few more dragons huddled inside the doorway, but they refused to come out. Reaching his branch-like hands above his head, Alazar grabbed onto the balcony that encircled the library. He let out a terrific roar as he pulled hard, bringing the upper floor down over the doorway, sealing the other attackers inside. The dragon threat had been eradicated.

Turning to look over his shoulder, Alazar's thoughts turned back to Madison.

36

Roots

Madison gasped at the sound of Dr. Alazar's loud scream. She could hear heavy objects crashing to the floor in the library and could only hope that the wicked man had met with an untimely death. She clambered over vines and squeezed between tree trunks as she made her way through the house. The vegetation had grown so thick, it made finding a way out nearly impossible.

After scrambling aimlessly around the mansion for some time, she found herself in a room that looked much like an office. It had barely been touched by the growth; however, the vines had penetrated the walls and were beginning to encroach on this area as well. In the center of the room was a desk with a phone and a computer. Madison dashed in and grabbed the receiver, but it was dead. Along the far wall was a counter with a small refrigerator and a coffee pot. To the right of the kitchenette was a small alcove with a window. Madison ran to it and threw up the sash. It was too high off the ground to jump.

She looked around. The sun was beginning to set. She had probably missed the Mars landing, she thought. Down the long driveway, she could see cars buzzing past on Marigold Avenue, but they were much too far to get anybody's attention. Pulling herself back into the window, she glanced around the room. That's when she noticed the sword.

Above a shelf of miniature dragon statues, an old Japanese Tachi samurai sword hung, mounted to an elegantly carved plaque along with its rosewood scabbard. Madison immediately went for the sword hoping to be able to hack her way through the thick vines that had grown throughout the hallways. She pulled over a chair to stand on and reached above the shelf to grab it, but a sharp pain stopped her.

"Ouch!" she hollered, pulling her arm back to cradle it. Blood oozed over her fingers. One of the miniature dragons had bitten her under the elbow. She hadn't realized that the small models had come to life as well. They screeched and shrieked at Madison in their tiny voices, like little baby dragons hungry for a meal. Madison grabbed a book and swung it across the shelf, knocking the creatures to the floor.

The sword didn't come loose easily. Madison yanked and pulled until the entire plaque ripped off the wall. The little dragons nipped at her ankles, like annoying chihuahuas, as she shook the sword to free it from its anchor. After a few kicks to the dragons and some hard pulls, the sword finally came free. She swung it hard, taking out the last few attacking creatures. "Take that, you little cretins," she growled.

Outside the office, Madison pushed through the thick growth. The sword made a whooshing sound as she swung it through the air, hacking up the leaves and vines that blocked her way through the hallways. It reminded her of the day she had used an old broomstick to attack the vines that had grown through the window of the old house in the woods. Only this time, the vines and sword were real, and there were dragons and madmen instead of owls.

Madison hacked her way back to the stairway, thinking the downstairs area would be less overgrown, and she could get outside from the lower level. Not realizing the hydra dragon she had left there earlier might have come to life as well, she opened the door.

Sure enough, three heads of terror leaped out at her. It snapped at Madison's sword as she wielded it awkwardly, having no understanding of the art of kendo. Though Madison's swings were clumsy, the sword still had a good sting, and the dragon backed off. She quickly pushed the door closed, catching one of its heads in the jamb. Leaning on the door with all her weight, she pushed as hard as she could until the neck snapped. The door slammed shut as the head fell to the floor.

The severed head sparked with blue rays of energy as it moved forward on its own volition. Madison shrieked as it snapped its teeth at her feet. Raising the end of the sword with its tip pointing down, she pushed it through the top of the hydra's head. The dragon groaned for a second, then went dark.

Madison leaned back against the wall and took a deep breath. After a short rest, she continued into the family room. Vines and shrubs had grown up around the TV and through the shelves of video games and DVDs, most of which had fallen to the floor. Beyond the family room, Madison could see daylight beaming through the trees in the breakfast room. She took two steps forward before she noticed something moving in the room and stopped short.

As soon as Madison entered the room, a couple dozen paper yellow jackets with straight pins for stingers took to flight. They came at her full force, ready to fight. Madison swung her sword haphazardly, but the insects were too small and dodged effortlessly around it. Before long, the bees began to sting, and

Madison took two direct hits on the arm. Swatting at the insects proved fruitless, and after several futile attempts to get past, she decided she was not leaving through that room.

She dodged out of the family room and into the service area. The spring-loaded door flopped closed as soon as she stepped through. On the other side, the bees pounded on the window, but their needles could not penetrate the glass. She blew out a huff of air.

Suddenly an incredible pain shot through her shoulder. She jerked her head in time to see a yellow jacket pulling its needle out of her arm. Reaching over, she grabbed the bee and tore it in half. Another yellow jacket buzzed past her head as she jumped out of the way. Madison lifted the sword and swung hard as the yellow jacket came in for the sting. The sword came down and split the paper insect in two.

"Huh," Madison said triumphantly. "I'm getting better at this."

She sneaked through the kitchen, watching for the bees, but they were too busy trying to get through the swinging door. On the other side of the room, Madison stepped out into the rear foyer. The door looked accessible. Madison rolled her eyes up and let out a sigh of relief. She was home free.

Stumbling to the door, she was already thinking about being back home. She couldn't wait to tell Lou all about what had happened. As she stepped forward, something large crashed through the great room sliding door. Wood flew across the foyer, and Madison's mouth dropped open. It was Dr. Alazar, the tree man.

"I've been looking for you," he growled.

Madison raised her sword. "I don't want to hurt you," she yelled back.

Ignoring what she said, Alazar reached back for momentum and swung his arm as hard as he could.

Madison stepped back and swung her sword in defense, cutting off his arm to what was once his elbow. Alazar screamed in pain.

"Ah‑ha!" Madison yelled triumphantly. "Let's see you fight with only one arm."

Alazar looked down at his missing limb and squinted his eyes. In seconds, a new arm burst out of the cut area, sending splinters of bark flying.

"Oh," Madison said as she braced herself for another blow.

Alazar took another swing at the girl, and Madison lifted her sword again, cutting his other arm off at about the same place. They could do this all day, she thought. She was too small, and her sword too short to do any real damage to the tree man. His arms were much too long for her to get in close and go for his body. She noticed, though, that Alazar had to concentrate a few seconds every time he generated a new limb. A few seconds was all she needed to get a good swing at a vulnerable spot.

Madison waited for Alazar to swing at her again, then she swiftly chopped another one of his limbs off. Keeping her momentum, she spun around as the tree man was regenerating his arm and sliced him through his waist.

Alazar screamed in agony as his anger welled up inside him like a volcano. He jumped up to swing at Madison again, but this time he charged at the same time, knocking her backward. She tripped over some vines and fell to the floor, dropping her sword. Alazar took advantage of her misfortune and reached out to crush the girl. He curled his long, woody fingers into a solid wood burl—a tree's version of a fist—and swung it down at Madison.

Rolling over at the last second, she managed to escape Alazar's fist by mere inches as it crashed to the floor. Splinters of wood flew as Alazar roared. Madison grabbed the sword and rolled back over as Alazar stood for another blow. Letting out a loud scream, she held up the only thing she had to protect herself—her sword. Alazar's fist came down on the point, jamming the blade deep inside his wooden burl. He jumped back, screeching in pain, pulling the sword from Madison's grip. She leaped up and ran toward the ballroom.

Alazar chased after her, crashing through the hallway. He ripped the vines and plants out of his way as he went, tearing down the support beams above each doorway to make room for his enormous size. Woodwork and plaster dropped to the floor in a cloud of dust.

The ballroom was once a vast empty space, but now it was overgrown with vines and trees. Madison jumped over ferns and bushes and dodged under branches as she weaved around the jungle-like growth. Alazar's immense strength gave him the ability to crash straight through the vegetation, yet it was still slowing him down.

Madison was at the rear door, ready to jump through when Alazar burst out of the growth. She ran as fast as she could into the changing rooms, but Alazar's arm grew long as he reached out for her. His long woody fingers curled around her body as he snatched her up. He pulled her back to look her in the eye. "Do you want to go for a little swim?" he growled as he carried her through the changing room.

Madison kicked and pushed against his clutches, but he was too strong for her. Inside the glass pool house, Alazar snarled at her, displaying his long brown wooden teeth. Showing no remorse, he plunged her into the water, holding her under as she kicked and pulled to get free. She held her breath until her lungs began to burn.

After a while, he pulled her back out just to gloat and see the terror on his victim's face. Madison gasped for air. "Now, I'll finish you," Alazar growled as he dunked her back into the pool.

Under the water, she could feel herself begin to get dizzy from lack of oxygen when suddenly Alazar's woody branches let loose. She quickly swam to the surface and sucked in the fresh air. Tossing her wet hair out of her eyes, she looked up to see that several vines had grown rapidly around Alazar, squeezing him tight. He struggled to free himself, giving Madison just enough time to climb out of the pool and bolt out the back door. It didn't take long for Alazar's great strength to break through the vines, but Madison was already outside and running around the pool house. She was finally out in the open air.

Before Madison could make it to safety, Alazar came crashing through the glass walls in pursuit. Madison bent down, throwing her arms over her head and ducking as large shards of glass whipped past her. Behind her, Alazar roared a horrific howl as his massive body shook the ground. He ran forward, stretching out his arms again, wrapping them around Madison's body, but his feet were becoming too heavy to lift. Sensing dirt beneath him, roots began to grow at a rapid rate.

Dropping Madison to the ground, he struggled hard to pull up his foot, bringing clumps of dirt with it. He took another step and pulled on his other leg, ripping it from the ground. With each step, his roots grew deeper until he was unable to walk any more. He roared in frustration, attempting to reach out for Madison again, but his arms were becoming rigid. The bark around his body thickened, and his limbs stiffened as he became more like a tree each second. He scowled at Madison and screamed her name, "Madison!" His face slowly hardened with his mouth open and became a permanent mark on the trunk.

Madison slowly rose to her feet and walked toward the tree. With each step, she prepared herself to run just in case Dr. Alazar began to move again, but everything that was once human was now tree. She stared at the wooden face etched into the bark. It was the face of a tormented soul and would never change as long as the tree grew. And it would live for many years.

37

Bird of Paradise

As Madison studied the giant oak tree now growing next to the pool house, her thoughts turned to Harold. She had to go back, she thought. The stone was still somewhere in the dining room. Leaving now was not an option in her mind.

Inside the house, Madison moved with caution around broken saplings and vines that hung from the ceiling and walls. Alazar had cleared a path back to the dining room when he had run through. She stumbled across the foyer and finally crawled between a tangled mass of vines and vegetation.

"Harold?" she called out. All she could see were branches and leaves.

"Harold?" she called again, and two eyes opened from within the twisted vines. "Is that you?"

"It's me," he grumbled.

"I'm so sorry I got you into this mess," Madison said as she scooched over a thick branch.

"No, I'm the one who should be sorry."

"For what?"

Harold sighed. "I didn't realize how much I was affecting everybody's lives. I thought nobody noticed the things I did. That nobody cared what I was going through. I guess I never realized what I really wanted was someone to sympathize with me. When people responded by neglecting me, instead of helping me, I became even more atrocious. I'm sorry I acted like a bully. I wish I could go back and do things differently."

"No," Madison stopped him. "I wish I saw things for what they were. A cry for help. The more of a bully you became, the less anybody showed you any sympathy at all. We all avoided you and shunned your need for attention."

"And the less people cared, the more of a bully I became," Harold finished her thought. "I was a runaway train and couldn't care less about anything in my way, not even a talented, pretty girl. And now look at me. I'm..." He turned his head the best he could. "I'm a plant. A useless plant."

Madison didn't know how to comfort him. After seeing what had happened to Dr. Alazar, she knew it would be over soon for Harold, too.

Vines grew from his body and throughout the entire room and were still reaching out through the ceiling and floor. Some of the vines had made their way out the broken window and were growing down the outside wall toward the ground.

"I'm glad the stone didn't harm *you*." Harold continued. "I think it knows that..."

"Knows what?" Madison asked.

"That there is something different about you."

"No, that's not true. I was just lucky to be behind the table when you hit it with the bat."

Harold slowly opened his leafy hand and revealed the onyx stone.

"You found it?" Madison yelped with joy.

Harold smiled. "I thought you would like that."

"But how?" Madison was so happy, she could hardly speak.

"I don't know," Harold answered. "I could feel it in the room, and I was able to call it to myself. It's weird."

Madison lifted the stone from his hand.

"I wish we could have known each other differently," Madison said. "I think we could have been friends."

Harold coughed when he laughed, shaking the leaves around him. "Imagine what Bryant and Chad would say if they could hear us right now?"

Madison smiled.

"They're good kids, Maddy. Tell them what happened here today. They'll appreciate it."

"I will," Madison promised.

"Oh, I almost forgot." Harold acted like he suddenly remembered. "I have something else for you." He uncurled his other hand, and a beautiful bird came forth.

Madison's eyes bulged with surprise. "It's my bird. The one that I drew, and you—"

"I know," Harold stopped her. "Only this one is real," he said. "It won't fade away when the stone isn't glowing."

The bird ruffled its pink feathers and looked up at Madison. It sang a beautiful chorus of notes then spread its bright white and orange wings. A crown of metallic blue and green feathers covered its head.

"It's beautiful," Madison cooed.

The bird lifted its wings, then flew off. Madison watched it fly up and around the room.

Outside the window, Harold's vines made their way down until they reached the dirt, then began to spread roots out into the soil.

"Maybe we can find a way to help you," Madison said as she watched the bird disappear through a hole in the ceiling. When the bird was gone, she looked back at Harold, and his eyes were closed. His body had become rigid and was now a permanent part of the plant. Madison noticed how peaceful his face looked, embedded in the vine's woody bark.

He was gone.

"I'll tell everybody how brave you were," she said as she slipped the onyx stone into her pocket and turned to leave. But she couldn't go. A sadness welled up inside her, and she found it difficult to walk away.

Turning back to the boy she'd known only as a bully, she leaned over and kissed his woody cheek. "That's for being a good kid," she whispered.

Leaving the dining room was more difficult than when she came in. Without her sword, she had to push her way through the jungle-like growth. *If this was how the Earth got its start*, Madison wondered, *it must have begun in the rain forest of South America or Africa.*

Outside the dining area, Madison crawled into the center of the foyer, where it was still open, although closing in fast. There was a clear path to the rear door, and Madison didn't hesitate. She hustled through the brush, stepping over vines and ferns growing along the floor. Suddenly Razor popped his head out of the thick weeds.

"Razor," Madison squealed. "I forgot you were still in here." She bent down and called him over, but he didn't come.

"What's wrong, boy?" Madison asked.

Razor looked up as a giant dragon head emerged from the leaves.

Madison stepped back. "You brought the dragon?" she asked as she stared at the monster. "Just like Harold asked... Thanks," she said sarcastically as she glanced back toward the dining room.

Madison was exhausted. She couldn't run anymore. At her wit's end, she just stood there as the dragon came closer. Before long, it was so close that she could see her reflection in its eye. But, for some reason, with razor standing next to the dragon showing no signs of anxiety, she felt calm, like she had nothing to worry about.

The dragon simply stared at the girl. Her reflection glimmered in his eye, then began to change. It was morphing, just like when Harold and Jim encountered the beast. Her heart pounded. She couldn't help wondering what devilish deed would be revealed. Would the punishment match that of the others? Her lower jaw quivered as she took deep breaths through her mouth, trying to remember her worse actions and how they compared with Harold's and Jim's.

Madison watched as her reflection slowly changed to become a little rabbit. She recognized it as the one she had saved from the boys a few weeks earlier. The dragon blinked his eyes, and the image was gone. It stepped back several feet and settled down on its hind legs. Slowly, its life energy faded until it was just a sculpture again. Madison cautiously walked up to the beast and touched its face. It was made of rubber.

"You're not evil after all," she spoke out loud. "You just *hate* evil."

Looking down at Razor, she smiled. "You... you did well. But, you probably don't have much energy charge left either." She slid her pack off and lowered it to the ground with the flap open.

"Come on, get in," she commanded in a gentle tone, and Razor hopped into the bag.

Suddenly there was a loud crash at the front door. Madison groaned as she prepared to run again. "What now?" she hissed. She threw her backpack over her shoulders and scrambled toward the rear foyer. The banging and crashing continued, and then there was the sound of wood being torn apart. She glanced back at the front door and saw light pouring in. Madison stopped and watched as two men dressed in official uniforms made their way inside the house. Someone started up a chainsaw and began hacking away at the trees. Advancing forward, the men were startled by the giant dragon. Madison yelled out, "Don't worry. It's not alive."

"Are you Madison Kleigh?" someone shouted over the whining of the motor.

"Yes," she answered.

"There's someone here to see you."

Madison's heart leaped when she saw her mother's face appear at the door.

"Mom!" she shouted and ran to her, stumbling over the vines that had grown across the floor.

"Madison," her mother called out with her arms open wide. Madison embraced her mother, hugging her harder than she ever had before.

"You're soaking wet," Ida said as she held her daughter. "Are you okay?" she asked, gently pushing Madison away so she could get a good look at her. "What happened here?"

"It's a long story, Mom," Madison said, pointing back at the carnage. "You're not going to believe this—"

"You'll be safer outside, ma'am," one of the officers interrupted, gesturing to the door. Ida nodded.

Outside, dozens of police and fire vehicles filled the driveway with their emergency lights flashing. Tree cutting crews rushed about, preparing large saws. The growth was spreading into the woods around the house.

Lou jumped out of the car and ran to Madison. "What did you do?" she shrieked, looking at the trees and vines now bulging from the windows and roof. "You ruined the house."

"That's not the half of it." Madison rambled. "You won't believe it. Dr. Alazar was an evil monster."

The girls chattered with excitement as an official-looking vehicle zipped around the circle and came to a screeching halt.

A man in uniform stepped out of the car. "Are you Ida Kleigh?"

He flashed a NASA badge. I'm Lieutenant Matt Johnson from Kennedy Space Center. I've been sent here to bring you back to talk to your husband."

"Mom," Madison shouted, remembering what Dr. Alazar had told her. "We have to warn Dad. Dr. Alazar said he had tampered with the ship. Dad's in danger."

"How do you know that?" Mr. Johnson asked her.

"Dr. Alazar told me," Madison repeated. "He was after the stone."

Ida's eyes rolled. "Madison, you're not still talking about that stupid stone, are you?"

"Yes, Mom, it has powers." She gestured to the house. "The stone did this."

Ida threw Mr. Johnson a worried look. "Is this true?"

"You'll hear all about it at the center," he said as he held the door open.

Ida held out her keys to Karen. "Could you take my car back home? I have to see what this is all about."

Karen nodded as she took them.

"Call me later," Lou shouted out.

"I will," Madison answered.

In a few seconds, they were headed down the driveway. "I'm never coming back to this place," Madison said.

As the car tooled down the road, Madison thought about what had happened.

"Hey, Mom?"

"Yes, Madison."

"Can I take up sword fighting?"

"Sword fighting?"

"Yeah, I want to learn how to fight with a sword."

Ida rubbed her forehead as if she had a headache coming on. "We'll talk about it later, okay?"

Madison nodded. "Um-hmm."

38

Mars

The first footprints left by man on Mars led away from the crater where the Excalibur's lander touched down. Michael Kleigh had been walking for just over an hour when the digital readout on his hand-held meter went over three-hundred. It hadn't moved much above fifty during his entire walk. He knelt down in the Martian dust and began to dig with a hand trowel. The words that mission coordinator, Ryan Newberry, had spoken, *complete your mission*, repeated in his mind as he dug.

The breathing apparatus on Michael Kleigh's spacesuit hissed with each breath as he worked. After an hour and a half, he had made a small mountain of dirt until his little shovel clinked against something hard. He reached into the hole and dug his gloved hand down around the object, pulling out a jet-black oblong stone about the size of an egg.

"Michael Kleigh to mission control," he said into his helmet radio. "I've located the object. I am returning to Arabia base now. I repeat… I have secured the object."

Halfway back to the ship, a voice came back on his radio. "Roger that, Kleigh. Store it onboard the lander on your return. The citizens of the United States are indebted to you. Be proud of what you have done for this great nation. We stand behind you. We salute you."

"Any last words for a doomed man?" Kleigh asked, knowing it will be another half an hour before he would receive an answer.

Back at the ship, Michael Kleigh sat on the rim of the crater, caressing the stone in his glove. In the distance, the tiny Martian moon, Phobos rose above the mountains while the sun hung in the sky over his shoulder. Everything was smaller on Mars in comparison to Earth, the sun, the moon, even the mountains felt small to Michael, though Olympus Mons was three times the height of Everest. He lay back against his mobile support pack and stared into the sky, trying to pick Mars's smallest moon, Deimos, from the background stars. Kleigh thought about what the names of the moons meant: *Fear and Panic. How appropriate.*

"Dad, It's Madison...," the somber voice announced over his radio. "I just wanted to say that I love you." Her voice went to a higher pitch as her throat tightened with emotion. "I wish you could come home. I miss you so much." There was a long pause. "Please come home, Dad." A single tear ran down her father's cheek as he listened. He could hear her sobbing in the background.

"Michael, It's Ida," his wife said, taking the microphone from her daughter. "Are you okay? We miss you here. Madison's been going stir crazy without you around. She's... well, her imagination has gone into overdrive since you've left. It's been hard with you gone, but we support you. We love you. Look, I don't care what they say, you go and fix that ship and get yourself home. If anybody can do it, you can. Now go, get that thing flying. We miss you, and we want you to come home... We need you... I need you. Do you hear me? Fix that ship."

"Warning, twenty minutes air remaining," the electronic voice announced from his suit. Michael

Kleigh sighed. He *could* fix the ship. He had the knowledge, but he could never do it in twenty minutes. Then there was the task of setting it upright. That would require a crane. If he had a rope and something substantial for leverage, like a tree, with Mars' one-third gravity, two people might be able to tip it upright, but Beckman was unconscious if he was even still alive. His situation was hopeless, and he needed a miracle if he was going to survive.

With little time left, Michael Kleigh searched for some profound words for people to remember him by. He took a deep breath and began.

"Today has been an extraordinary day," he started out. "And I wish that it could end in a good way. Ida, Madison, I'm doing something no other person has ever had the opportunity to do. Today I am living my dream, a very big dream. And I hope one day, you'll live yours. I'm sorry I won't be there to see it. I never thought that I would be standing on Mars, watching the sun come up, and broadcasting to the entire world.

"How can I top Armstrong's 'One small step for man, one giant leap for mankind'? Though I took a much bigger leap, it's always the first one who gets the credit; always the first one they remember. All I've done here today was take one more small step for man and one more giant leap for mankind, one of many yet to come.

"Ida Kleigh, I am so in love with you. And I want nothing more than to be back home with you. And you, too, Madison. Keep going on those crazy adventures of yours. Someday, maybe you will come here and see the amazing things that I am seeing right now. And then, maybe you can bring me home. Goodbye, everybody. Today a good man dies. Tomorrow many more will live."

He rubbed the stone in his hands. He knew that he would not survive long enough to receive any response.

39

A Message from Earth

After sending her message, and before her father's last statement arrived, Madison ran from the communications room, sobbing. Out in the hallway, she dropped back against the wall and slid to the floor. It was the last chance she was ever going to have to say something to her father, and she couldn't think of what to say other than *please come home*.

She had so many wonderful memories with her father: kayaking the Silver River, riding bikes along the West Orange Trail. There were so many father-daughter moments to remember. Hate welled up inside her as she sat on the floor, crying. She wanted nothing more to do with NASA or space. All she wanted now was for her father to come home.

From the hallway, Madison could hear people talking inside an office. It was evident to her that they were discussing the possibilities of retrieving the samples her father had gathered on Mars. They were mostly concerned about one particular item: the Terra Stone. Madison stopped her crying so she could listen.

"...what if he broke the stone, it could release its energy and produce an atmosphere."

"We don't know what would happen. You saw the devastation the stone has caused in Korolyov. From what we can see, nobody who had contact with it has survived."

"What about Kleigh's neighborhood? The kid survived."

"But we don't know how much of the stone's power was released, or if she was even with the stone when it happened. Hell, we don't even know if the thing produces oxygen, and what about the thin atmosphere? It could take years for the stone to produce a livable environment."

"If our theories are correct, and that is how life started on Earth, there couldn't have been any air here either."

"But we don't know that. We'd be destroying the most important discovery in all human history."

"We better make a decision soon, he is running out of air."

"We need to study the stone, and that's not going to happen if Kleigh breaks it open on Mars. We need it in one piece."

"How much time does he have?"

"Not much. He could be dead by the time the next radio message gets to him."

Outside in the hallway, Madison's anger grew. These people were discussing her father's fate like he was some sort of puppet. But she was just a thirteen-year-old kid who was expected to stay out of the way as the adults plotted and schemed, making decisions that made their lives easier with no regard for how it would affect others.

The last time this happened and Madison had kept her feelings to herself, the real Razor had died. He would be alive today if people gave her the chance to prove herself. Even the stone couldn't help him now. But perhaps, the stone could help her father. She was told not to interfere, but there comes a time when one must disobey, and this was Madison's time.

With determination fueled by resentment, she got up off the floor and stormed into the room. Her eyes flashed with anger.

A woman noticed her come in. "Are you lost, child?"

"He wasn't sent to be the first man on Mars," Madison said softly.

"I'm sorry, what did you say?"

Madison spoke up. "My father's mission. It wasn't just to be the first man on Mars, was it?" she asked with fire in her eyes.

"I don't know what you're talking about, dear," the woman said with a fake smile.

"You sent him to get another stone."

"Stone? What stone?" the woman asked.

Madison couldn't believe how easy they found it to lie.

"Look," the woman's face twisted as she glanced at the other scientists, "It's Madison, right?" she whispered.

"I think so," another one answered.

"Look, Madison—"

"You don't even know my name," Madison cut in. "You don't care about our family or my father. All you care about is getting your stupid stone." Madison stormed out the door. The scientists in the room glanced at each other with concerned expressions on their faces.

Madison paused in the hallway, remembering something she had said to Lou weeks ago.

"I know what the stone's purpose is. It creates life!"

She remembered something else Lou had said, "We know that the stone is somehow connected to our minds."

Harold had said, "You're not a perfect person, Madison. There's something about you, and the stone knows what that is. You'll find out sooner or later."

Even Jim had given her some important clues, "Your father will bring back the stone from Mars,"

Madison remembered something else Jim had asked, "Did you ever wonder how life began on Earth? Where all the trees and plants and animals came from? Everybody wants that stone."

Everybody, Madison thought, *including the United States government*. And according to Madison, they were just as evil as Dr. Alazar himself, their minds warped by the desire for power, the power of the Terra Stone.

"Are you okay?" A voice came from behind her. The scientists had left their room.

Madison turned around sharply. "What did you tell my Dad to do?"

"Listen, your father works for us. He has agreed to help us."

"You told him to find the stone, didn't you?"

"What stone are you talking about?" he asked.

"Didn't you?" Madison shouted.

Ida heard her daughter's distressed voice and came out into the hallway. "What's going on, Maddy?"

Madison turned to her mother. "I know how to save Dad," she said.

Ida's eyes lit up. "How?"

Madison glanced down the hall to the communications room. "This way."

The scientists became alarmed. "Where is she going?"

Madison began to run.

"You can't go in there," one of them yelled.

Startled by Madison's abrupt entrance, the communications operator jumped to his feet. "Hey,

Madison, what's going on?" he asked, but she ignored him and scrambled for the radio.

"Hey!" he bellowed. "You need to be authorized." Madison grabbed the microphone and switched on the transmitter. "Dad!" she yelled into the device.

"Put that down," the man ordered as he jumped from his station. Madison continued to ignore him.

"Break the stone. Can you hear me? Break the stone."

Madison screeched when two men grabbed her and pulled her back away from the equipment, but she refused to let go of the mic. "Break it, Dad, break it," she yelled out before the microphone was yanked from her hands. Madison struggled against their grip.

"Madison," her mother yelled, trying to calm her daughter down. "This is not going to help your father. You got your message through, now it's up to him."

Madison relaxed, and the security officers let her loose.

They led her and her mother back to Ryan Newberry's office. Ryan sat down next to Madison, who insisted on standing.

"Madison, if we don't find that stone at the Gordon Mansion, then we need the one your father found on Mars."

"Oh, I'm sorry, what stone would that be?" Madison said sarcastically.

"Look, we are under orders to keep the stone secret. That stone is more important than you realize. I'm sure your father has become very emotional right now and might not be thinking clearly. We need you to get on that radio and tell your father not to break it. He'll listen to you when he hears your voice."

Madison wiped a tear from her eye.

"Can you do that for me?" Newberry asked.

"You're asking her to tell her father to choose the stone over his own life. I think that's too much to ask a thirteen-year-old," Ida said.

"Madison," Newberry said gently. "Breaking the stone could release enough energy to terraform the entire planet. Do you think anybody would survive that? I wish we could fly up there and pick him up. I really do, but it'll take years to get another ship and crew out there. What do you say?"

Madison snuffed her nose and nodded.

40

Wind and Rain

"Break the stone, Dad. Break the stone, now," Madison's distressed voice echoed through Michael's radio fifteen minutes later.

"Maddy? What are they doing to you?" he asked, knowing his question will be irrelevant fifteen minutes from now.

He glanced down at the stone in his hand. "My God, the stone, it's glowing bright blue," he spoke out loud, which went over the radio.

"Break the stone, Dad," kept ringing in his mind. He would be disobeying a direct order. His career would be over, but being stranded on Mars with only minutes of air remaining, his life was going to end anyhow. Michael glared at the stone through the glass of his helmet. *What do you know that I don't, Madison?* he wondered.

After giving it some careful thought, Michael Kleigh decided to set the stone on a hard surface and try to break it. He picked up a good size red Martian rock, lifted it high, then slammed it down, but it crumbled around the onyx stone. The little black rock didn't suffer even the tiniest scratch. Michael stared in awe as its blue glow reflected off his helmet. "What are you?" he whispered under his breath.

He fumbled around for a larger, denser rock and repeated his experiment, bringing it down hard on the black egg. The large rock split in two over the little stone, which still showed no signs of damage. He made his way back to the ship and unraveled the tool kit. Inside was a medium-size crescent wrench, which he lugged back to the stone he had left a short distance past the crater's rim. After several more attempts to crack open the rock, he sat down on the ground to think. He needed something more substantial, he thought as he studied the wrench in his hands.

"Warning, five minutes air remaining," his automated suit warned.

Michael slid back down the crater wall and entered the ship. This time, he came back with a solid metal cylinder about three feet long. After trying so many times to break the stone, and failing, he began to lose his sense of caution, and this time he stood directly in front of the rock, lifting the canister above his head with both hands. With all his strength, he brought the solid metal cylinder down onto the small stone.

Even in Mars' low gravity, the weight of the canister was enough to split the rock in two. At that moment, an enormous burst of energy shot from the stone at the speed of light, and the canister was projected straight into the sky. The shockwave instantly knocked Michael back at least thirty feet into the thin atmosphere, over a large boulder, and into the crater, past the ship.

Michael Kleigh lay stunned below the protective wall of the crater as a wind storm blew with tremendous force on the surface. When he was finally about to open his eyes, all he could see was white. His retinas had been burned with light as bright as the sun, causing temporary blindness. Feeling around with his hands, he was able to prop himself up against a rock.

Even though his airtight helmet, he could hear the rushing wind.

"Warning, sixty seconds air remaining," the voice inside his suit buzzed again. He tried to look around to get an idea of how far he had tumbled from the spacecraft when he noticed something strange on his spacesuit. He struggled with the foreign matter, trying to toss it off before he realized what it was that had attached itself to his suit. He fumbled around, trying to figure out if his suit had been compromised as his eyesight slowly returned. It appeared to be a vine. Looking down at his legs, he saw they were covered in leaves and other plant life. At first, he thought he was seeing things due to an eye injury, but when he reached down, he could feel the plants. He grabbed one and plucked it off. *This is impossible*, he told himself.

Michael Kleigh struggled to stand in the strong wind. As his eyesight returned, he looked up the side of the crater and saw more vines growing over the rim. Saplings, ferns, and vines made their way down the side of the crater at unrealistic speed. He tried to take a step but was hindered by the growth, now taking over his spacesuit. Panicking, he began to pluck the growth off as fast as he could. With every stem he pulled off, two more seemed to take its place. He was running out of time.

Soon, drops of water began pelting his face shield. *Rain?* he thought. *It's raining on Mars.* Long flashes of lightning arched across the Martian sky as Michael continued ripping plants from his body.

"Let there be light," he said out loud.

"Warning, thirty seconds air remaining," the electronic voice came back. Michael decided his best option was to climb back to the lander and borrow some air from Beckman.

From the top of the crater wall, a twisting whirlwind swept down, scattering dust and sand into the thin atmosphere. Michael Kleigh struggled against the wind as he climbed the hill for the safety of the lander. He fought the storm, one step at a time, reaching out for support from the large boulders around him. The ground shook under his feet, and large rocks tumbled down the slope. One unusually large boulder headed straight for the ship, missing it by only a few feet. Michael Kleigh fell to his knees.

His thoughts went back to his daughter. "Madison," he called out. "What did you get me into?" An apple-sized rock was heaved by the wind and slammed into the side of his helmet, shattering the shield, exposing his face to Mars' atmosphere. He tried holding his breath, but the spacecraft was too far. Finally, unable to go without breathing any longer, he sucked in, expecting to get a lung full of carbon dioxide, but instead, he was breathing clean fresh air.

"This is impossible," Michael Kleigh said out loud as he gasped in deep breaths of oxygen. There was still a large amount of carbon dioxide in the air, making him feel light-headed, but he was getting enough oxygen to survive.

The plants continued to grow on his spacesuit, making it difficult to walk. Sitting on a rock, he once again began pulling the stalks from his pressure suit. Vines began growing down his legs and across his chest as he tried to keep up with removing the growth. Eventually, the plant life had become embedded in his suit, which began to tear apart when he pulled out the weeds.

Finally, feeling quite unsure of himself, he decided to remove his pressure suit entirely. It was the strangest feeling to be standing on Mars in his white undergarment. Uncertain of how long the stone would be able to sustain this atmosphere, Michael rushed back to the ship.

On the rim of the crater, Michael Kleigh could see saplings growing into trees as large vines draped over the edge, growing downward. Ferns, flowers, and other leafy plants sprang from the sterile soil in a miraculous growth of life from nothing. Small insects burst forth from some of the buds and flew out across the sky.

"I must be hallucinating!" Michael said to himself as he rubbed his arms and legs. "I'm still in my spacesuit, and I've run out of air. Now my brain is starving for oxygen, and I'm seeing things." He reached down and pinched his leg. It felt real enough.

The wind howled as Michael made his way to the ship, this time instead of stumbling over rocks and loose dirt, he was stumbling over vines and tangled growth. When he finally reached the craft, he found it was covered in vines and plants. Being so close to the rim of the crater, he couldn't fight the urge to go to the top and look over the edge, so he continued on in his stocking feet.

At the top, he cautiously raised his head above the rocks. The wind was still strong, but there were now many trees to help block it. What he saw was a jungle of twisted vines and plants. He couldn't believe his eyes. He had received the miracle he had wished for.

After a few minutes of gawking, a hand reached down and touched Michael's shoulder. He jumped back in a panic as he spun around. Facing him was pilot Francis Beckman, still in his spacesuit but not wearing a helmet. A patch of dried blood covered the side of his face. "You scared the crap out of me," Michael yelped.

"What's going on?" Beckman asked. "When did we get back to Earth? Was I out that long?"

Kleigh laughed. "We're not on Earth. We're still on Mars."

Beckman looked around. "What are you talking about? Mars doesn't have any plant life."

"It does now," Kleigh yelled over the sound of rushing wind.

"I don't understand. How hard did I hit my head?"

"I broke the stone," Kleigh answered.

"You did what?"

"I broke the stone, and this happened," Kleigh said, gesturing to the trees.

"We were under strict orders. What is mission control going to say?"

"It was that or die," Kleigh answered. "The hull had been compromised. We were out of air."

The two men had to continually step out of the vines and plants that grew around their legs as they talked.

"How long do you think this will last?" Beckman asked.

"There's no way of knowing."

"We probably should get back to the ship."

"It doesn't matter," Kleigh reminded him. "The hull isn't air-tight. We would die just as quickly in there as we would out here. We're at the mercy of the stone."

"Have you alerted mission control of our situation?" Beckman asked.

"No, my suit has been damaged. Is your radio working?"

"My helmet is in the ship."

He looked down into the crater. They could barely see the lander through the leaves. "Let's get back then," Kleigh said with a sigh.

The two astronauts clambered down the crater wall, crawling through the mass of tangled vines and trees until they reached the hatch of their little ship.

Once inside, they activated the onboard radio. "This is Mars lander calling the Excalibur, do you read, Hankins?"

"Loud and clear, lander, what's going on down there? I've been trying to call you for half an hour. I'm reading a vicious storm in your area, can you confirm? I repeat, what's your situation?"

"The situation is green," Kleigh relayed back to Hankins. "I repeat, the situation is green." Glancing outside the window of the craft, he continued, "Literally."

"Have you retrieved the object?"

"Affirmative. The object has been brought back to the lander," Kleigh answered.

"Has it been secured?" Hankins asked.

"Negative. Condition of the object is unknown."

"Come again? The condition of the object is unknown?

"Affirmative. Condition unknown, it's been lost in the storm. We have taken shelter inside the lander. We will continue our search as soon as outside conditions allow it." Kleigh spoke into the radio.

"What are your oxygen levels? Your telemetry data shows your tanks are empty. How are you breathing down there?"

Kleigh and Beckman laughed as they looked out the lander's windows. "The stone is providing us with a breathable atmosphere," Kleigh answered.

"Come again?"

"I repeat, the stone is providing us with a sustainable atmosphere."

41

Razor's Last Stand

Inside the communications room, Cagan Paxton switched on the transmitter and handed the microphone to Madison as two security officers looked on. Ryan Newberry nodded to her. Madison picked up the receiver and got ready to press the talk button, but she was immediately interrupted by a conversation between her father and the Excalibur, which had taken place on Mars fifteen minutes earlier.

Unsure of what to do, Madison looked over at Paxton for instructions.

"Just hang on for a minute," he said.

The radio conversation between Kleigh and Hankins continued as the little group in the communications room listened in.

Madison and her mother exchanged glances as they listened to her father explain that he had broken the stone and there were now plants growing on Mars.

Paxton picked up his phone and dialed out. After a short delay, he said only one quick sentence. "The Terra Stone's been compromised." He hung up the phone and instructed security to have the Kleigh family removed from the communications room.

"Where are you taking us?" Ida asked.

They led the two of them back to Ryan Newberry's office, where they waited another half hour.

Madison anxiously swung her legs as she sat waiting for news about her father. Her mother sat beside her with a worried look on her face.

"It appears that your father has taken your advice, Madison," Newberry said with a sigh as he walked into the room.

"Is he okay?"

"He is alive."

Madison couldn't contain a burst of excitement.

"He reported there are oxygen and rain on Mars," Newberry continued, "along with an out-of-control growth of plant life."

Madison's face almost cracked from her big smile. "I told you so."

"Don't celebrate yet," Newberry went on. "We still haven't found a way to bring him home. All you did was buy us a little time. We don't know what the consequences of his actions will be."

"Consequences?" Ida asked.

"We're interfering with the delicate balance of the universe. We don't know what effects it will have."

"Haven't you always been talking about the possibilities of terraforming Mars? Michael just sent you light years into the future."

Ryan Newberry gave her a stern look. "After years of research, perhaps, but not in one day."

"You're just angry because you didn't get the stone," Madison chimed in.

"Yes, Madison. A very unpleasant side effect. That stone would have helped us in many ways. It could have helped us solve major problems we are facing here on Earth. Mars may have a beautiful environment now, but it's not useful to anybody here, and I don't think there are many families who can afford the six billion dollars it would cost to move there."

"Is my Dad going to be in trouble?"

"That hasn't been decided yet."

Madison paced back and forth with her fingers wrapped around the stone in her pocket.

Ryan Newberry let out a sigh, "Look, we're searching the Gordon mansion now. We're hoping that there will be enough of that stone left to do the research we need. I understand why you did what you did."

Madison looked down at the floor. "They won't find anything."

"What?"

Madison looked up at the man. "They won't find the stone."

Newberry leaned forward on his desk. "How do you know that?"

Madison glanced away, avoiding eye contact.

"Maddy?" her mother asked. "Do you know where the stone is?"

Madison nodded.

"Do you have the stone, Madison?" Newberry asked.

"I need it," she said.

"If you have the stone, you have to let us know. That thing is very dangerous."

"No, not if you know how to use it," Madison told them.

"What do you mean, *know how to use it?*" Newberry asked. "What do you need the stone for?"

Madison slipped off her backpack and pulled out the picture of Razor.

Ida rolled her eyes. "Madison, don't do this now."

"Wait," Newberry put out his hand to stop Ida. "Let her finish."

Madison laid the picture of Razor onto the table as two of the scientists came in to watch. She reached into her pocket and pulled out the onyx stone. The scientists gasped. "She's got the stone?"

Madison blew on the stone, and it glowed bright blue.

"It's reacting to the carbon dioxide," one of the scientists blurted out.

Unsure if she should be giving her secrets out, she shook the stone, and it began to spark with energy at the chip.

"You've done this before?" Newberry asked Madison.

"Uh-huh, lots of times," she answered as she dropped the stone onto the picture. Her mother stood up from her chair to get a better view. The scientists stepped back as blue waves of energy flowed out over the drawing. Gasps and exclamations filled the room when Razor lifted himself from the table and stood on all fours.

"Madison!" her mother squealed. "Is this what you've been trying to tell me?"

"Yes, Mom. The stone brings things to life. Razor will die if you take the stone away from me."

"Does this mean everything you said was true?"

Madison nodded.

"Oh, Madison." Ida reached out and embraced her daughter. "I'm so sorry."

"I'm sorry, too, Mom. I couldn't let anybody take the stone away from me. I promised Razor he would be alive forever."

"Oh my gosh," Ida held Madison out to look at her. "Those dragons were really alive?"

Madison nodded. Ida pulled her in her tight. "I'm so sorry I didn't believe you."

"And Dr. Alazar," Madison continued.

Ryan Newberry became very serious. "Dr. Alazar? Lauro Alazar?"

Madison nodded.

"What about Dr. Alazar?"

"He did something to the spaceship."

Pulling up a chair, Newberry pointed to the security team and waved them over. "I want you to tell me everything you know about Dr. Alazar," he said to Madison.

She had a mouthful to say, and finally, people were beginning to treat her with a little respect. One of the scientists brought over a soda. "Thank you," she said as she began telling her story that ten minutes ago would have been taken for the babbling exaggerations of a child looking for attention. Everybody stood with wide eyes as they hung on every word she had to say from Jim with his gun, the yellow jackets, and Harold turning into a large vine to Alazar becoming an oak tree.

Ryan Newberry sucked on his finger after receiving a nasty paper cut from Razor.

"Sorry about that," Madison chuckled. "He's a little skittish with new people.

"He's remarkable, Madison." Noticing the holes, tear, and wrinkles in the cat's tail, he asked," What happened here?"

"He's been through a lot," Madison answered.

"How long will he..." Newberry didn't know what to call it. "...be alive before you have to... you know... activate the stone again?"

"About an hour, I think. I haven't timed it," Madison answered. She leaned forward, and Razor rubbed on her face.

"There's something I still don't understand," Ida spoke up. "Who sent the stone?"

"Now that is a mystery. We may never know. Obviously, the sender knew there was someone at NASA that couldn't be trusted, but they trusted your husband. I imagine they figured it wouldn't be opened for at least another six months, so it would be safe. I really don't think it was ever intended for Madison to get it. Just a mere coincidence that it came on her birthday."

"An awfully big coincidence," Ida added.

Newberry glanced up at her. "I'm sorry," he said as he shook his head. "I can't let her keep it."

Ida nodded. "I understand."

He reached out his open palm in the same manner Jim and Alazar had done back at the mansion. Madison's hand trembled as she relinquished her onyx stone. She couldn't help feeling she was making a mistake.

42

One Last Goodbye

One of the scientists whom Madison knew as Sammy walked into Newberry's office. He glanced down at Razor, laying across Madison's lap as he walked by. If Sammy hadn't known better, he would have thought it was just a drawing cut from a piece of paper. And soon, it would be just that.

Madison could feel Razor getting lighter as the energy slowly drained away. She stroked his paper body, worried that she would never see him alive again. She just had to get to that stone at least one last time.

Behind a glass door, Madison could see Newberry talking with Matt Johnson, the man who had picked them up at the mansion earlier. After a few moments, Mr. Newberry left the office and hurried past her and her mother into the hall. He tried his best to hide the blue chest, which held the onyx stone as he rushed by, but Madison was drawn to that little box like a moth to a porch light on a summer night.

She had been keeping a mental note of where it was all evening. Every time it was moved, she kept a watchful eye, making excuses to go to the bathroom or get a drink, just to follow it around. This time it was being carried into the hall by Ryan Newberry.

"Mom, I'm thirsty. Can I go into the lounge and get a drink from the water cooler?"

"Again? You've been there four times already."

"I know, but my mouth is dry from being chased by dragons all day."

Ida sighed as she nodded. "Hurry back."

Madison jumped to her feet.

"Leave your cat here," Ida started to say, but Madison was already out the door.

She stepped into the hallway just in time to see Newberry enter the small lounge at the end of the hall. "Perfect," she said to herself. It was the same place she had told her mother she would be. Holding her cat by her side, Madison rushed to the lounge and pushed the door open, but Newberry was nowhere to be seen. Across the room were an outside door and a large window. She stood Razor up on a table in the center of the room, then zipped over and glanced through the glass. Newberry was reaching into the back seat of a gray car.

"Oh, no, Razor..." Madison turned toward the cat. "He's leaving with the stone." Razor's eyelids began to droop as he wavered back and forth, slowly dropping to his knees. Madison ran over to the table and gently cradled him in her arms. "Razor, no," she whispered as she looked into his face.

His eyes slowly closed, and his body uncurled into a rigid piece of flat paper. Madison lifted him up and rubbed her face against his. She massaged his paper ear between her fingers as a tear dripped from her cheek onto his. "You need more energy," she sniffed. "But how?"

Suddenly the outside door opened, and Newberry rushed in. "Keys, keys, where are the keys?" he mumbled to himself as he hurried through the lounge into the hallway. Madison's eyes lit up.

Once outside, Madison ran to the gray car and yanked the back door open. Sitting on the seat was the little blue box. She smiled big as she climbed into the car and closed the door. Laying Razor on the seat, she snapped the clasp and lifted the lid of the box. Cradled in its foam cutout, the onyx stone rested as if it were waiting for her. *Razor can live for another hour,* she thought, as she reached for the stone.

It was the muffled sound of the building's lounge door closing that caused Madison to glance up through the back window. Her heart leapt to her throat when she saw Mr. Newberry heading for the car, almost running. Something was unsettling about the look on his face.

She let out a squeal, then squeezed down onto the floor, pulling a blanket over herself only seconds before Newberry jumped into the driver's seat and started the engine. He threw the car into reverse and twisted around to look out the rear window. In his haste, he did not notice the paper cat lying on the back seat.

As Newberry took off down the road, Madison peered out from under the blanket. Through a small opening, she could see the blue chest sitting on the back seat. She slowly reached up to retrieve the box but had to retreat when Newberry stretched his arm around and began feeling for it without taking his eyes off the road.

Madison gasped as she watched his hand feel around the seat, missing Razor by inches. Finally, he touched the box and grabbed it up, pulling it up to the front. Hidden under the blanket, she could see a devilish grin spread across his face as he glared at the stone.

Concentrating on crossing an intersection, Newberry set the chest down on the passenger seat and turned the wheel. Madison took advantage of the distraction and quickly retrieved Razor from the back seat. Her mind raced, wondering how she was going to explain what she was doing in the back of the car.

Unfortunately, she was unable to think her way out of her predicament. She was going to have to admit she had done something wrong and reveal herself. And the longer she waited, the more trouble she would be in. She let out a heavy sigh. *What am I going to say?* she wondered as she prepared to get up. Suddenly Newberry's mobile rang, and Madison sank back down to the floor. *It's probably Mom*, she thought. *Now I'm really in for it.*

"N'yuberri govorit," Newberry spoke into the phone. "U menya yest' tovar. YA uzhe yedu v aeroport "

Madison froze. "That's Russian," she whispered, then slapped her hand over her mouth. Her heart pounded. *Newberry speaks Russian?* she asked herself. *He's not transporting the stone for NASA. He's stealing it.*

Matt Johnson rushed into Newberry's office. "Excuse me," Ida said as she waved him down. "Matt?"

"Yes," he said as he shuffled through papers on the desk.

"Have you seen Madison? She went to get a drink of water."

A couple of security officers suddenly stormed into the room.

"Is something wrong? Have you heard from my husband?" Ida continued to press, but the men appeared to have other concerns on their minds.

"Just a moment, Ida," Johnson said.

"Did he say where he was going?" one of the security officers asked.

"No, he didn't," Johnson answered.

"What's happening?" Ida asked.

"Can you take her to the lounge and get her some coffee or something?" Johnson said, pointing to the security team.

"Please come this way, ma'am," one of the officers said.

"That's my husband up there. I have the right to know what's going on."

"This doesn't concern your husband," the man answered. "It's about that stone your daughter brought here."

"What about the stone?" Ida asked as she stumbled out into the hallway, being urged by the security officer. Looking up and down the corridor, she began to show distress. "Madison?" she called out. "Where's my daughter?"

"Where did you see her last?" the officer asked.

"She went to the lounge to get a drink."

Another security personnel ran up. "Newberry's car is gone, sir," he said out of breath.

"Damn," Johnson grumbled. "And he took the only person who knew about Dr. Alazar." He looked up at Ida. "I guess this does concern you after all." Pointing to one of the officers, "Go check the bathrooms, find that girl."

"Ryan Newberry was in on it too?" one of the officers asked.

"It looks that way. Get me Officer Spenser on the phone. Now!" he barked.

"What about Madison?" Ida blurted out.

"We're doing the best we can," Johnson yelled.

Ida stared at him. "She's my daughter," she said. "If she's in danger, I need to know."

I'm sorry," Johnson said. "I shouldn't have yelled. "Does she have a cell phone?"

Ida dropped her hands to her sides. "She has one, but she isn't very good at keeping it charged up."

"We'll do everything we can. We'll find her."

Ida allowed the officer to lead her away.

"Spenser's on the phone," a young man said as he popped his head around the corner. "Line three."

"Gerald?" Johnson queried as he picked up the phone. "We have a problem. I need a car stopped."

- - -

Newberry's phone rang again. He picked it up, looked at the number, and threw it back down into the console. "I don't need to speak to anybody at NASA anymore," he grumbled.

Still hiding under the covers, Madison could see the little blue chest sitting on the passenger seat with the lid partially open. She knew what she had to do. The stone was her only hope. Biting her lip, she slowly reached for the box.

Ryan Newberry concentrated on his driving, keeping a wary eye on the other vehicles. He was hoping to avoid any run-in with the authorities. An airline ticket stuck out of his front shirt pocket. Soon he would be on his way to Russia with a prize worthy of a reward that would set him up for the rest of his life.

At first, he hadn't noticed the little hand reaching for the box, but eventually, he caught the movement in the corner of his eye and glanced over. The car swerved across the lane as Newberry jerked the wheel, surprised by the unexpected appearance of someone's hand. "What the he—" he blurted out.

He reached down to grab the box as he steered the car back into its lane. Madison latched onto it as well, which started a tug-of-war battle between the two of them. The car swerved again as Newberry struggled to keep hold of the blue chest, but Madison was not about to give it up. She tugged it back, but being stronger, Newberry managed to yank it from her hands.

He veered the car back into its lane again as he glanced at the box. The stone was gone. It had fallen out during the struggle. "I know that's you, Madison, you little pest," he ranted. "You should have stayed home."

Cutting off another vehicle, Newberry swerved into the right lane. He wanted to pull over and yank Madison from his car, but he needed a secluded area to do it, which was not easy to find along Route One. Not wanting to draw attention to himself, he kept driving while feeling around for the stone.

Madison could see where the black rock had fallen and wedged itself between the seat and the center console, just out of Newberry's sight. Taking a chance, she reached out to snatch it up, but Ryan grabbed her wrist. Though the man's grip was strong, she refused to let go of the stone. He began banging her hand against the console, forcing her to drop it back into the passenger seat.

Suddenly there was a loud rumble, and the car bounced violently. Newberry let go of Madison's wrist in time to grab the wheel with both hands and steer the vehicle back onto the pavement from the shoulder of the road. The other drivers honked at him and made obscene gestures as the sped by. Newberry was getting angry and decided he would turn off at the next intersection to rid himself of this menace once and for all. As he approached the exit, he noticed a state trooper in his rearview mirror.

...

Trooper Margaret Florentine noticed the gray sedan swerving erratically as it sped down the road and decided to pull the driver over for questioning. Unaware of the seriousness of the situation, she didn't expect what happened next. The vehicle made a sudden turn onto the onramp of route 528 toward I-95 and picked up speed. Florentine got on the radio and called in a 10-100, hot pursuit.

The siren on trooper Florentine's patrol car wailed as she chased the speeding sedan. She tried to comprehend what the driver was trying to do so that she could predict his actions and stop the chase safely. However, all her training wasn't enough to deal with behavior this erratic.

Inside the sedan, Madison once again had the onyx stone in her hand and managed to squeeze herself back behind the driver's seat. Newberry did his best to reach behind his seat and grab at the girl, but she was able to stay out of his grasp.

"What are you going to do now?" he bellowed. "Jump out of a speeding car?" In anger, he yanked the wheel back and forth, jerking the car across the highway. The tires squealed as the car swerved from side to side. Madison screeched as she was tossed back and forth across the back of the vehicle.

Madison held on to the stone with one hand and the door handle with the other. Terrified beyond all reason, she finally did the one thing that always seemed to help her in troubled situations. She blew on the stone.

43

Stop in the Name of the Law

The phone rang in the director's office back at the NASA space center. Anxiously, Matt snatched it up. "Johnson here."

Hearing the phone, Ida ran in, "Did they find her?"

Matt held up his forefinger, giving the *one moment* signal. "Gerald! What do you have for me?"

Ida wrung her hands as she waited.

"Great... Is the girl with him...? Keep me posted." Hanging up the phone, he said to Ida, "The state police are following a gray sedan down route one. They believe it's our defector."

"Is Madison alright?"

"They didn't say who was in the car. They probably won't know until they stop him."

"What do you mean, *stop him?* How—"

Matt reached out and touched Ida's hand. "She'll be okay."

"No!" Ryan Newberry screamed as he watched the stone glow bright blue in his rearview mirror. He jerked the car onto the cloverleaf of the I-95 interchange, squealing the tires. Madison slid across the back of the car, banging her hand with the stone in it against the passenger seat. The rock flew through the air and cracked against the dashboard, sending out blue waves of energy across the entire front of the vehicle.

Newberry watched in horror as the dashboard was inatantly engulfed by green weeds and grass. Vines began to push through the air vents, popping the louver covers out as they grew. Ryan frantically began plucking the growth from the dashboard and tossing it out the window as he drove.

Seeing greenery being tossed out of the car, trooper Florentine assumed the driver was disposing of an illegal substance. She could have never imagined how wrong she was.

In the back seat, Madison held on tight as she watched the emerging vines become thicker as they grew. Through the rear window, she could see the flashing lights of the police car. She closed her eyes and wished hard as though she was praying, "Please stop, please stop," she mumbled.

Interrupting her anxious thoughts, a woody vine made its way around the front seat and began to curl around her leg. Madison screeched and began kicking at the plant, crushing its stalk. Soon another vine crept over the top of the seat as the jungle weeds and ferns began to overtake the interior of the car.

The vehicle swerved from lane to lane as Newberry fought the plant life from entangling itself in the steering wheel. Unwilling to move his feet from the pedals, he had given the vines a chance to coil themselves up his legs. Moving into every crevice, the plants pushed themselves through the air vents into the engine compartment. The passenger side window burst out as vines began their assault of the exterior of the sedan. In desperation, Newberry engaged the windshield wipers as vines encroached upon the front of the car. They grew up around the armatures, snapping the rubber blades off as they slapped across the windshield.

Following behind with her siren blaring, Trooper Florentine was dumbfounded. The vehicle she was chasing now had large green vines and leaves spewing from its windows. The plants were quickly engulfing the entire car.

"Come again?" the dispatcher responded to her call. "You say the vehicle you're pursuing has plant life sprouting from its windows?"

"Affirmative, and not just a few leaves. There's a jungle growing along the roof of the vehicle." At that moment, the rear window of the sedan burst out, providing Trooper Florentine with her first clear view of the inside of the car. She could see a young girl fighting off the vines. "Baker-5-2 calling. Code eight, I repeat, code eight. There's a juvenile in the vehicle."

The tires chopped through stems and leaves, sending shreds of greenery spinning into the air as plants grew over the fenders. Inside the car, Newberry continued struggling to keep the vehicle on the road. Red warnings lit up on the dashboard as twisting flora made its way into the operations of the engine. It wasn't long before the sedan began slowing down. Newberry slammed his foot on the gas pedal to no avail, and the car finally rolled to a stop.

Approaching with caution, Trooper Florentine stepped up to the driver's door with her pistol drawn. "Out of the car, now!" she shouted, but there was no response. Looking into the open window, she could see why. Like a boa constrictor, vines had wrapped themselves around Newberry to the point where he couldn't move.

"Sorry officer, I'm unable to acquiesce," Newberry answered as a leafy vine sprouted along his cheek and covered his mouth.

Florentine holstered her weapon and proceeded to help Madison out of the vehicle. She pulled hard on the back door until it ripped free from the vines, and Madison stumbled out. "Are you alright?" the trooper asked.

Madison nodded.

"What's your name, sweetie?" Florentine continued, but before Madison could answer, the trooper stepped back and reached for her gun again.

Madison jerked her head to see what frightened the woman and saw Razor stepping through the broken rear window. "Don't worry. It's just my cat," she said.

"Your cat?" Florentine asked nervously. "He's a little thin."

"I know this looks strange," Madison went on, "...but—"

She was interrupted by a loud hiss just before the hood of the car popped open, spewing out a myriad of jungle-like plants as if it had suddenly vomited.

"Eww!" The trooper's face twisted in disgust.

Two more patrol cars raced to the scene, followed shortly by Matt Johnson in one of NASA's official vehicles.

Ida jumped from the vehicle and embraced her daughter.

"Okay, where is it?" Mr. Johnson asked, sounding suspicious.

Madison pointed to the car, "In there, someplace."

Johnson walked up to the driver's door of the gray sedan and laughed. Newberry did his best to turn his head and look him in the eye, but the vines held him back.

The other officers stood around, scratching their heads. "Should we call for the Jaws of Life?" one of them asked. "Or a gardener?"

Ida knelt down to speak to Madison. "Don't scare me like that again, okay. Tell me before you run off. You can trust me."

Madison nodded.

"We heard from your father," Ida continued. "They got the ship fixed. He's coming home."

Madison's eyes began to tear. "He's okay?"

Ida nodded, trying not to cry herself.

Madison threw her arms around her mother and hugged her hard.

44

A New Promise

Madison and Lou cleared away an area in the back yard large enough to set up her new tent. Up and down the neighborhood chainsaws could be heard as neighbors chopped away the daily new growth. Vines and plants covered the back lawn, and new trees filled the woods so thick it was difficult to walk through.

"This one is a lot bigger than your old one," Lou said as she watched Madison roll out the tent.

"Mom got it for me after the old one was ripped up by the wild plants in our yard."

"How much longer will this stuff keep growing?" Lou asked.

"Well, it took over a year for the plants in Korolyov to stop," Madison answered as she slipped the fiberglass rods through their sleeves. "It doesn't seem to be as bad here, though. In Russia, they had to evacuate the city. Could you hand me that pole over there?"

Lou picked up the tent pole and reached out to Madison with it. "I saw two more of your blue and orange butterflies today."

"Yeah, I saw one yesterday. They're all over the place," Madison said.

Lou laughed. "We should name them the Madison Kleigh butterfly. After all, you invented them."

"Well," Madison thought for a while. "I've been calling them Blue Razor Butterflies."

"After your cat?" Lou asked.

"Yeah, it's my way of keeping his memory alive. He's one of the reasons why we have those butterflies now."

"I like that," Lou said. "I'll tell everybody that's what they're called, and maybe the name will stick."

Lou held the tent in place as Madison pulled the side out and set the poles into their pockets.

"There, all ready for a night out in the jungle," she said as she wiped the sweat from her forehead. Go get your sleeping bag, and I'll meet you back here in an hour."

The two girls ran off to their respective homes.

Later that evening, Madison and Lou lay on their sleeping bags, looking up from the front of their tent.

"I never thought that one day I'd be sleeping in a jungle," Lou said.

"Neither did I," Madison agreed as she pointed above the tent. "It's too bad we can't see much of the sky anymore with all these trees."

The girls stared upward. "Maybe we'll spot another Blue Razor," Lou said.

"Or a pink bird," Madison added.

"You know that pact we made with each other on your birthday?"

"Yeah, what of it?"

"I think we should renew it," Lou said.

"Renew it?" Madison shifted onto her side. "But, the stone is gone."

"I know, but we should make one without the stone." Lou sat up, crossing her legs in front of herself. "We'll promise that we will be friends forever and that we won't leave each other."

Madison pulled out her sketchpad and a pencil.

"Don't write anything bad this time," Lou continued.

"What should we write?"

"I think we should make a list of promises." Lou reached for the pad. "I'll go first." She spoke out loud as she wrote. "I promise never to leave my best friend behind again, no matter how bad things get."

"Oh, oh, me next," Madison grabbed onto the sketchpad.

"Wait, I'm not finished writing." Lou scribbled down her last few words just before Madison impatiently pulled the pad away.

Madison grabbed for the pencil, too, but Lou refused to give it up. "I need to write your first promise for you, something to do with patience," she giggled as she held the pencil out so Madison couldn't reach it.

"Okay, be that way," Madison said and reached into her backpack for a different one. She hunched over the pad and began to write. "I promise..." she started to say but went quiet. She quickly hid what she was writing when Lou leaned over to see.

"What are you writing?" she asked.

Madison giggled. "You'll see."

"No fair, I read mine out loud as I wrote it."

Madison turned her back, but Lou reached around and grasped onto the pad.

"Wait!" Madison screeched. "I'm not finished."

"I want to see," Lou squealed as she tugged on the drawing pad.

Madison held on just long enough to finish her promise, although the penmanship was a bit choppy due to the struggle.

With the pad now in her possession, Lou read out loud what Madison had written. "I promise to let Lou get eaten by the dragon next time."

Madison laughed.

"Come on, be serious. Besides, the dragon never ate you anyhow. Even though I did write that it would."

"Then that means these pacts don't work very well."

"They work if we write things we really mean to do."

"Okay, I'll be serious," Madison said as she took the pad from Lou. "I promise to share everything with my best friend, Lou, and not hog things for myself," she spoke as she wrote.

Lou grabbed for the pad. "Me next. I have something else to add."

"Wait, I want to write another one."

"No, it's my turn. You just wrote that you wouldn't hog things." As Lou reached out for the sketchpad, her foot got tangled in her blanket, yanking it across the tent floor. A stack of playing cards went flying.

"Hey! Watch it," an annoyed voice grumbled from the back of the tent.

Lou glanced up. "Sorry, I didn't mean it. What are you guys playing anyhow?"

"Rummy five-hundred," Chad answered. "What are you two *fighting* about?"

"We're listing promises to each other."

"Like, you'll stop fighting over stupid things," Bryant added as he stuffed his face with a fist full of potato chips.

"Yeah, something like that, or eating less junk food. That's what you should put on the list."

"That's girl stuff. I don't want anything to do with it."

"Well," Madison continued. "You should at least promise not to shoot any more animals with your BB gun."

"You write it, and I'll sign it."

"No, you need to write it," Lou added. "We're all writing promises that make us better people. It's what Harold would have wanted."

Chad reached out for the pad. "I'll do it for Harold." He sat quietly as he wrote, then handed it back to Madison, who anxiously read it to herself, expecting some smart-aleck remark.

Her mischievous smirk melted into a serious expression. "Do you really mean it?"

Chad scrunched his shoulders and began picking up the cards.

Madison held the pad out for Lou to see, but Bryant snatched it out of her hands. "Give me that," he spat out. Bryant let out an exaggerated laugh as he read it, then tossed the sketchbook back as he rolled onto his back. "That'll be the day," he snickered.

Lou picked up the pad and read it softly as Chad began to beat Bryant with his pillow. "I promise never to bully anybody again." She looked up at the two boys, now in the middle of a severe pillow fight. A big smile crept across her face as she pulled out her own pillow and joined the battle. Before long, Madison was sucked in. Laughs, giggles, and screeches emanated from the tent as the four friends continued to roughhouse. Playing cards, potato chips, and feathers flew through the air.

The shenanigans came to a sudden halt when Madison's mother popped her head into the tent. "I hope this isn't going to continue all night."

"No, Mom. We'll behave."

"Good. Then I won't have to get my own pillow."

"You can if you want to," Madison giggled.

"I have something better."

Madison couldn't imagine what her mother could have been talking about. But, when she reached in with something in her hand, Madison gasped, and her eyes grew wide. "Where did you get him?" she shrieked. Her mother was holding a little kitten about the size of a softball.

"He was wandering around the yard, lost. I thought maybe you could care for him until we found his mother."

"What if we can't find his mother?" Madison asked.

"Then I guess you'll have to be his foster mom."

"Do you mean it?" Madison asked excitedly. She lifted the kitten up and rubbed her face against him.

Her mother smiled as she nodded. "I'll go get some tuna fish," she said, then disappeared outside the tent flap.

"O-M-G," Lou screeched. "He's so adorable."

"He's not made of paper, is he?" Bryant blurted out.

"No, he's not paper." Madison scoffed.

The kitten waddled across the sleeping bags as the girls cooed over him. Even Chad and Bryant couldn't help making affectionate sounds to coax the cat to play with them.

"He's so cute," Madison doted. "He looks just like the Razor I drew."

Lou noticed that the kitten's stubby tail was bent in a few places. She laughed. "Look, even his tail is wrinkled."

Madison laughed too. "Exactly like Razor," she said.

At that moment, a light bulb went on in both the girls' heads. Madison jerked her head up to stare at Lou, who did the same. They both gasped as a thought entered their minds. "You don't think—"

"Just like your butterfly," Lou interrupted.

"And my bird," Madison added.

The girls stared at the kitten. Its tail was bent like a lightning bolt.

45

Home Again

Madison walked through the old house in the woods. Plants and vines had grown up inside the building spreading around each room. She pushed past large leaves until she found the little office. *Good,* she thought. *It hasn't been destroyed.* The window had been broken out, and a large vine extended into the house, clinging to the ceiling, but the room was still in pretty good condition. Madison reached down and lifted the old scrapbook from the floor. She set it on the desk and began thumbing through the pages.

"Hello, Madison," a low, throaty voice flowed from the doorway.

Startled, Madison gasped, jerking her head to look behind her. An old man with gray hair stood in the hallway.

"Grandpa Osborne!" Madison yelled and ran into his arms. "What are you doing here?"

"I think the more appropriate question is, *what are you doing here?*"

"Come in, look at what I found."

Madison led her grandfather into the small office and pulled out the newspaper clippings from the scrapbook.

"Look at this, Grandpa." She pointed to the article.

"On September twelfth, nineteen-fifty-nine, Russia sent a space probe to the moon."

"Yes, I know. I was seventeen years old back then."

"Don't you find that rather odd?"

"Not at all. They were trying to see if they could send an object to the moon."

"Why?"

Her grandfather shrugged his shoulders. "Just to see if it could be done, I suppose."

"And then spend years sending ships to try to get it back?"

Her grandfather stood up and chuckled. "I see now. This is about the stone, isn't it?"

Madison breathed out an exasperated sigh. "You've been talking to Mom, haven't you?" She turned away and fidgeted with the newspaper.

"Oh, don't worry," he said as he bent over and whispered. "I'm her father. I don't have to listen to her either," he laughed.

Madison smiled. "Look at this article, *Soviet rocket hits moon after 35 hours.* Look where it landed, right near the sea of Tranquility. That's where Apollo eleven landed.

"Yes, that's correct."

Madison pulled out another newspaper. "Luna 15 Lands near Apollo Site. The entire moon and they both end up in the same area on the same day?"

Her grandfather nodded. "Yes, that is quite a coincidence."

"And look at this one," Madison pulled out another yellowed newspaper article. "Terra Stone Discovery a Myth."

Madison looked up at her grandfather. "That's what the scientists at NASA called my onyx stone."

"Slow down there. You're moving way too fast for my old brain to keep up."

"You know what I think?"

"What do you think?"

"I think Russia was trying to do to the moon what my Dad did to Mars, but it didn't work. And when they found out that the US was going to the moon, they wanted to get there first so that they could get the stone back before the Americans found it."

"You sound like your grandmother's father."

"My grandmother's father?"

"Yes, your *great* grandfather. He's the one who found the Terra stone originally."

"He did? Where? When?"

"He found it at a dig in South America."

Madison thought for a while, trying to make sense of everything. "How did the Russians get it?"

"They stole it," her grandfather answered. "Once everybody deemed it to be a worthless stone, people didn't care about protecting it any longer. Your great grandfather had always suspected it was more than it appeared, but nobody believed him." He grunted. "Not even me."

"Somebody in Russia believed him," Madison said.

Her grandfather nodded with understanding. "Yes, evidently."

Madison walked over to the window and looked up into the sky. "They'll believe him now."

"That's why he didn't tell anybody about the second stone."

"The second stone?"

"Yes, he found two stones originally."

"What happened to the second stone?"

Her grandfather smiled. "That's what I came here to find out."

"Here? In this house?" Madison looked around the room. "Did the person who lived here know about the stone?"

"Yes, he did," her grandfather answered.

"Wait here," Madison said as she darted out the door. Her grandfather picked up the album and studied the cover. He ran his hand over the cloth as if it were a lost friend.

"Look at this," Madison said upon returning to the room. She was carrying the picture of the family that had been hanging in the hallway. "I think these are the people who lived here. They look familiar, don't they?"

Her grandfather took the frame into his hands and blew off some dust. His eyes glassed over as he examined it. "Yes, they do."

"Do you know who they are?" Madison asked.

Her grandfather nodded. "This picture is over thirty years old."

"Who are they?"

"You don't recognize your mother?"

Madison took another look at the photograph. Her brow wrinkled as she thought. "That's not my mother."

"Not the woman," her grandfather said. "The girl. She was five years old when this picture was taken."

Madison stared at the picture.

Her grandfather tapped his finger over the image of the man. "That's me."

Madison looked into his eyes. "Why is there a picture of you in this old house?"

Her grandfather laughed. "It's my house." He looked around. "At least it used to be."

Madison gasped. She couldn't believe what she was hearing. "Why didn't Mom ever tell me?"

"Oh, I suppose it's because she doesn't like the past. Especially when it's sad."

"Why did you leave?"

Her grandfather pointed to the woman in the picture. "Your grandmother."

Madison took another look. "That's my grandmother?"

"Yes, you never knew her. She went missing before you were born... during our last research assignment in Brazil. I thought she was dead."

"Wait a minute," Madison said eagerly. "Did you say great-grandpa found the stone in South America?"

Her grandfather nodded. "Yes, I believe so."

Madison glanced at the floor as she thought. "That's where he found the stone I have," she mumbled.

Her grandfather gave her a sideways glance. "What did you say?"

"I said that's where he found the stone I have."

"You have a stone from your great-grandfather's collection?"

"Yes, Uncle Robert gave it to me."

Her grandfather grunted. "I should have known."

"What's wrong?"

"Those stones were all supposed to be turned over to the government."

"Then who sent me the terra stone?"

"Nobody sent you the stone. I sent it to your father."

"You?"

Her grandfather laughed. "*O, what a tangled web we weave when first we practice to deceive.* Sir Walter Scott, by the way. It was just by chance that I was called in to help in Korolyov last year. They figured I would have some insight since I had connections with your great grandfather, who had discovered the stone. Of course, I couldn't provide any information that would help stop the growth, and since the Russian government was eager to keep the situation secret, I was able to stay and help. I already knew the cause of the entire ordeal. I could only guess that they wanted me where they could keep an eye on me." He leaned over and lowered his voice. "That's just between you and me, understand?"

Madison nodded her head. She glanced out the window. "When did you live here?"

"Before you were born. Your grandmother's family used to own the entire area up to the rock wall on the other side of the woods."

"I feel sorry for them."

"Oh, why?"

"They had to be neighbors with the Gordon's."

Her grandfather laughed. "They *were* the Gordon's."

"What? How is that possible?"

"Your grandmother's father was Charles Gordon."

"You mean I'm related to Harold Gordon?"

This amused her grandfather. "I'm afraid so. He's your cousin. Well... third cousin, I guess. His great grandfather was one of the Gorden kids, like your great-grandfather. They were brothers." He laughed.

"What's so funny?"

"All these years and the two families are still feuding. The best part is, you don't even know about it. Although, if it weren't for the Gordon side of the family, your parents never would have met."

"What do you mean?"

"One of the Gordon kids married a..." he shook his fist. "What was his name...?" Madison waited with anticipation as her grandfather tried to remember. "Newberry!" he blurted out. "Reginald Newberry. He worked for NASA in the early days; in the sixties, I think it was. He's the one who introduced your parents to each other.

"Newberry? But he was working for Russia."

"Like I said," her grandfather continued. "The families have been feuding for years. You'll understand when you get older."

Madison stared at the picture of her grandparents with her mother. The things her grandfather had been telling her was too much to take in at one time.

"Madison," her grandfather sighed. "I'm going away for a little while."

"But you just got back from Russia."

"I know, but." He pulled a folded magazine page from his pocket and held it out for Madison to see. It was a photo of a woman.

"She looks just like Mom," Madison said, holding the magazine page up to the family photo.

"Yes, too much to be a coincidence."

"Who is she?"

"I think she's your aunt."

"I have an aunt in Brazil?"

"I don't know. But if you do, she'll know what happened to your grandmother. I have to go and find out."

46

Splashdown

Five months later...

The news of Excalibur's miraculous return home spread across the globe as reporters continually hounded the astronauts and NASA. They were especially interested in the way Kleigh and Beckman were able to launch the Mars lander after tipping it back into a vertical position using the new vegetation now growing on the planet.

Information Madison had provided NASA about Dr. Alazar had been helpful in repairing the malfunctioning gimbal. By remaining in their pressure suits, the men had been able to rendezvous with the Excalibur without the need to repair the hull breach. Once the men had been safely returned to the orbiter, they had been able to jettison the lander module and head home. Five months later, the Orion space capsule had floated down on its parachutes into the Pacific Ocean.

Michael Kleigh, Brad Hankins, and Francis Beckman had been kept in quarantine for a week after returning from Mars and were required to stay on base in Houston for two more weeks.

The very first day the men had been able to leave isolation, Madison ran into her father's arms.

"There was no keeping her away," Ida said. "We're going to have to stay in a hotel all week so we can make daily trips to see you."

"You should see my new kitten, Dad," Madison rambled on.

Michael looked directly at Ida. "A kitten?"

Ida nodded her head.

"But, I thought—"

"He's so adorable," Madison interrupted. "He even has a bent tail, just like the cat I drew."

The three of them walked the grounds of Johnson Space Center and talked for hours.

"So, who's this Jim guy?" her father asked.

"Oh, he was just some jerk who tried to take advantage of Mom," Madison answered.

Ida wrapped her arm around her husband and put her head on his shoulder. "I'm just glad you're home, that's all," she said. "I'm glad to have my family back." She smiled at Madison.

"I missed you so much, Dad," Madison said as she reached to give her father another hug. As she embraced him, her backpack fell to the ground, but she paid no attention to it. As it tumbled to the pavement, the top flap sprung open and her paper drawing of Razor slid part way out.

The paper cat fluttered in the breeze. Its eye, colored with green pencil, stared into the blue sky.

47

And then there was Light

Back at home, Madison hugged her father before going up to bed. "Good night, Dad. I'm glad you're home safe." She kissed her mother and bounded up the stairs with the kitten in her arms.

In her room, Madison pulled Razor from her backpack and set him on the edge of her bed, where he always liked to sleep. "Good night, boy. I miss you," she said, then kissed his face. "I wish you could be alive again."

She opened her closet door and pulled her nightshirt from its drawer. Looking up at the top shelf, she noticed that the lid on her stone collection had come open. She pulled the wooden box down and looked inside. Her entire collection was there, including the onyx stone that looked just like the real one from space. Madison pulled it from the box and examined it.

There were no marks on it anywhere. Its surface was perfect, with no cracks or chips. She glanced over at her paper drawing, then blew on the stone. Nothing happened. She sighed as she replaced the stone and closed the clasp on the box. She slid it back onto the top shelf and closed the closet door. "I had to try," she mumbled to herself.

Madison slid under the covers and turned off her bedside light. Being tired from a long, busy day, she fell asleep in minutes.

As Madison slept, the wooden box inside her closet popped open again. Inside, the onyx stone began to glow. A soft blue light illuminated the closet, sending out rays around the door. A thin beam of light cut the darkness like a knife, falling across the foot of Madison's bed and across the paper cat. It lasted only a few seconds then faded to darkness.

Razor lifted his head and looked around. Madison stirred in her sleep, rolling over with a sigh.

*****

Did you like this book?
Tell your friends.

Follow Jeffrey David Montanye:
@JeffreyDMontanye
Twitter: @JDMontanye

www.JeffreyDMontanye.com

Other Books by Jeffrey David Montanye

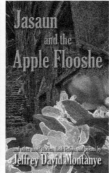